IN THE TENNESSEE MOUNTAINS

BY

CHARLES EGBERT CRADDOCK

1912

CONTENTS.

DRIFTING DOWN LOST CREEK.

I.

High above Lost Creek Valley towers a wilderness of pine. So dense is this growth that it masks the mountain whence it springs. Even when the Cumberland spurs, to the east, are gaunt and bare in the wintry wind, their deciduous forests denuded, their crags unveiled and grimly beetling, Pine Mountain remains a sombre, changeless mystery; its clifty heights are hidden, its chasms and abysses lurk unseen. Whether the skies are blue, or gray, the dark, austere line of its summit limits the horizon. It stands against the west like a barrier. It seemed to Cynthia Ware that nothing which went beyond this barrier ever came back again. One by one the days passed over it, and in splendid apotheosis, in purple and crimson and gold, they were received into the heavens, and returned no more. She beheld love go hence, and many a hope. Even Lost Creek itself, meandering for miles between the ranges, suddenly sinks into the earth, tunnels an unknown channel beneath the mountain, and is never seen again. She often watched the floating leaves, a nettle here and there, the broken wing of a moth, and wondered whither these trifles were borne, on the elegiac current. She came to fancy that her life was like them, worthless in itself and without a mission; drifting down Lost Creek, to vanish vaguely in the mountains.

Yet her life had not always been thus destitute of pleasure and purpose. There was a time—and she remembered it well—when she found no analogies in Lost Creek. Then she saw only a stream gayly dandering down the valley, with the laurel and the pawpaw close in to its banks, and the kildeer's nest in the sand.

Before it takes that desperate plunge into the unexplored caverns of the mountain, Lost Creek lends its aid to divers

1

jobs of very prosaic work. Further up the valley it turns a mill-wheel, and on Mondays it is wont to assist in the family wash. A fire of pine-knots, kindled beside it on a flat rock, would twine long, lucent white flames about the huge kettle in which the clothes were boiled. Through the steam the distant landscape flickered, ethereal, dream-like. The garments, laid across a bench and beaten white with a wooden paddle, would flutter hilariously in the wind. Deep in some willowy tangle the water-thrush might sing. Ever and anon from the heights above vibrated the clinking of a hand-hammer and the clanking of a sledge. This iterative sound used to pulse like a lyric in Cynthia's heart. But her mother, one day, took up her testimony against it.

"I do declar', it sets me plumb catawampus ter hev ter listen ter them blacksmiths, up yander ter thar shop, at thar everlastin' chink-chank an' chink-chank, considerin' the tales I hearn 'bout 'em, when I war down ter the quiltin' at M'ria's house in the Cove."

She paused to prod the boiling clothes with a long stick. She was a tall woman, fifty years of age, perhaps, but seeming much older. So gaunt she was, so toothless, haggard, and disheveled, that but for her lazy step and languid interest she might have suggested one of Macbeth's witches, as she hovered about the great cauldron.

"They 'lowed down yander ter M'ria's house ez this hyar Evander Price hev kem ter be the headin'est, no 'count critter in the kentry! They 'lowed ez he hev been a-foolin' round Pete Blenkins's forge, a-workin' fur him ez a striker, till he thinks hisself ez good a blacksmith ez Pete, an' better. An' all of a suddenty this same 'Vander Price riz up an' made a consarn ter bake bread in, sech ez hed never been seen in the mountings afore. They 'lowed down ter M'ria's ez they dunno what he patterned arter. The Evil One must hev revealed the contrivance ter him. But they say it did cook

2

bread in less 'n haffen the time that the reg'lar oven takes; leastwise his granny's bread, 'kase his mother air a toler'ble sensible woman, an' would tech no sech foolish fixin'. But his granny 'lowed ez she didn't hev long ter live, nohow, an' mought ez well please the chil'ren whilst she war spared. So she resked a batch o' her salt-risin' bread on the consarn, an' she do say it riz like all possessed, an' eat toler'ble short. An' that banged critter 'Vander war so proud o' his contrivance that he showed it ter everybody ez kem by the shop. An' when two valley men rid by, an' one o' thar beastis cast a shoe, 'Vander hed ter take out his contraption fur them ter gape over, too. An' they ups an' says they hed seen the like afore a-many a time; sech ovens war common in the valley towns. An' when they fund out ez 'Vander hed never hearn on sech, but jes' got the idee out 'n his own foolishness, they jes' stared at one another. They tole the boy ez he oughter take hisself an' his peartness in workin' in iron down yander ter some o' the valley towns, whar he'd find out what other folks hed been doin' in metal, an' git a good hank on his knack fur new notions. But 'Vander, he clung ter the mountings. They 'lowed down yander at M'ria's quiltin' ez 'Vander fairly tuk ter the woods with grief through other folks hevin' made sech contraptions ez his'n, afore he war born."

The girl stopped short in her work of pounding the clothes, and, leaning the paddle on the bench, looked up toward the forge with her luminous brown eyes full of grave compassion. Her calico sun-bonnet was thrust half off her head. Its cavernous recesses made a background of many shades of brown for her auburn hair, which of a brilliant, rich tint, highly esteemed of late years in civilization, but in the mountains still accounted a capital defect. There was nothing as gayly colored in all the woods, except perhaps a red-bird, that carried his tufted topknot so bravely through shade and sheen that he might have been the transmigrated spirit of an Indian, still roaming in the old hunting-ground. The beech shadows, delicately green, imparted a more ethereal fairness to her fair face, and her sombre brown homespun dress heightened the effect by contrast. Her mother noted an unwonted flush upon her cheek, and recommenced with a deep, astute purpose.

"They 'lowed down yander in the Cove, ter M'ria's quiltin', ez this hyar 'Vander Price hev kem ter be mighty difficult, sence he hev been so gin over ter pride in his oven an' sech. They 'lowed ez even Pete Blenkins air fairly afeard o' him. Pete hisself hev always been knowed ez a powerful evil man, an' what 'twixt drink an' deviltry mos' folks hev been keerful ter gin him elbow-room. But this hyar 'Vander Price hectors round an' jaws back so sharp ez Pete hev got ter be truly mealy-mouthed where 'Vander be. They 'lowed down yander at M'ria's quiltin' ez one day Pete an' 'Vander bed a piece o' iron a-twixt 'em on the anvil, an' Pete would tap, same ez common, with the hand-hammer on the hot metal ter show Vander whar ter strike with the sledge. An' Pete got toler'ble bouncin', an' kep' faultin' Vander,—jes' like he use ter quar'l with his t'other striker, till the man would bide with him no more. All at wunst 'Vander hefted the sledge, an' gin Pete the ch'ice ter take it on his skull-bone, or show more manners. An' Pete showed 'em."

There was a long pause. Lost Creek sounded some broken minor chords, as it dashed against the rocks on its headlong way. The wild grapes were blooming. Their fragrance, so delicate yet so pervasive, suggested some exquisite unseen presence—the dryads were surely abroad! The beech-trees stretched down their silver branches and green shadows. Through rifts in the foliage shimmered glimpses of a vast array of sunny parallel mountains, converging and converging, till they seemed to meet far away in one long, level line, so ideally blue that it looked less like earth than

4

heaven. The pine-knots flamed and glistered under the great wash-kettle. A tree-toad was persistently calling for rain, in the dry distance. The girl, gravely impassive, beat the clothes with the heavy paddle. Her mother shortly ceased to prod the white heaps in the boiling water, and presently took up the thread of her discourse.

"An' 'Vander hev got ter be a mighty suddint man. I hearn tell, when I war down ter M'ria's house ter the quiltin', ez how in that sorter fight an' scrimmage they hed at the mill, las' month, he war powerful ill-conducted. Nobody hed thought of hevin' much of a fight,—thar hed been jes' a few licks passed a-twixt the men thar; but the fust finger ez war laid on this boy, he jes' lit out an' fit like a catamount. Right an' lef' he lay about him with his fists, an' he drawed his huntin' knife on some of 'em. The men at the mill war in no wise pleased with him."

"'Pears-like ter me ez 'Vander air a peaceable boy enough, ef he ain't jawed at, an' air lef' be," drawled Cynthia.

Her mother was embarrassed for a moment. Then, with a look both sly and wise, she made an admission,—a qualified admission. "Waal, wimmen—ef—ef—ef they air young an' toler'ble hard-headed *yit*, air likely ter jaw *some*, ennyhow. An' a gal oughtn't ter marry a man ez hev sot his heart on bein' lef' in peace. He's apt ter be a mighty sour an' disapp'inted critter."

This sudden turn to the conversation invested all that had been said with new meaning, and revealed a subtle diplomatic intention. The girl seemed deliberately to review it, as she paused in her work. Then, with a rising flush, "I ain't studyin' 'bout marryin' nobody," she asserted staidly. "I hev laid off ter live single."

Mrs. Ware had overshot the mark, but she retorted, gallantly reckless, "That's what yer aunt Malviny useter declar' fur gospel sure, when she war a gal. An' she hev got ten chil'ren, an' hev buried two husbands, an' ef all they say air true she's tollin' in the third man now. She's a mighty spry, good-featured woman an' a fust-rate manager, yer aunt Malviny air, an' both her husbands lef' her su'thin',—cows, or wagons, or land. An' they war quiet men when they war alive, an' stays whar they air put, now that they air dead; not like old Parson Hoodenpyle what his wife hears stumpin' round the house an' preachin' every night, though she air ez deef ez a post, an' he hev been in glory twenty year,—twenty year, an' better. Yer aunt Malviny hed luck, so mebbe 't ain't no killin' complaint fur a gal ter git ter talkin' like a fool about marryin' an' sech. Leastwise, I ain't minded ter sorrow."

She looked at her daughter with a gay grin, which, distorted by her toothless gums and the wreathing steam from the kettle, enhanced her witch-like aspect and was spuriously malevolent. She did not notice the stir of an approach through the brambly tangles of the heights above until it was close at hand; as she turned, she thought only of the mountain cattle,—to see the red cow's picturesque head and crumpled horns thrust over the sassafras bushes, or to hear the brindle's clanking bell. It was certainly less unexpected to Cynthia when a young mountaineer, clad in brown jeans trousers and a checked homespun shirt, emerged upon the rocky slope. He still wore his blacksmith's leather apron, and his powerful corded hammer-arm was bare beneath his tightly rolled sleeve. He was tall and heavily built; his sun-burned face was square, with a strong lower jaw, and his features were accented by fine lines of charcoal, as if the whole were a clever sketch. His black eyes held fierce intimations, but there was mobility of expression about them that suggested changing impulses, strong but fleeting. He was like his forge fire: though the heat might be intense for a time, it fluctuated with the breath of the bellows. Just now he was meekly quailing before the old woman, whom he evidently had not thought to find here. It was as apt an illustration as might be, perhaps, of the inferiority of strength to finesse. She seemed an inconsiderable adversary, as haggard, lean, and prematurely aged she swayed on her prodding-stick about the huge kettle; but she was as a veritable David to this big young Goliath, though she too flung hardly more than a pebble at him.

"Laws-a-me!" she cried, in shrill, toothless glee; "ef hyar ain't 'Vander Price! What brung ye down hyar along o' we-uns, Vander?" she continued, with simulated anxiety. "Hev that thar red heifer o' our'n lept over the fence agin, an' got inter Pete's corn? Waal, sir, ef she ain't the headin'est heifer!"

"I hain't seen none o' yer heifer, ez I knows on," replied the young blacksmith, with gruff, drawling deprecation. Then he tried to regain his natural manner. "I kem down hyar," he remarked in an off-hand way, "ter git a drink o' water." He glanced furtively at the girl; then looked quickly away at the gallant red-bird, still gayly parading among the leaves.

The old woman grinned with delight. "Now, ef that ain't s'prisin'," she declared. "Ef we hed knowed ez Lost Creek war a-goin' dry over yander a-nigh the shop, so ye an' Pete would hev ter kem hyar thirstin' fur water, we-uns would hev brung su'thin' down hyar ter drink out'n. We-uns hain't got no gourd hyar, hev we, Cynthy?"

"'Thout it air the little gourd with the saft soap in it," said Cynthia, confused and blushing.

Her mother broke into a high, loud laugh. "Ye ain't wantin' ter gin 'Vander the soap-gourd ter drink out'n, Cynthy! Leastwise, I ain't goin' ter gin it ter Pete. Fur I s'pose ef ye hev ter kem a haffen mile ter git a drink, 'Vander, ez surely Pete 'll hev ter kem, too. Waal, waal, who would hev b'lieved ez Lost Creek would go dry nigh the shop, an' yit be ascuttlin' along like that, hyar-abouts!" and she pointed with her bony finger at the swift flow of the water.

He was forced to abandon his clumsy pretense of thirst. "Lost Creek ain't gone dry nowhar, ez I knows on," he admitted, mechanically rolling the sleeve of his hammer-arm up and down as he talked. "It air toler'ble high,—higher 'n I ever see it afore. 'T war jes' night afore las' ez two men got a kyart sunk in a quicksand, whilst fordin' the creek. An' one o' thar wheels kem off, an' they hed right smart scufflin' ter keep thar load from washin' out'n the kyart an' driftin' clean away. Leastwise, that was how they telled it ter me. They war valley men, I'm a-thinkin'. They 'lowed ter me ez they hed ter cut thar beastis out 'n the traces. They loaded him up with the goods an' fotched him ter the shop."

Mrs. Ware forebore her ready gibes in her interest in the country-side gossip. She ceased to prod the boiling clothes. She hung motionless on the stick. "I s'pose they 'lowed, mebbe, ez what sort'n goods they hed," she hazarded, seeing a peddler in the dim perspective of a prosaic imagination.

"They lef' some along o' we-uns ter keep till they kem back agin. They 'lowed ez they could travel better ef thar beastis war eased some of his load. They hed some o' all sorts o' truck. They 'lowed ez they war aimin' ter sot up a store over yander ter the Settlemint on Milksick Mounting. They lef' right smart o' truck up yander in the shed a-hint the shop; 'pears like ter me it air a kyart-load itself. I promised ter keer fur it till they kem back again."

Certainly, so far as Cynthia was concerned, the sharpness of wits and the acerbity of temper ascribed generally to the red-haired gentry could be accounted no slander. The flame-colored halo about her face, emblazoned upon the dusky depths of her old brown bonnet, was not more fervid than an angry glow overspreading her delicate cheek, and an intense fiery spark suddenly a-light in her brown eyes.

8

"Pete Blenkins mus' be sodden with drink, I'm a-thinkin'!" she cried impatiently. "Like ez not them men will 'low ez the truck ain't all thar, when they kem back. An' then thar'll be a tremenjious scrimmage ter the shop, an' somebody'll git hurt, an' mebbe killed."

"Waal, Cynthy," exclaimed her mother, in tantalizing glee, "air you-uns goin' ter ache when Pete's head gits bruk? That's powerful 'commodatin' in ye, cornsiderin' ez he hev got a wife, an' chil'ren ez old ez ye be. Waal sorrow fur Pete, ef ye air so minded."

The angry spark in Cynthia's eyes died out as suddenly as it kindled. She began to beat the wet clothes heavily with the paddle, and her manner was that of having withdrawn herself from the conversation. The young blacksmith had flushed, too, and he laughed a little, but demurely. Then, as he still rolled and unrolled the sleeve of his hammer-arm, his wonted gravity returned.

"Pete hain't got nothin' ter do with it, nohow," he averred. "Pete hev been away fur two weeks an' better: he hev gone ter see his uncle Joshua, over yander on Caney Fork. He 'lowed ez apple-jack grows powerful fine in them parts."

"Then who war holpin' at the forge ter-day?" asked Mrs. Ware, surprised. "I 'lowed I hearn the hand-hammer an' sledge too, same ez common."

There was a change among the lines of charcoal that seemed to define his features. He looked humbled, ashamed. "I hed my brother a-strikin' fur me," he said at last.

"Why, 'Vander," exclaimed the old woman shrilly, "that thar boy's a plumb idjit! Ye oughtn't trust him along o' that sledge! He'd jes' ez lief maul ye on the head with it ez maul the hot iron. Ye know he air ez strong ez a ox; an' the critter's fursaken in his mind."

"I knows that," Evander admitted. "I wouldn't hev done it, ef I hedn't been a-workin' on a new fixin' ez I hev jes' thought up, an' I war jes' *obligated* ter hev somebody ter strike fur me. An' laws-a-massy, 'Lijah wouldn't harm nobody. The critter war ez peart an' lively ez a June-bug,—so proud ter be allowed ter work around like folks!" He stopped short in sudden amazement: something stood in his eyes that had no habit there; its presence stupefied him. For a moment he could not speak, and he stood silently gazing at that long, level blue line, in which the converging mountains met,—so delicately azure, so ethereally suggestive, that it seemed to him like the Promised Land that Moses viewed. "The critter air mighty aggervatin' mos'ly ter the folks at our house," he continued, "but they hectors him. He treats me well."

"An ill word is spoke 'bout him ginerally round the mounting," said the old woman, who had filled and lighted her pipe, and was now trying to crowd down the charge, so to speak, without scorching too severely her callous fore-finger. "I hev hearn folks 'low ez he hev got so turrible crazy ez he oughter be sent away an' shet up in jail. An' it 'pears like ter me ez that word air jestice. The critter's fursaken."

"Fursaken or no fursaken, he ain't goin' ter be jailed fur nothin',—'ceptin' that the hand o' the Lord air laid too heavy on him. I can't lighten its weight. I'm mortial myself. The rider says thar's some holp in prayer. I hain't seen it yit, though I hev been toler'ble busy lately a-workin' in metal, one way an' another. What good air it goin' ter do the mounting ter hev 'Lijah jailed, stiddier goin' round the woods a-talkin' ter the grasshoppers an' squir'ls, ez seem ter actially know the critter, an' bein' ez happy ez they air, 'ceptin' when he gits it inter his noodle, like he sometimes do, ez he ain't edzactly like other folks be?" He paused. Those strange visitants trembled again upon his smoke-blackened lids. "Fursaken or no," he cried impulsively, "the man ez tries ter git him jailed will 'low ez he air fursaken his own self, afore I gits done with him!"

"'Vander Price," said the old woman rebukingly, "ye talk like ye hain't got good sense yerself." She sat down on a rock embedded in the ferns by Lost Creek, and pulled deliberately at her long cob-pipe. Then she too turned her faded eyes upon the vast landscape, in which she had seen no change, save the changing season and the waxing or the waning of the day, since first her life had opened upon it. That level line of pale blue in the poetic distance had become faintly roseate. The great bronze-green ranges nearer at hand were assuming a royal purple. Shadows went skulking down the valley. Across the amber zenith an eagle was flying homeward. Her mechanical glance followed the sweeping, majestic curves, as the bird dropped to its nest in the wild fastnesses of Pine Mountain, that towered, rugged and severe of outline, against the crimson west. A cow-bell jangled in the laurel.

"Old Suke's a-comin' home ez partic'lar an' percise ez ef she hed her calf thar yit. I hev traded Suke's calf ter my married daughter M'ria,—her ez married Amos Baker, in the Cove. The old brindle can't somehow onderstan' the natur' o' the bargain, an' kems up every night moo-ing, mighty disapp'inted. 'Twarn't much shakes of a calf, nohow, an' I stood toler'ble well arter the trade."

She looked up at the young man with a leer of self-gratulation. He still lingered, but the unsophisticated mother in the mountains can be as much an obstacle to anything in the nature of love-making, when the youth is not approved, as the expert tactician of a drawing-room. He had only the poor consolation of helping Cynthia to carry in the load of stiff, dry clothes to the log cabin, ambushed behind the beech-trees, hard by in the gorge. The house had a very unconfiding aspect; all its belongings seemed huddled about

11

it for safe-keeping. The beehives stood almost under the eaves; the ash-hopper was visible close in the rear; the rain-barrel affiliated with the damp wall; the chickens were going to roost in an althea bush beside the porch; the boughs of the cherry and plum and crab-apple trees were thickly interlaced above the path that led from the rickety rail fence, and among their roots flag-lilies, lark-spur, and devil-in-the-bush mingled in a floral mosaic. The old woman went through the gate first. But even this inadvertence could not profit the loitering young people. "Law, Cynthy," she exclaimed, pointing at a loose-jointed elderly mountaineer, who was seated beneath the hop vines on the little porch, while a gaunt gray mare, with the plow-gear still upon her, cropped the grass close by, "yander is yer daddy, ez empty ez a gourd, I 'll be bound! Hurry an' git supper, child. Time's a-wastin',—time's a-wastin'!"

When Evander was half-way up the steep slope, he turned and looked down at the embowered little house, that itself turned its face upward, looking as it were to the mountain's summit. How it nestled there in the gorge! He had seen it often and often before, but whenever he thought of it afterward it was as it appeared to him now: the darkling valley below it, the mountains behind it, the sunset sky still flaring above it, though stars had blossomed out here and there, and the sweet June night seemed full of their fragrance. He could distinguish for a good while the gate, the rickety fence, the path beneath the trees. The vista ended in the open door, with the broad flare of the fire illumining the puncheon floor and the group of boisterous tow-headed children; in the midst was the girl, with her bright hair and light figure, with her round arms bare, and her deft hand stirring the batter for bread in a wooden bowl. She looked the very genius of home, and so he long remembered her.

The door closed at last, and he slowly resumed his way along the steep slope. The scene that had just vanished seemed yet vividly present before him. The gathering gloom made less impression. He took scant heed of external objects, and plodded on mechanically. He was very near the forge when his senses were roused by some inexplicable inward monition. He stood still to listen: only the insects droning in the chestnut-oaks, only the wind astir in the laurel. The night possessed the earth. The mountains were sunk in an indistinguishable gloom, save where the horizontal line of their summits asserted itself against an infinitely clear sky. But for a hunter's horn, faintly wound and faintly echoed in Lost Creek Valley, he might have seemed the only human creature in all the vast wilderness. He saw through the pine boughs the red moon rising. The needles caught the glister, and shone like a golden fringe. They overhung dusky, angular shadows that he knew was the little shanty of a blacksmith shop. In its dark recesses was a dull red point of light, where the forge fire still smouldered. Suddenly it was momentarily eclipsed. Something had passed before it.

"'Lijah!" he called out, in vague alarm. There was no answer. The red spark now gleamed distinct.

"Look-a-hyar, boy, what be you-uns a-doin' of thar?" he asked, beset with a strange anxiety and a growing fear of he knew not what.

Still no answer.

It was a terrible weapon he had put into the idiot's hand that day,—that heavy sledge of his. He grew cold when he remembered poor Elijah's pleasure in useful work, in his great strength gone to waste, in the ponderous implement that he so lightly wielded. He might well have returned to-night, with some vague, distraught idea of handling it again. And what vague, distraught idea kept him skulking there with it?

13

"Foolin' along o' that new straw-cutter ter-day will be my ruin, I'm afeard," Evander muttered ruefully. Then the sudden drops broke out on his brow. "I pray ter mercy," he exclaimed fervently, "the boy hain't been a-sp'ilin' o' that thar new straw-cutter!"

This fear dominated all others. He strode hastily forward. "Come out o' thar, 'Lijah!" he cried roughly.

There were moving shadows in the great barn-like door,—three—four—The moon was behind the forge, and he could not count them. They were advancing shadows. A hand was laid upon his arm. A drawling voice broke languidly on the night. "I'm up an' down sorry ter hev ter arrest you-uns, 'Vander, bein' ez we air neighbors an' mos'ly toler'ble friendly; but law is law, an' ye air my prisoner," and the constable of the district paused in the exercise of his functions to gnaw off a chew of tobacco with teeth which seemed to have grown blunt in years of that practice; then he leisurely resumed: "I war jes' sayin' ter the sheriff an' dep'ty hyar,"—indicating the figures in the door-way,—"ez we-uns hed better lay low till we seen how many o' you-uns war out hyar; else I wouldn't hev kep' ye waitin' so long."

The young mountaineer's amazement at last expressed itself in words. "Ye hev surely los' yer senses, Jubal Tynes! What air ye arrestin' of me fur?"

"Fur receivin' of stolen goods,—the shed back yander air full of 'em. I dunno whether ye holped ter rob the cross-roads store or no; but yander's the goods in the shed o' the shop, an' Pete's been away two weeks, an' better; so 'twar obleeged ter be you-uns ez received 'em."

Evander, in a tumult of haste, told his story. The constable laughed lazily, with his quid between his teeth. "Mebbe so,—mebbe so; but that's fur the jedge an' jury ter study over. Them men never tuk thar kyart no furder. 'Twar never stuck in no quicksand in Lost Creek. They knowed the sheriff war on thar track, an' they stove up thar kyart, an' sent the spokes an' shafts an' sech a-driftin' down Lost Creek, thinkin' 'twould be swallered inter the mounting an' never be seen agin. But jes' whar Lost Creek sinks under the mounting the drift war cotched. We fund it thar, an' knowed ez all we hed ter do war ter trace 'em up Lost Creek. An' hyar we be! The goods hev been identified this very hour by the man ez owns 'em. I hope ye never holped ter burglarize the store, too; but 'tain't fur me ter say. Ye hev ter kem along o' we-uns, whether ye like it or no," and he laid a heavy hand on his prisoner's shoulder.

The next moment he was reeling from a powerful blow planted between the eyes. It even felled the stalwart constable, for it was so suddenly dealt. But Jubal Tynes was on his feet in an instant, rushing forward with a bull-like bellow. Once more he measured his length upon the ground,—close to the anvil this time, for the position of all the group had changed in the fracas. He did not rise again; the second blow was struck with the ponderous sledge. As the men hastened to lift him, they were much hindered by the ecstatic capers of the idiot brother, who seemed to have been concealed in the shop. The prisoner made no attempt at flight, although, in the confusion, he was forgotten for the time by the officers, and had some chance of escape. He appeared frightened and very meek; and when he saw that there was blood upon the sledge, and they said brains, too, he declared that he was sorry he had done it.

"*I* done it!" cried the idiot joyfully. "Jube sha'n't fight 'Vander! *I* done it!" and he was so boisterously grotesque and wild that the men lost their wits while he was about; so they turned him roughly out of the forge, and closed the doors upon him. At last he went away, although for a time

15

he beat loudly upon the shutter, and called piteously for Evander.

It was a great opportunity for old Dr. Patton, who lived six miles down the valley, and zealously he improved it. He often felt that in this healthful country, where he was born, and where bucolic taste and local attachment still kept him, he was rather a medical theorist than a medical practitioner, so few and slight were the demands upon the resources of his science. He was as one who has long pondered the unsuggestive details of the map of a region, and who suddenly sees before him its glowing, vivid landscape.

"A beautiful fracture!" he protested with rapture,—"a beautiful fracture!"

Through all the country-side were circulated his cheerful accounts of patients who had survived fracture of the skull. Among the simple mountaineers his learned talk of the trephine gave rise to the startling report that he intended to put a linchpin into Jubal Tynes's head. It was rumored, too, that the unfortunate man's brains had "in an' about leaked haffen out;" and many freely prompted Providence by the suggestion that "ef Jube war ready ter die it war high time he war taken," as, having been known as a hasty and choleric man, it was predicted that he would "make a most survigrus idjit."

"Cur'ous enough ter me ter find out ez Jube ever hed brains," commented Mrs. Ware. "'Twar well enough ter let some of 'em leak out ter prove it. He hev never showed he hed brains no other way, ez I knows on. Now," she added, "somebody oughter tap 'Vander's head, an' mebbe they'll find him pervided, too. Wonders will never cease! Nobody would hev accused Jube o' sech. Folks'll hev ter respec' them brains. 'Vander done him that favior in splitting his head open."

"'Twarn't 'Vander's deed!" Cynthia declared passionately. She reiterated this phrase a hundred times a day, as she went about her household tasks. "'Twarn't 'Vander's deed!" How could she prove that it was not, she asked herself as often,— and prove that against his own word?

For she herself had heard him acknowledge the crime. The new day had hardly broken when, driving her cow, she came by the blacksmith's shop, all unconscious as yet of the tragedy it had housed. A vague prescience of dawn was on the landscape; dim and spectral, it stood but half revealed in the doubtful light. The stars were gone; even the sidereal outline of the great Scorpio had crept away. But the gibbous moon still swung above the dark and melancholy forests of Pine Mountain, and its golden chalice spilled a dreamy glamour all adown the lustrous mists in Lost Creek Valley. Ever and anon the crags reverberated with the shrill clamor of a watch-dog at a cabin in the Cove; for there was an unwonted stir upon the mountain's brink. The tramp of horses, the roll of wheels, the voices of the officers at the forge, busily canvassing their preparations for departure, sounded along the steeps. The sight of the excited group was as phenomenal to old Suke as to Cynthia, and the cow stopped short in her shambling run, and turned aside into the blooming laurel with a muttered low and with crouching horns. Early wayfarers along the road had been attracted by the unusual commotion. A rude slide drawn by a yoke of oxen stood beneath the great pine that overhung the forge, while the driver was breathlessly listening to the story from the deputy sheriff. A lad, mounted on a lank gray mare, let the sorry brute crop, unrebuked, the sassafras leaves by the wayside, while he turned half round in his saddle, with a white horror on his face, to see the spot pointed out on which Jubal Tynes had fallen. The wounded man had been removed to the nearest house, but the ground was still dank with blood, and this heightened the dramatic effects of the

17

recital. The sheriff's posse and their horses were picturesquely grouped about the open barn-like door, and the wagon laden with the plunder stood hard by. It had been discovered, when they were on the point of departure, that one of the animals had cast a shoe, and the prisoner was released that he might replace it.

When Evander kindled the forge fire he felt that it was for the last time. The heavy sighing of the bellows burst forth, as if charged with a conscious grief. As the fire alternately flared and faded, it illumined with long, evanescent red rays the dusky interior of the shop: the horseshoes hanging upon a rod in the window, the plowshares and bars of iron ranged against the wall, the barrel of water in the corner, the smoky hood and the anvil, the dark spot on the ground, and the face of the blacksmith himself, as he worked the bellows with one hand, while the other held the tongs with the red-hot horseshoe in the fire. It was a pale face. Somehow, all the old spirit seemed spent. Its wonted suggestions of a dogged temper and latent fierceness were effaced. It bore marks of patient resignation, that might have been wrought by a life-time of self-sacrifice, rather than by one imperious impulse, as potent as it was irrevocable. The face appeared in some sort sublimated.

The bellows ceased to sigh, the anvil began to sing, the ringing staccato of the hammer punctuated the droning story of the deputy sheriff, still rehearsing the sensation of the hour to the increasing crowd about the door. The girl stood listening, half hidden in the blooming laurel. Her senses seemed strangely sharpened, despite the amazement, the incredulity, that possessed her. She even heard the old cow cropping the scanty grass at her feet, and saw every casual movement of the big brindled head. She was conscious of the splendid herald of a new day flaunting in the east. Against this gorgeous presence of crimson and gold, brightening and brightening till only the rising sun could outdazzle it, she noted the romantic outlines of the Cumberland crags and woody heights, and marveled how near they appeared. She was sensible of the fragrance of the dewy azaleas, and she heard the melancholy song of the pines, for the wind was astir. She marked the grimaces of the idiot, looking like a dim and ugly dream in the dark recesses of the forge. His face was filled now with strange, wild triumph, and now with partisan anger for his brother's sake; for Evander was more than once harshly upbraided.

"An' so yer tantrums hev brung ye ter this eend, at last, 'Vander Price!" exclaimed an old man indignantly. "I misdoubted ye when I hearn how ye fit, that day, yander ter the mill; an' they do say ez even Pete Blenkins air plumb afeard ter jaw at ye, nowadays, on 'count o' yer fightin' an' quar'lin' ways. An' now ye hev gone an' bodaciously slaughtered pore Jubal Tynes! From what I hev hearn tell, I jedge he air obleeged ter die. Then nothin' kin save ye!"

The girl burst suddenly forth from the flowering splendors of the laurel. "'Twarn't 'Vander's deed!" she cried, perfect faith in every tone. "'Vander, 'Vander, who did it? Who did it?" she reiterated imperiously.

Her cheeks were aflame. An eager expectancy glittered in her wide brown eyes. Her auburn hair flaunted to the breeze as brilliantly as those golden harbingers of the sun. Her bonnet had fallen to the ground, and her milk-piggin was rolling away. The metallic staccato of the hammer was silenced. A vibratory echo trembled for an instant on the air. The group had turned in slow surprise. The blacksmith looked mutely at her. But the idiot was laughing triumphantly, almost sanely, and pointing at the sledge to call her attention to its significant stains. The sheriff had laid the implement carefully aside, that it might be produced in court in case Jubal Tynes should pass beyond the point of affording, for

Dr. Patton's satisfaction, a gratifying instance of survival from fracture of the skull, and die in a commonplace fashion which is of no interest to the books or the profession.

"'Twarn't 'Vander's deed! It *couldn't* be!" she declared passionately.

For the first time he faltered. There was a pause. He could not speak.

"*I* done it!" cried the idiot, in shrill glee.

Then Evander regained his voice. "'Twar me ez done it," he said huskily, turning away to the anvil with a gesture of dull despair. "*I* done it!"

Fainting is not a common demonstration in the mountains. It seemed to the bewildered group as if the girl had suddenly dropped dead. She revived under the water and cinders dashed into her face from the barrel where the steel was tempered. But life returned enfeebled and vapid. That vivid consciousness and intensity of emotion had reached a climax of sensibility, and now she experienced the reaction. It was in a sort of lethargy that she watched their preparations to depart, while she sat upon a rock at the verge of the clearing. As the wagon trundled away down the road, laden with the stolen goods, one of the posse looked back at her with some compassion, and observed to a companion that she seemed to take it considerably to heart, and sagely opined that she and 'Vander "must hev been a-keepin' company tergether some. But then," he argued, "she's a downright good-lookin' gal, ef she do be so red-headed. An' thar air plenty likely boys left in the mountings yit; an' ef thar ain't, she can jes' send down the valley a piece fur me!" and he laughed, and went away quite cheerful, despite his compassion. The horsemen were in frantic impatience to be off, and presently they were speeding in single file along the sandy mountain road.

Cynthia sat there until late in the day, wistfully gazing down the long green vista where they had disappeared. She could not believe that Evander had really gone. Something, she felt sure, would happen to bring them back. Once and again she thought she heard the beat of hoofs,—of distant hoofs. It was only the melancholy wind in the melancholy pines.

They were laden with snow before she heard aught of him. Beneath them, instead of the dusky vistas the summer had explored, were long reaches of ghastly white undulations, whence the boles rose dark and drear. The Cumberland range, bleak and bare, with its leafless trees and frowning cliffs, stretched out long, parallel spurs, one above another, one beyond another, tier upon tier, till they appeared to meet in one distant level line somewhat grayer than the gray sky, somewhat more desolate of aspect than all the rest of the desolate world. When the wind rose, Pine Mountain mourned with a mighty voice. Cynthia had known that voice since her birth. But what new meaning in its threnody! Sometimes the forest was dumb; the sun glittered frigidly, and the pines, every tiny needle encased in ice, shone like a wilderness of gleaming rays. The crags were begirt with gigantic icicles; the air was crystalline and cold, and the only sound was the clinking of the hand-hammer and the clanking of the sledge from the forge on the mountain's brink. For there was a new striker there, of whom Pete Blenkins did not stand in awe. He felt peculiarly able to cope with the world in general since his experience had been enriched by a recent trip to Sparta. He had been subpoenaed by the prosecution in the case of the State of Tennessee versus Evander Price, to tell the jury all he knew of the violent temper of his quondam striker, which he did with much gusto and self-importance, and pocketed his fee with circumspect dignity.

"'Vander looks toler'ble skimpy an' jail-bleached,—so Pete Blenkins say," remarked Mrs. Ware, as she sat smoking her pipe in the chimney corner, while Cynthia stood before the warping bars, winding the party-colored yarn upon the equidistant pegs of the great frame. "Pete 'lowed ter me ez he hed tole you-uns ez 'Vander say he air powerful sorry he would never l'arn ter write, when he went ter the school at the Notch. 'Vander say he never knowed ez he would have a use for sech. But law! the critter hed better be studyin' 'bout the opportunities he hev wasted fur grace; fur they say now ez Jube Tynes air bound ter die. An' he will fur true, ef old Dr. Patton air the man I take him fur."

"'T warn't 'Vander's deed," said Cynthia, her practiced hands still busily investing the warping bars with a homely rainbow of scarlet and blue and saffron yarn. It added an embellishment to the little room, which was already bright with the firelight and the sunset streaming in at the windows, and the festoons of red pepper and pop-corn and peltry swinging from the rafters.

"Waal, waal, hev it so," said her mother, in acquiescent dissent,—"hev it so! But 't war his deed receivin' of the stolen goods; leastwise, the jury b'lieved so. Pete say, though, ez they wouldn't hev been so sure, ef it warn't fur 'Vander's resistin' arrest an' in an' about haffen killin' Jubal Tynes. Pete say ez 'Vander's name fur fightin' an' sech seemed ter hev sot the jury powerful agin him."

"An' thar war nobody thar ez would gin a good word fur him!" cried the girl, dropping her hands with a gesture of poignant despair.

"'T warn't in reason ez thar could be," said Mrs. Ware. "'Vander's lawyer never summonsed but a few of the slack-jawed boys from the Settlemint ter prove his good character, an' Pete said they 'peared awk'ard in thar minds an' flustrated, an' spoke more agin 'Vander 'n fur him. Pete 'lows

22

ez they hed ter be paid thar witness-fee by the State, too, on account of 'Vander hevin' no money ter fetch witnesses an' sech ter Sparty. His dad an' mam air mighty shiftless— always war,—an' they hev got that hulking idjit ter eat 'em out'n house an' home. They hev been mightily put ter it this winter ter live along, 'thout 'Vander ter holp 'em, like he uster. But they war no ways anxious 'bout his trial, 'kase Squair Bates tole 'em ez the jedge would app'int a lawyer ter defend 'Vander, ez he hed no money ter hire a lawyer fur hisself. An' the jedge app'inted a young lawyer thar; an' Pete 'lowed ez that young lawyer made the trial the same ez a gander-pullin' fur the 'torney-gineral. Pete say ez that young lawyer's ways tickled the 'torney-gineral haffen ter death. Pete say the 'torney-gineral jes' sot out ter devil that young lawyer, an' he done it. Pete say the young lawyer hed never hed more 'n one or two cases afore, an' he acted so foolish that the 'torney-gineral kep' all the folks laffin' at him. The jury laffed, an' so did the jedge. I reckon 'Vander thought 'twar mighty pore fun. Pete say ez 'Vander's lawyer furgot a heap ez he oughter hev remembered, an' fairly ruined 'Vander's chances. Arter the trial the 'torney-gineral 'lowed ter Pete ez the State hed hed a mighty shaky case agin 'Vander. But I reckon he jes' said that ter make his own smartness in winnin' it seem more s'prisn'. 'Vander war powerful interrupted by thar laffin' an' the game they made o' his lawyer, an' said he didn't want no appeal. He 'lowed he hed seen enough o' jestice. He 'lowed ez he'd take the seven years in the pen'tiary that the jury gin him, fur fear at the nex' trial they'd gin him twenty-seven; though the 'torney-gineral say ef Jube dies they will fetch him out agin, an' try him fur that. The 'torney-gineral 'lowed ter Pete ez 'Vander war a fool not ter move fur a new trial an' appeal, an' sech. He 'lowed ez 'Vander war a derned ignorant man. An' all the folks round the court-house gin thar opinion ez 'Vander hev got less gumption 'bout'n the law o' the land than enny man

23

they ever see, 'cept that young lawyer he hed ter defend him. Pete air powerful sati'fied with *his* performin' in Sparty. He ups an' 'lows ez they paid him a dollar a day fur a witness-fee, an' treated him mighty perlite,—the jedge an' jury too."

How Cynthia lived through that winter of despair was a mystery to her afterward. Often, as she sat brooding over the midnight embers, she sought to picture to herself some detail of the life that Evander was leading so far away. The storm would beat heavily on the roof of the log cabin, the mountain wind sob through the sighing pines; ever and anon a wolf might howl in the sombre depths of Lost Creek Valley. But Evander had become a stranger to her imagination. She could not construct even a vague *status* that would answer for the problematic mode of life of the "valley folks" who dwelt in Nashville, or in the penitentiary hard by. She began to appreciate that it was a narrow existence within the limits of Lost Creek Valley, and that to its simple denizens the world beyond was a foreign world, full of strange habitudes and alien complications. Thus it came to pass that he was no longer even a vision. Because of this subtle bereavement she would fall to sobbing drearily beside the dreary, dying fire,—only because of this, for she never wondered if her image to him had also grown remote. How she pitied him, so lonely, so strange, so forlorn, as he must be! Did he yearn for the mountains? Could he see them in the spirit? Surely in his dreams, surely in some kindly illusion, he might still behold that fair land which touched the sky: the golden splendors of the sunshine sifting through the pines; flying shadows of clouds as fleet racing above the distant ranges; untrodden woodland nooks beside singing cascades; or some lonely pool, whence the gray deer bounded away through the red sumach leaves.

Sombre though the present was, the future seemed darker still, clouded by the long and terrible suspense concerning the wounded officer's fate and the crime that Evander had acknowledged.

"He *couldn't* hev done it," she argued futilely. "'Twarn't his deed."

She grew pale and thin, and her strength failed with her failing spirit, and her mother querulously commented on the change.

"An' sech a hard winter ez we-uns air a-tus-slin' with; an' that thar ewe a-dyin' ez M'ria traded fur my little calf, ez war wuth forty sech dead critters; an' hyar be Cynthy lookin' like she hed fairly pegged out forty year ago, an' been raised from the grave,—an' all jes' 'kase 'Vander Price hev got ter be a evil man, an' air locked up in the pen'tiary. It beats my time! He never said nothin' 'bout marryin', nohow, ez I knows on. I never would hev b'lieved you-uns would hev turned off Jeemes Blake, ez hev got a good grist-mill o' his own an' a mighty desirable widder-woman fur a mother, jes' account of 'Vander Price. An' 'Vander will never kem back ter Pine Mounting no more'n Lost Creek will."

Cynthia's color flared up for a moment. Then she sedately replied, "I hev tole Jeemes Blake, and I hev tole you-uns, ez I count on livin' single."

"I'll be bound ye never tole 'Vander that word!" cried the astute old woman. "Waal, waal, waal!" she continued, in exclamatory disapproval, as she leaned to the fire and scooped up a live coal into the bowl of her pipe, "a gal is a aggervatin' contrivance, ennyhow, in the world! But I jes' up an' tole Jeemes ez ye hed got ter lookin' so peaked an' mournful, like some critter ez war shot an' creepin' away ter die somewhar, an' he hedn't los' much, arter all." She puffed vigorously at her pipe; then, with a change of tone, "An' Jeemes air mighty slack-jawed ter his elders, too! He tuk me up ez sharp. He 'lowed ez he hed no fault ter find with yer looks. He said ye war pritty enough fur him. Then my dander riz, an' I spoke up, an' says, 'Mebbe so, Jeemes, mebbe so, fur ye air in no wise pritty yerself.' An' then he gin me no more of his jaw, but arter he hed sot a while longer he said, 'Far'well,' toler'ble perlite, an' put out."

After a long time the snow slipped gradually from the mountain top, and the drifts in the deep abysses melted, and heavy rains came on. The mists clung, shroud-like, to Pine Mountain. The distant ranges seemed to withdraw themselves into indefinite space, and for weeks Cynthia was bereft of their familiar presence. Myriads of streamlets, channeling the gullies and swirling among the bowlders, were flowing down the steeps to join Lost Creek, on its way to its mysterious sepulchre beneath the mountains.

And at last the spring opened. A vivid green tipped the sombre plumes of the pines. The dull gray mists etherealized to a silver gauze, and glistened above the mellowing landscape. The wild cherry was blooming far and near. From the summit of the mountain could be seen for many a mile the dirt-road in the valley,—a tawny streak of color on every hilltop, or winding by every fallow field and rocky slope. A wild, new hope was suddenly astir in Cynthia's heart; a new energy fired her blood. It may have been only the recuperative power of youth asserting itself. To her it was as if she had heard the voice of the Lord; and she arose and followed it.

II.

Following the voice of the Lord, Cynthia took her way along a sandy bridle-path that penetrates the dense forests of Pine Mountain. The soft spring wind, fluttering in beneath her sun-bonnet, found the first wild-rose blooming on her thin cheek. A new light shone like a steadfast star in her deep brown eyes. "I hev took a-holt," she said resolutely, "an' I'll never gin it up. 'Twarn't his deed, an' I'll prove that, agin his own word. I dunno how,—but I'll prove it."

The woods seemed to open at last, for the brink of the ridge was close at hand. As the trees were marshaled down the steep declivity, she could see above their heads the wide and splendid mountain landscape, with the benediction of the spring upon it, with the lofty peace of the unclouded sky above it, with an impressive silence pervading it that was akin to a holy solemnity.

There was a rocky, barren slope to the left, and among the brambly ledges sheep were feeding. As the flock caught her attention she experienced a certain satisfaction. "They hed sheep in the Lord's life-time," she observed. "He gins a word 'bout'n them more'n enny other critter."

And she sat down on a rock, among the harmless creatures, and was less lonely and forlorn.

A little log house surmounted the slope. It was quaintly awry, like most of the mountaineers' cabins, and the ridgepole, with its irregularly projecting clapboards serrating the sky behind it, described a negligently oblique line. Its clay chimney had a leaning tendency, and was propped to its duty by a long pole. There was a lofty martin-house, whence the birds whirled fitfully. The rail fence inclosing the dooryard was only a few steps from the porch. There rested the genial afternoon sunshine. It revealed the spinning-wheel that stood near the wall; the shelf close to the door, with a pail of water and a gourd for the incidentally thirsty; the idle churn, its dasher on another shelf to dry; a rooster strutting familiarly in at the open door; and a newly hatched brood picking about among the legs of the splint-bottomed chairs, under the guidance of a matronly old "Dominicky hen." In one of the chairs sat a man, emaciated, pallid, swathed in many gay-colored quilts, and piping querulously in a high, piercing key to a worn and weary woman, who came to the fence and looked down the hill as he feebly pointed.

"Cynthy—Cynthy Ware!" she called out, "air that you-uns?"

Cynthia hesitated, then arose and went forward a few steps. "It be me," she said, as if making an admission.

"Kem up hyar. Jube's wantin' ter know why ye hain't been hyar ter inquire arter him." The woman waited at the gate, and opened it for her visitor. She looked hardly less worn and exhausted than the broken image of a man in the chair. "Jube counts up every critter in the mountings ez kems ter inquire arter him," she added, in a lower voice. "'Pears-like ter me ez it air about time fur worldly pride ter hev loosed a-holt on him; but Satan kin foster guile whar thar ain't enough life left fur nuthin' else, an' pore Jube hev never been so gin over ter the glory o' this world ez now."

"He 'pears ter be gittin' on some," said the girl, although she hardly recognized in the puny, pallid apparition among the muffling quilts the bluff and hale mountaineer she had known.

"Fust-rate!" weakly piped out the constable. "I eat a haffen pone o' bread fur dinner!" Then he turned querulously to his wife: "Jane Elmiry, ain't ye goin' ter git me that thar fraish aig ter whip up in whiskey, like the doctor said?"

"'T ain't time yit, Jube," replied the patient wife. "The doctor 'lowed ez the aig must be spang fraish; an' ez old Topknot lays ter the minit every day, I'm a-waitin' on her."

The wasted limbs under the quilts squirmed around vivaciously. "An' yander's the darned critter," he cried, spying old Topknot leisurely pecking about under a lilac bush, "a-feedin' around ez complacent an' sati'fied ez ef I warn't a-settin' hyar waitin' on her lazy bones! Cynthy, I'm jes' a-honing arter suthin' ter eat all the time, an' that's what makes me 'low ez I'm gittin' well; though Jane Elmiry"—he glared fiercely at his meek wife, "hev somehows los' her knack at cookin', an' sometimes I can't eat my vittles when they air fetched ter me."

He fell back in his chair, his tangled, over-grown hair hardly distinguishable from his tangled, over-grown beard. His eyes roved restlessly about the quiet landscape. A mist was gathering over the eastern ranges; shot with the sunlight, it was but a silken and filmy suggestion of vapor. A line of vivid green in the valley marked the course of Lost Creek by the willows and herbage fringing its banks. A gilded bee, with a languorous drone, drifted in and out of the little porch, and the shadow of the locust above it was beginning to lengthen. The tree was in bloom, and Cynthia picked up a fallen spray as she sat down on the step. He glanced casually at her; then, with the egotism of an invalid, his mind reverted to himself.

"Why hain't ye been hyar ter inquire arter me, Cynthy,—you-uns, or yer dad, or yer mam, or somebody? I hain't been lef' ter suffer, though, 'thout folkses axin' arter me, I tell ye! The miller hev been hyar day arter day. Baker Teal, what keeps the store yander ter the Settlemint, hev rid over reg'lar. Tom Peters kems ez sartain ez the sun. An' the jestice o' the peace"—he winked weakly in triumph, "Squair Bates—hev been hyar nigh on ter wunst a week. The sheriff or one o' the dep'ties hain't been sca'ce round hyar, nuther. An' some other folkses—I name no names—sends me all the liquor I kin drink from a still ez they say grows in a hollow rock round hyar somewhar. They sends me all I kin drink, an' Jane Elmiry, too. I don't want but a little, but Jane Elmiry air a tremenjious toper, ye know!" He laughed in a shrill falsetto at his joke, and his wife smiled, but faintly, for she realized the invalid's pleasant mood was brief. "Ef I hed a-knowed how pop'lar I be, I'd hev run fur jestice o' the peace stiddier constable. But nex' time thar'll be a differ; that hain't the las' election this world will ever see, Cynthy." Then, as his eyes fell upon her once more, he remembered his question. "Why n't ye been hyar ter inquire arter me?"

The girl was confused by his changed aspect, his eager, restless talk, his fierce girding at his patient wife, and lost what scanty tact she might have otherwise claimed.

"The folkses ez rid by hyar tole us how ye be a-gittin' on. An' we-uns 'lowed ez mebbe ye wouldn't want ter see us, bein' ez we war always sech friends with 'Vander, an'"—

The woman stopped her by a hasty gesture and a look of terror. They did not escape the invalid's notice.

"What ails ye, Jane Elmiry?" he cried, angrily. "Ye act like ye war *de*stracted!"

A sudden fit of coughing impeded his utterance, and gave his wife the opportunity for a whispered aside. "He ain't spoke 'Vander's name sence he war hurt. The doctor said he warn't ter talk about his a-gittin' hurt, an' the man ez done it. The doctor 'lowed 't would fever him an' put him out'n his head, an' he must jes' think 'bout'n gittin' well all the time, an' sech."

Jubal Tynes had recovered his voice and his temper. "I hain't got no grudge agin' 'Vander," he declared, in his old, bluff way, "nur 'Vander's friends, nuther. It air jes' that dad-burned idjit, 'Lijah, ez I *de*spise. Jane Elmiry, ain't that old Topknot ez I hear a-cack-lin'? Waal, waal, sir, dad-burn that thar lazy, idle poultry! Air she a-stalkin' round the yard yit? Go, Jane Elmiry, an' see whar she be. Ef she ain't got sense enough ter git on her nest an lay a aig when desirable, she hain't got sense enough ter keep out'n a chicken pie."

"I mought skeer her off'n her nest," his wife remonstrated.

30

But the imperious invalid insisted. She rose reluctantly, and as she stepped off the porch she cast an imploring glance at Cynthia.

The girl was trembling. The mere mention of the deed to its victim had unnerved her. She felt it was perhaps a safe transition from the subject to talk about the idiot brother. "I hev hearn folks 'low ez 'Lijah oughter be locked up, but I dunno," she said.

The man fixed a concentrated gaze upon her. "Waal, ain't he?"

"'Lijah ain't locked up," she faltered, bewildered.

His face fell. Unaccountably enough, his pride seemed grievously cut down.

"Waal, 'Lijah ain't 'sponsible, I know," he reasoned; "but bein' ez he treated me this way, an' me a important off'cer o' the law, 'pears-like 'twould a-been more respec'ful ef they hed committed him ter jail ez insane, or sent him ter the 'sylum,—fur they take some crazies at the State's expense." He paused thoughtfully. He was mortified, hurt. "But shucks!" he exclaimed presently, "let him treat haffen the county ez he done me, ef he wants ter. I ain't a-keerin'."

Cynthia's head was awhirl. She could hardly credit her senses.

"How war it that 'Lijah treated you-uns?" she gasped.

In his turn he stared, amazed.

"Cynthy, 'pears-like ye hev los' yer mind! How did 'Lijah treat me? Waal, 'Lijah whacked me on the head with his brother's sledge, an' split my skull, an' the folks say some o' my brains oozed out. I hev got more of 'em now, though, than ye hev. Ye look plumb bereft. What ails the gal?"

31

"Air ye sure—sure ez that war the happening of it?—kase 'Vander tells a differ. He 'lowed ez 't war *him* ez hit ye with the sledge. An' nobody suspicioned 'Lijah."

Jubal Tynes looked very near death now. His pallid face was framed in long elf-locks; he thrust his head forward, till his emaciated throat and neck were distinctly visible; his lower jaw dropped in astonishment.

"God A'mighty!" he ejaculated, "why hev 'Vander tole sech a lie? *Sure!* Why, I *seen* 'Lijah! 'Vander never teched the sledge. An' 'Vander never teched me."

"Ye hev furgot, mebbe," she urged, feverishly. "'T war in the dark."

"Listen at the gal argufyin' with me!" he exclaimed, angrily. "I *seen* 'Lijah, I tell ye, in the light o' the forge fire. 'T war n't more 'n a few coals, but ez 'Lijah swung his arm it fanned the fire, an' it lept up. I seen his face in the glow, an' the sledge in his hand. 'Lijah war hid a-hint the hood. 'Vander war t' other side o' the anvil. I gripped with 'Lijah. I seen him plain. He hit me twict. I never los' my senses till the second lick. Then I drapped. What ails 'Vander, ter tell sech a lie? Ef I hed a-died, stiddier gittin' well so powerful peart, they'd hev hung him, sure."

"Mebbe he thought they'd hang 'Lijah!" she gasped, appalled at the magnitude of the sacrifice.

"'Lijah ain't 'sponsible ter the law," said Jubal Tynes, with his magisterial aspect, "bein' ez he air a ravin' crazy, ez oughter be locked up."

"I reckon 'Vander never knowed ez that war true," she rejoined, reflectively. "The 'torney-gineral tole Pete Blenkins, when 'Vander war convicted of receivin' of stolen goods, ez how 'Vander war toler'ble ignorant, an' knowed powerful little 'bout the law o' the land. He done it, I reckon, ter pertect the idjit."

Jubal Tynes made no rejoinder. He had fallen back in his chair, so frail, so exhausted by the unwonted excitement, that she was alarmed anew, realizing how brief his time might be.

"Jubal Tynes," she said, leaning forward and looking up at him imploringly, "ef I war ter tell what ye hev tole me, nobody would believe me, 'kase—'kase 'Vander an' me hev kep' company some. Hedn't ye better tell it ter the Squair ez how 'Vander never hit ye, but said he did, ter git the blame shet o' the idjit 'Lijah, ez ain't 'sponsible, nohows? Ain't thar no way ter make it safe fur 'Vander? They 'lowed he wouldn't hev been convicted of receivin' of stolen goods 'ceptin' fur the way the jury thought he behaved 'bout resistin' arrest an' hittin' ye with the sledge."

The sick man's eyes were aflame. "Ye 'low ez I'm goin' ter die, Cynthy Ware!" he cried, with sudden energy. "I'll gin ye ter onderstand ez I feel ez strong ez a ox! I won't do nuthin' fur 'Vander. Let him stand or fall by the lie he hev tole! I feel ez solid ez Pine Mounting! I won't do nuthin' ez ef I war a-goin' ter die,—like ez ef I war a chicken with the pip—an' whar air that ole hen ez war nominated ter lay a aig, ter whip up in whiskey, an' ain't done it?"

A sudden wild cackling broke upon the air. The red rooster, standing by the gate, stretched up his long neck to listen, and lifted his voice in jubilant sympathy. Jubal Tynes looked around at Cynthia with a laugh. Then his brow darkened, and his mind reverted to his refusal.

"Ye jes' onderstand," he reiterated, "ez I won't do nuthin' like ez ef I war goin' ter die."

She got home as best she could, weeping and wringing her hands much of the way, feeling baffled and bruised, and aghast at the terrible perplexities that crowded about her.

Jubal Tynes had a bad night. He was restless and fretful, and sometimes, when he had been still for a while, and seemed about to sink into slumber, he would start up abruptly, declaring that he could not "git shet of studying 'bout 'n 'Vander, an' 'Lijah, an' the sledge," and violently wishing that Cynthia Ware had died before she ever came interrupting him about 'Vander, and 'Lijah, and the sledge. Toward morning exhaustion prevailed. He sank into a deep, dreamless sleep, from which he woke refreshed and interested in the matter of breakfast.

That day a report went the excited rounds of the mountain that he had made a sworn statement before Squire Bates, denying that Evander Price had resisted arrest, exonerating him of all connection with the injuries supposed to have been received at his hands, and inculpating only the idiot Elijah. This was supplemented by Dr. Patton's affidavit as to his patient's mental soundness and responsibility.

It roused Cynthia's flagging spirit to an ecstasy of energy. Her strength was as fictitious as the strength of delirium, but it sufficed. Opposition could not baffle it. Obstacles but multiplied its expedients. She remembered that the trained and astute attorney for the State had declared to Pete Blenkins, after the trial, that the prosecution had no case against Evander Price for receiving stolen goods, and must have failed but for the prejudice of the jury. It was proved to them by his own confession that he had resisted arrest and assaulted the officer of the law, and circumstantial evidence had a light task, with this auxiliary, to establish other charges. Now, she thought, if the jury that convicted him, the judge that sentenced him, and the governor of the State were cognizant of this stupendous self-sacrifice to

34

fraternal affection, could they, would they, still take seven years of his life from him? At least, they should know of it,—she had resolved on that. She hardly appreciated the difficulty of the task before her. She was densely ignorant. She lived in a primitive community. Such a paper as a petition for executive clemency had never been drawn within its experience. She could not have discovered that this proceeding was practicable, except for the pride of office and legal lore of Jubal Tynes. He joyed in displaying his learning; but beyond the fact that such a paper was possible, and sometimes successful, and that she had better see the lawyer at the Settlement about it, he suggested nothing of value. And so she tramped a matter of ten miles along the heavy, sandy road, through the dense and lonely woods; and weary, but flushed with joyous hope, she came upon the surprised lawyer at the Settlement. This was a man who built the great structure of justice upon a foundation of fees. He listened to her, noted the poverty of her aspect, and recommended her to secure the coöperation of the convict's immediate relatives. And so, patiently back again, along the dank and darkening mountain road.

The home of her lover was not an inviting abode. When she had turned from the thoroughfare into a vagrant, irresponsible-looking path, winding about in the depths of the forest, it might have seemed that in a group which presently met her eyes, the animals were the more emotional, alert, and intelligent element. The hounds came huddling over the rickety fence, and bounded about her in tumultuous recognition. An old sow, with a litter of shrill soprano pigs, started up from a clump of weeds, in maternal anxiety and doubt of the intruder's intentions. The calf peered between the rails in mild wonder at this break in the monotony. An old man sat motionless on the fence, with as sober and business-like an aspect as if he did it for a salary. The porch was occupied by an indiscriminate collection of

35

household effects,—cooking utensils, garments, broken chairs,—and an untidy, disheveled woman. An old crone, visible within the door, was leisurely preparing the evening meal. Cynthia's heart warmed at the sight of the familiar place. The tears started to her sympathetic eyes. "I hev kem ter tell ye all 'bout'n 'Vander!" she cried impulsively, when she was welcomed to a chair and a view of the weed-grown "gyarden-spot."

But the disclosure of her scheme did not waken responsive enthusiasm. The old man, still dutifully riding the fence, conservatively declared that the law of the land was a "mighty tetchy contrivance," and he didn't feel called on to meddle with it. "They mought jail the whole fambly, ez fur ez I know, an' then who would work the gyarden-spot, ez air thrivin' now, an' the peas fullin' up cornsider'ble?"

Mrs. Price had "no call ter holp sot the law on 'Lijah agin 'Vander's word. I dunno what the folks would do ter 'Lijah ef Jube died, sence he hev swore ez he hev done afore Squair Bates. Some tole me ez 'Lijah air purtected by bein' a idjit but I ain't sati'fied 'bout'n that. 'Lijah war sane enough ter be toler'ble skeered when he hearn bout'n it all, an' hev tuk ter shettin' hisself up in the shed-room when strangers kem about." And indeed Cynthia had an unpleasant impression that the idiot was looking out suspiciously at her from a crack in the door, but he precipitately slammed it when she turned her head to make sure. The old crone paused in her preparations for supper, that she might apply all her faculties to argument. "It don't 'pear ter reason how the gov'nor will pardon 'Vander fur receivin' of stolen goods jes' 'kase 't warn't him ez bruk Jube Tynes's head," she declared. "Vander war jailed fur *receivin' stolen goods*,—nobody never keered nothin' fur Jube Tynes's head! *I* hev knowed the Tynes fambly time out'n mind," she continued, raising her voice in shrill contempt. "I knowed Jubal Tynes, an' his daddy afore him. An' now ter kem talkin' ter me 'bout the gov'nor o' Tennessee keerin' fur Jube Tynes's nicked head. *I* don't keer nothin' 'bout Jube Tynes's nicked head; an' let 'em tell the gov'nor that fur *me*, an' see what he will think then!"

Poor Cynthia! It had never occurred to her to account herself gifted beyond her fellows and her opportunities. The simple events of their primitive lives had never before elicited the contrast. It gave her no satisfaction. She only experienced a vague, miserable wonder that she should have perceptions beyond their range of vision, should be susceptible of emotions which they could never share. She realized that she could get no material aid here, and she went away at last without asking for it.

Her little all was indeed little,—a few chickens, some "spun-truck," a sheep that she had nursed from an orphaned lamb, a "cag" of apple-vinegar, and a bag of dried fruit,—but it had its value to the mountain lawyer; and when he realized that this was indeed "all" he drew the petition in consideration thereof, and appended the affidavits of Jubal Tynes and Dr. Patton.

"She ain't got a red head on her for nothin'," he said to himself, in admiration of her astuteness in insisting that, as a part of his services, he should furnish her with a list of the jury that convicted Evander Price.

"For every man of 'em hev got ter sot his name ter that thar petition," she averred.

He even offered, when his energy and interest were aroused, to take the paper with him to Sparta when he next attended circuit court. There, he promised, he would secure some influential signatures from the members of the bar and other prominent citizens.

When she was fairly gone he forgot his energy and interest. He kept the paper three months. He did not once offer it for a signature. And when she demanded its return, it was mislaid, lost.

Oratory is a legal requisite in that region. He might have taken some fine points from her unconscious eloquence, inspired by love and grief and despair, her scathing arraignment of his selfish neglect, her upbraidings and alternate appeals. It overwhelmed him, in some sort, and yet he was roused into activity unusual enough to revive the lost document. She went away with it, leaving him in rueful meditation. "She *hain't* got a red head on her for nothin'," he said, remembering her pungent rhetoric.

But as he glanced out of the door, and saw her trudging down the road, all her grace and pliant swaying languor lost in convulsive, awkward haste and a feeble, jerky gait, he laughed.

For poor Cynthia had become in some sort a grotesque figure. Only Time can pose a crusader to picturesque advantage. The man or woman with a great and noble purpose carries about with it a pitiful little personality that reflects none of its lustre. Cynthia's devotion, her courage, her endurance in righting this wrong, were not so readily apparent when, in the valley, she went tramping from one juror's house to another's as were her travel-stained garments, her wild, eager eye, her incoherent, anxious speech, her bare, swollen feet,—for sometimes she was fain to carry her coarse shoes in her hands for relief in the long journeyings. Her father had refused to aid "sech a fool yerrand," and locked up his mare in the barn. Without a qualm, he had beheld Cynthia set out resolutely on foot. "She'll be back afore the cows kem home," he said, with a laughing nod at his wife. But they came lowing home and clanking their mellow bells in many and many a red sunset before they again found Cynthia waiting for them on the banks of Lost Creek.

The descent to a lower level was a painful experience to the little mountaineer. She was "sifflicated" by the denser atmosphere of the "valley country," and exhausted by the heat; but when she could think only of her mission she was hopeful, elated, and joyously kept on her thorny way. Sometimes, however, the dogs barked at her, and the children hooted after her, and the men and women she met looked askance upon her, and made her humbly conscious of her disheveled, dusty attire, her awkward, hobbling gait, her lean, hungry, worn aspect. Occasionally they asked for her story, and listened incredulously and with sarcastic comments. Once, as she started again down the road, she heard her late interlocutor call out to some one at the back of the house, "Becky, take them clothes in off 'n the line, an' take 'em in quick!"

And though her physical sufferings were great, she had some tears to shed for sorrow's sake.

Always she got a night's lodging at the house of one or another of the twelve jurymen, whose names were gradually affixed to the petition. But they too had questions that were hard to answer. "Are you kin of his?" they would ask, impressed by her hardships and her self-immolation. And when she would answer, "No," she would fancy that the shelter they gave her was not in confidence, but for mere humanity. And she shrank sensitively from these supposititious suspicions. They were poor men, mostly, but one of them stopped his plowing to lend her his horse to the next house, and another gave her a lift of ten miles in his wagon, as it was on his way. He it was who told her, in rehearsing the country-side gossip, that the governor was canvassing the State for reëlection, and had made an appointment to speak at Sparta the following day.

A new idea flashed into her mind. Her sudden resolution fairly frightened her. She cowered before it, as they drove along between the fields of yellowing corn, all in the gairish sunshine, spreading so broadly over the broad plain. That night she lay awake thinking of it, while the cold drops started upon her brow. Before daybreak she was up and trudging along the road to Sparta. It was still early when she entered the little town of the mountain bench, set in the flickering mists and chill, matutinal sunshine, and encompassed on every hand by the mighty ranges. A flag floated from the roof of the court-house, and there was an unusual stir in the streets. Excited groups were talking at every corner, and among a knot of men, standing near, one riveted her attention. He had been spoken of in her hearing as the governor of the State. Bold with the realization of the opportunity, she pushed through the staring crowd and thrust the much-thumbed petition into his hand. He cast a surprised glance upon her, then looked at the paper. "All right; I'll examine it," he said hastily, and folding it he turned away. In his political career he had studied many faces; unconsciously an adept, he may have deciphered those subtle hieroglyphics of character, and despite her ignorance, her poverty, and the low, criminal atmosphere of her mission, read in her eyes the dignity of her endeavor, the nobility of her nature, and the prosaic martyrdom of her toilsome experience. He turned suddenly back to reassure her. "Rely on it," he said heartily, "I'll do what I can."

Her pilgrimage was accomplished; there was nothing more but to turn her face to the mountains. It seemed to her at times as if she should never reach them. They were weary hours before she came upon Lost Creek, loitering down the sunlit valley to vanish in the grewsome caverns beneath the range. The sumach leaves were crimsoning along its banks. The scarlet-oak emblazoned the mountain side. Above the encompassing heights the sky was blue, and the mountain

40

air tasted like wine. Never a crag or chasm so sombre but flaunted some swaying vine or long tendriled moss, gilded and gleaming yellow. Buckeyes were falling, and the ashy "Indian pipes" silvered the roots of the trees. In every marshy spot glowed the scarlet cardinal-flower, and the goldenrod had sceptred the season. Now and again the forest quiet was broken by the patter of acorns from the chestnut-oaks, and the mountain swine were abroad for the plenteous mast. Overhead she heard the faint, weird cry of wild geese winging southward. The whole aspect of the scene was changed, save only Pine Mountain. There it stood, solemn, majestic, mysterious, masked by its impenetrable growth, and hung about with duskier shadows wherever a ravine indented the slope. The spirit within it was chanting softly, softly. For the moment she felt the supreme exaltation of the mountains. It lifted her heart. And when a sudden fluctuating red glare shot out over the murky shades, and the dull sighing of the bellows reached her ear from the forge on the mountain's brink, and the air was presently vibrating with the clinking of the hand-hammer and the clanking of the sledge, and the crags clamored with the old familiar echoes, she realized that she had done all she had sought to do; that she had gone forth helpless but for her own brave spirit; that she had returned helpful, and hopeful, and that here was her home, and she loved it.

This enabled her to better endure the anger and reproaches of her relatives and the curiosity and covert suspicion of the whole country-side.

Evander's people regarded the situation with grave misgivings. "I hope ter the mercy-seat," quavered old man Price, "ez Cynthy Ware hain't gone an' actually sot the gov'nor o' Tennessee more' n ever agin that pore critter; but I misdoubts,"—he shook his head piteously, as he perched on the fence,—"I misdoubts."

"An' the insurance o' that thar gal!" cried Mrs. Price. "She never had no call ter meddle with 'Vander."

Cynthia's mother entertained this view, also, but for a different reason. "'Twar no consarn o' Cynthy's, nohow," she said, advising with her daughter Maria. "Cynthy air neither kith nor kin o' 'Vander, who air safer an' likelier in the pen'tiary 'n ennywhar else, 'kase it leaves her no ch'ice but Jeemes Blake, ez she hed better take whilst he air in the mind fur it an' whilst she kin git him."

Jubal Tynes wished he could have foreseen that she would meet the governor, for he could have told her exactly what to say; and this, he was confident, would have secured the pardon.

And it was clearly the opinion of the "mounting," expressed in the choice coteries assembled at the mill, the blacksmith's shop, the Settlement, and the still-house, that a "young gal like Cynthy" had transcended all the bounds of propriety in this "wild junketing after gov'nors an' sech through all the valley country, whar she warn't knowed from a gate-post, nor her dad nuther."

There were, however, doubters, who disparaged the whole account of the journey as a fable, and circulated a whisper that the petition had never been presented.

This increased to open incredulity as time wore on, to ridicule, to taunts, for no word came of the petition for pardon and no word of the prisoner.

The bleak winter wore away; spring budded and bloomed into summer; summer was ripening into autumn, and every day, as the corn yellowed and thickly swathed ears hung far from the stalk, and the drone of the locust was loud in the grass, and the deep, slumberous glow of the sunshine suffused every open spot, Cynthia, with the return of the season, was vividly reminded of her weary ploddings, with

42

bleeding feet and aching head, between such fields along the lengthening valley roads. And the physical anguish she remembered seemed light—seemed naught—to the anguish of suspense which racked her now. Sometimes she felt impelled to a new endeavor. Then her strong common sense checked the useless impulse. She had done all that could be done. She had planted the seed. She had worked and watched, and beheld it spring up and put forth and grow into fair proportions; only time might bring its full fruition.

The autumn was waning; cold rains set in, and veined the rocky chasms with alien torrents; the birds had all flown, when suddenly the Indian summer, with its golden haze and its great red sun, its purple distances and its languorous joy, its balsamic perfumes and its vagrant day-dreams, slipped down upon the gorgeous crimson woods, and filled them with its glamour and its poetry.

One of these days—a perfect day—a great sensation pervaded Pine Mountain. Word went the rounds that a certain notorious horse thief, who had served out his term in the peni tentiary, had stopped at the blacksmith shop on his way home, glad enough of the prospect of being there once more; "an' ez pious in speech ez the rider, mighty nigh," said the dwellers about Pine Mountain, unfamiliar with his aspect as a penitent and discounting his repentance. It was a long story he had to tell about himself, and he enjoyed posing as the central figure in the curious crowd that had gathered about him. He seemed for the time less like a criminal than a great traveler, so strange and full of interest to the simple mountaineers were his experiences and the places he had seen. He stood leaning against the anvil, as he talked, looking out through the barn-like door upon the amplitude of the great landscape before him; its mountains so dimly, delicately blue in the distance, so deeply red and brown and yellow nearer at hand, and still closer shaded off by the dark plumy boughs of the pines on either side of the ravine above which the forge was perched. Deep in the valley, between them all, Lost Creek hied along, veining the purple haze with lines of palpitating silver. It was only when the material for personal narration was quite exhausted that he entered, though with less zest, on other themes.

"Waal,—now, 'Vander Price," he drawled, shifting his great cowhide boots one above another. "I war 'stonished when I hearn ez 'Vander war in fur receivin' of stolen goods. Shucks!"—his little black eyes twinkled beneath the drooping brim of a white wool hat, and his wide, flat face seemed wider and flatter for a contemptuous grin,—"I can't onderstand how a man kin git his own cornsent ter go cornsortin' with them ez breaks inter stores and dwellin's an' sech, an' hankerin' arter store-fixin's an' store-truck. Live-stock air a differ. The beastis air temptin', partic'lar ef they air young an' hev got toler'ble paces." Perhaps a change in the faces of his audience admonished him, for he qualified: "The beastis air temptin'—*ter the ungodly*. I hev gin over sech doin's myself, 'kase we hed a toler'ble chaplain yander in the valley" (he alluded thus equivocally to his late abode), "an' I sot under the preachin' a good while. But store-truck!— shucks! Waal, the gyards 'lowed ez 'Vander war a turrible feller ter take keer on, when they war a-fetchin' him down ter Nashvul. He jes' seemed desolated. One minit he'd fairly cry ez ef every sob would take his life; an' the nex' he'd be squarin' off ez savage, an' tryin' ter hit the gyards in the head. He war ironed, hand an' foot."

There was no murmur of sympathy. All listened with stolid curiosity, except Cynthia, who was leaning against the open door. The tears forced their way, and silently flowed, unheeded, down her cheeks. She fixed her brown eyes upon the man as he went on:—

44

"But when they struck the railroad, an' the critter seen the iron engine ez runs by steam, like I war a-tellin' ye about, he jes' stood rooted ter the spot in amaze; they could sca'cely git him budged away from thar. They 'lowed they hed never seen sech joy ez when he war travelin' on the steam-kyars a-hint it. When they went a-skeetin' along ez fast an' ez steady ez a tur-r-key-buzzard kin fly, 'Vander would jes' look fust at one o' the gyards an' then at the t'other, a-smilin' an' tickled nearly out 'n his senses. An' wunst he said, 'Ef this ain't the glory o' God revealed in the work o' man, what is?' The gyards 'lowed he acted so cur'ous they would hev b'lieved he war a plumb idjit, ef it hedn't a-been fur what happened arterward at the Pen."

"Waal, what war it ez happened at the Pen?" demanded Pete Blenkins. His red face, suffused with the glow of the smouldering forge-fire, was a little wistful, as if he grudged his quondam striker these unique sensations.

"They put him right inter the forge at the Pen, an' he tuk ter the work like a pig ter carrots." The ex-convict paused for a moment, and cast his eye disparagingly about the primitive smithy. "They do a power o' work thar, Pete, ez you-uns never drempt of."

"Shucks!" rejoined Pete incredulously, yet a trifle ill at ease.

"'Vander war a good blacksmith fur the mountings, but they sot him ter l'arnin' thar. They 'lowed, though, ez he war pearter'n the peartest. He got ter be powerful pop'lar with all the gyards an' authorities, an' sech. He war plumb welded ter his work—he sets more store by metal than by grace. He 'lowed ter me ez he wouldn't hev missed bein' thar fur nuthin'! 'Vander air a powerful cur'ous critter: he 'lowed ter me ez one year in the forge at the Pen war wuth a hundred years in the mountings ter him."

Poor Cynthia! Her eyes, large, luminous, and sweet, with the holy rapture of a listening saint, were fixed upon the speaker's evil, uncouth face. Evander had not then been so unhappy!

"But when they hired out the convict labor ter some iron works' folks, 'Vander war glad ter go, 'kase he'd git ter l'arn more yit 'bout workin' in iron an' sech. An' he war powerful outed when he hed ter kem back, arter ten months, from them works. He hed tuk his stand in metal thar, too. An' he hed fixed some sort'n contrivance ter head rivets quicker'n cheaper'n it air ginerally done; an' he war afeard ter try ter git it 'patented,' ez he calls it, 'kase he b'lieved the Pen could claim it ez convict labor,—though some said not. Leastwise, he determined ter hold on ter his idee till his term war out. But he war powerful interrupted in his mind fur fear somebody else would think up the idee, too, an' patent it fust. He war powerful irked by the Pen arter he kem back from the iron works. He 'lowed ter me ez he war fairly crazed ter git back ter 'em. He 'lowed ez he hed ruther see that thar big shed an' the red hot puddler's balls a-trundlin' about, an' all the wheels a-whurlin', an' the big shears a-bitin' the metal ez nip, an' the tremenjious hammer a-poundin' away, an' all the dark night around split with lines o' fire, than to see the hills o' heaven! It 'pears to me mo' like hell! But jes' when 'Vander war honing arter them works ez ef it would kill him ter bide away from thar, his pardon kem. He fairly lept an' shouted fur joy!"

"His pardon!" cried Cynthia.

"Air 'Vander pardoned fur true?" exclaimed a chorus of mountaineers.

The ex-convict stared about him in surprise. "Ain't you-uns knowed that afore? 'Vander hev been out'n the Pen a year."

46

A year! A vague, chilly premonition thrilled through Cynthia. "Whar be he now?" she asked.

"Yander ter them iron works. He lit out straight. I seen him las' week, when I war travelin' from my cousin Jerry's house, whar I went ez soon ez I got out'n the Pen. The steam-kyars stopped at a station ez be nigh them iron works, an' I met up with 'Vander on the platform. That's how I fund out all I hev been a-tellin' ye, 'kase we didn't hev no time ter talk whilst we war in the Pen; they don't allow no chin-choppin' thar. When 'Vander war released, the folks at the iron works tuk him ter work on weges, an' gin him eighty dollars a month."

There was an outburst of incredulity. "Waal, sir!" "Tim'thy, ye kerry that mouth o' yourn too wide open, an' it leaks out all sorts o' lies!" "We-uns know ye of old, Tim'thy!" "Pine Mounting haint furgot ye yit!"

"I wouldn't gin eighty dollars fur 'Vander Price, hide, horns, an' tallow!" declared Pete Blenkins, folding his big arms over his leathern apron, and looking about with the air of a man who has placed his valuation at extremely liberal limits.

"I knowed ye wouldn't b'lieve that, but it air gospel-true," protested the ex-convict. "Thar is more money a-goin' in the valley 'n thar is in the mountings, an' folks pays more fur work. Besides that, 'Vander hev got a patent, ez he calls it, fur his rivet contrivance, an' he 'lows ez it hev paid him some a'ready. It'll sorter stiffen up the backbone o' that word ef I tell ye ez he 'lowed ez he hed jes' sent two hunderd dollars ter Squair Bates ter lift the mortgage off'n old man Price's house an' land, an' two hunderd dollars more ter be gin ter his dad ez a present. An' Squair Bates acted 'cordin' ter 'Vander's word, an' lifted the mortgage, an' handed old man Price the balance. An' what do ye s'pose old man Price done with the money? He went right out an' buried it in the woods, fur fear he'd be pulled out'n his bed fur it, some dark

47

night, by lawless ones. He'll never find it agin, I reckon. The idjit hed more sense. I seen 'Lijah diggin' fur it, ez I rid by thar ter-day."

"Did 'Vander 'low when he air comin' back ter Pine Mounting?" asked Pete Blenkins. "He hev been gone two year an' a half now."

"I axed him that word. An' he said he mought kem back ter see his folks nex' year, mebbe, or the year arter that. But I misdoubts. He air so powerful tuk up with metal an' iron, an' sech, an' so keen 'bout his 'ventions, ez he calls 'em, ez he seemed mighty glad ter git shet o' the mountings. 'Vander 'lows ez you-uns dunno nothin' 'bout iron up hyar, Pete."

It was too plain. Cynthia could not deceive herself. He had forgotten her. His genius, once fairly evoked, possessed him, and faithfully his ambitions served it. His love, in comparison, was but a little thing, and he left it in the mountains,—the mountains that he did not regret, that had barred him so long from all he valued, that had freed him at last only through the prison doors. His love had been an unavowed love, and there was no duty broken. For the first time she wondered if he ever knew that she cared for him,— if he never remembered. And then she was suddenly moved to ask, "Did he 'low ter you-uns who got his pardon fur him?"

"I axed that word when las' I seen him, an' the critter said he actually hed never tuk time ter think 'bout'n that. He 'lowed he war so tickled ter git away from the Pen'tiary right straight ter the iron works an' the consarn he hed made ter head rivets so peart, ez he never wondered 'bout'n it. He made sure, though, now he had kem ter study 'bout'n it, ez his dad hed done it, or it mought hev been gin him fur good conduc' an' sech."

"'Twar Cynthy hyar ez done some of it," explained Pete Blenkins, "though Jubal Tynes stirred himself right smart."

As Cynthia walked slowly back to her home in the gorge, she did not feel that she had lavished a noble exaltation and a fine courage in vain; that the subtlest essence of a most ethereal elation was expended as the motive power of a result that was at last flat, and sordid, and most material. She did not murmur at the cruelty of fate that she should be grieving for his woes while he was so happy, so blithely busy. She did not regret her self-immolation. She did not grudge all that love had given him; she rejoiced that it was so sufficient, so nobly ample. She grudged only the wasted feeling, and she was humbled when she thought of it.

The sun had gone down, but the light yet lingered. The evening star trembled above Pine Mountain. Massive and darkling it stood against the red west. How far, ah, how far, stretched that mellow crimson glow, all adown Lost Creek Valley, and over the vast mountain solitudes on either hand! Even the eastern ranges were rich with this legacy of the dead and gone day, and purple and splendid they lay beneath the rising moon. She looked at it with full and shining eyes.

"I dunno how he kin make out ter furgit the mountings," she said; and then she went on, hearing the crisp leaves rustling beneath her tread, and the sharp bark of a fox in the silence of the night-shadowed valley.

Mrs. Ware had predicted bitter things of Cynthia's future, more perhaps in anger than with discreet foresight. Now, when her prophecy was in some sort verified, she shrank from it, as if with the word she had conjured up the fact. And her pride was touched in that her daughter should have been given the "go-by," as she phrased it. All the mountain—nay, all the valley—would know of it. "Law, Cynthy," she exclaimed, aghast, when the girl had rehearsed the news, "what be ye a-goin' ter do?"

"I'm a-goin' ter weavin'," said Cynthia. She already had the shuttle in her hand. It was a useful expression for a broken heart, as she was expert at the loom.

She became so very skillful, with practice, that it was generally understood to be mere pastime when she would go to help a neighbor through the weaving of the cloth for the children's clothes. She went about much on this mission: for although there were children at home, the work was less than the industry, and she seemed "ter hev a craze fur stirrin' about, an' war a toler'ble oneasy critter." She was said to have "broken some sence 'Vander gin her the go-by, like he done," and was spoken of at the age of twenty-one as a "settled single woman;" for early marriages are the rule in the mountains. When first her father and then her mother died, she cared for all the household, and the world went on much the same. The monotony of her tragedy made it unobtrusive. Perhaps no one on Pine Mountain remembered aright how it had all come about, when after an absence of ten years Evander Price suddenly reappeared among them.

Old man Price had, in the course of nature, ceased to sit upon the fence,—he could hardly be said to have lived. The fence itself was decrepit; the house was falling to decay. The money which Evander had sent from time to time, that it might be kept comfortable, had been safely buried in various localities and in separate installments, as the remittances had come. To this day the youth of Pine Mountain, when afflicted with spasms of industry and, as unaccustomed, the lust for gold, dig for it in likely spots as unavailingly as the idiot once sought it. Evander took the family with him to his valley home, and left the little hut for the owl and the gopher to hide within, for the red-berried vines to twine about the rotting logs, for the porch to fall in the wind, for silence to enter therein and make it a dwelling-place.

"How will yer wife like ter put up with the idjit?" asked Pete Blenkins of his old striker.

"She'll be *obleeged* ter like it!" retorted Evander, with an angry flash in his eyes, presaging contest.

It revealed the one dark point in his prospects. The mountaineers were not so slow-witted as to overlook it, but Evander had come to be the sort of man whom one hardly likes to question. He had a traveling companion, however, who hailed from the same neighborhood, and who talked learnedly of coal measures, and prodded and digged and bought leagues of land for a song,—much of it dearly bought. He let fall a hint that in marrying, Evander had contrived to handicap himself. "He would do wonders but for that woman!"

His mountain auditors could hardly grasp the finer points of the incompatibility; they could but dimly appreciate that the kindling scintilla of a discovery in mechanics, more delicately poised on practicability than a sunbeam on a cobweb, could have a tragic extinction in a woman's inopportune peevishness or selfish exactions.

In Evander's admiration of knowledge and all its infinite radiations, he had been attracted by a woman far superior to himself in education and social position, although not in this world's goods. She was the telegraph operator at the station near the iron works. She had felt that there was a touch of romance and self-abnegation in her fancy for him, and this titillated her more tutored imagination. His genius was held in high repute at the iron works, and she had believed him a rough diamond. She did not realize how she could have appreciated polished facets and a brilliant lustre and a conventional setting until it was too late. Then she began to think this genius of hers uncouth, and she presently doubted if her jewel were genuine. For although of refined instincts, he had been rudely reared, while she was in some sort inured

51

to table manners and toilet etiquette and English grammar. She could not be content with his intrinsic worth, but longed for him to prove his value to the world, that it might not think she had thrown herself away. In moments of disappointment and depression his prison record bore heavily upon her, and there was a breach when, in petulance, she had once asked, If he were indeed innocent in receiving the stolen goods, why had he not proved it? And she urged him to much striving to be rich; and she would fain travel the old beaten road to wealth in the iron business, and scorned experiments and new ideas and inventions, that took money out without the certainty of putting it in. And she had been taught, and was an adept in specious argument. He could not answer her; he could only keep doggedly on his own way; but obstinacy is a poor substitute for ardor. Though he had done much, he had done less than he had expected,—far, far less in financial results than she had expected. His ambitions were still hot within him, but they were worldly ambitions now. They scorched his more delicate sensibilities, and seared his freshest perceptions, and set his heart afire with sordid hopes. He was often harassed by a lurking doubt of his powers; he vaguely sought to measure them; and he began to fear that this in itself was a sign of the approach to their limits. He could still lift his eyes to great heights, but alas for the wings,—alas!

He had changed greatly: he had become nervous, anxious, concentrated, yet not less affectionate. He said much about his wife to his old friends, and never a word but loyal praise. "Em'ly air school-l'arned fur true, an' kin talk ekal ter the rider."

The idiot 'Lijah was welcome at his side, and the ancient yellow cur, that used to trot nimbly after him in the old days, rejoiced to limp feebly at his heels. He came over, one morning, and sat on the rickety little porch with Cynthia, and talked of her father and mother; but he had forgotten the mare, whose death she also mentioned, and the fact that old Suke's third calf was traded to M'ria Baker. His recollections were all vague, although at some reminiscence of hers he laughed jovially, and 'lowed that "in them days, Cynthy, ye an' me hed a right smart notion of keeping company tergether." He did not notice how pale she was, and that there was often a slight spasmodic contraction of her features. She was busy with her spinning-wheel, as she placidly replied, "Yes,—though I always 'lowed ez I counted on livin' single."

It was only a fragmentary attention that he accorded her. He was full of his plans and anxious about rains, lest a rise in Caney Fork should detain him in the mountains; and he often turned and surveyed the vast landscape with a hard, callous glance of worldly utility. He saw only weather signs. The language of the mountains had become a dead language. Oh, how should he read the poem that the opalescent mist traced in an illuminated text along the dark, gigantic growths of Pine Mountain!

At length he was gone, and forever, and Cynthia's heart adjusted itself anew. Sometimes, to be sure, it seems to her that the years of her life are like the floating leaves drifting down Lost Creek, valueless and purposeless, and vaguely vanishing in the mountains. Then she remembers that the sequestered subterranean current is charged with its own inscrutable, imperative mission, and she ceases to question and regret, and bravely does the work nearest her hand, and has glimpses of its influence in the widening lives of others, and finds in these a placid content.

A-PLAYIN' OF OLD SLEDGE AT THE SETTLEMINT.

"I hev hearn tell ez how them thar boys rides thar horses over hyar ter the Settlemint nigh on ter every night in the week ter play kyerds,—'Old Sledge' they calls it; an' thar goin's-on air jes' scandalous,—jes' a-drinkin' of apple-jack, an' a-bettin' of thar money."

It was a lonely place: a sheer precipice on one side of the road that curved to its verge; on the other, an ascent so abrupt that the tall stems of the pines seemed laid upon the ground as they were marshaled in serried columns up the slope. No broad landscape was to be seen from this great projecting ledge of the mountain; the valley was merely a little basin, walled in on every side by the meeting ranges that rose so high as to intercept all distant prospect, and narrow the world to the contracted area bounded by the sharp lines of their wooded summits, cut hard and clear against the blue sky. But for the road, it would have seemed impossible that these wild steeps should be the chosen haunt of aught save deer, or bear, or fox; and certainly the instinct of the eagle built that eyrie called the Settlement, still higher, far above the towering pine forest. It might be accounted a tribute to the enterprise of Old Sledge that mountain barriers proved neither let nor hindrance, and here in the fastnesses was held that vivacious sway, potent alike to fascinate and to scandalize.

In the middle of the stony road stood a group of roughly clad mountaineers, each in an attitude of sluggish disinclination to the allotted task of mending the highway, leaning lazily upon a grubbing-hoe or sorry spade,—except, indeed, the overseer, who was upheld by the single crowbar furnished by the county, the only sound implement in use among the party. The provident dispensation of the law,

54

leaving the care of the road to the tender mercies of its able-bodied neighbors over eighteen and under forty-five years of age, was a godsend to the Settlement and to the inhabitants of the tributary region, in that even if it failed of the immediate design of securing a tolerable passway through the woods, it served the far more important purpose of drawing together the diversely scattered settlers, and affording them unwonted conversational facilities. These meetings were well attended, although their results were often sadly inadequate. To-day the usual complement of laborers was on hand, except the three boys whose scandalous susceptibility to the mingled charms of Old Sledge and apple-jack had occasioned comment.

"They'll hev ter be fined, ef they don't take keer an' come an' work," remarked the overseer of the road, one Tobe Rains, who reveled in a little brief authority.

"From what I hev hearn tell 'bout thar go-in's-on, none of 'em is a-goin' ter hev nuthin' ter pay fines with, when they gits done with thar foolin' an' sech," said Abner Blake, a man of weight and importance, and the eldest of the party.

It did not seem to occur to any of the group that the losses among the three card-players served to enrich one of the number, and that the deplorable wholesale insolvency shadowed forth was not likely to ensue in substance. Perhaps their fatuity in this regard arose from the fact that fining the derelict was not an actuality, although sometimes of avail as a threat.

"An' we hev ter leave everythink whar it fell down, an' come hyar ter do thar work fur 'em,—a-fixin' up of this hyar road fur them ter travel," exclaimed Tobe Rains, attempting to chafe himself into a rage. "It's got ter quit,—that's what I say; this hyar way of doin' hev got ter quit." By way of lending verisimilitude to the industrial figure of rhetoric, he lifted his hammer and dealt an ineffectual blow at a large bowlder. Then he picked up his crowbar, and, leaning heavily on the implement, resigned himself to the piquant interest of gossip. "An' thar's that Josiah Tait," he continued, "a settled married man, a-behavin' no better 'n them fool boys. He hain't struck a lick of work fur nigh on ter a month,—'ceptin' a-goin' huntin' with the t'others, every wunst in a while. He hev jes' pulled through at the little eend of the horn. I never sot much store by him, nohow, though when he war married ter Melindy Price, nigh 'bout a year ago, the folks all 'lowed ez she war a-doin' mighty well ter git him, ez he war toler'ble well off through his folks all bein' dead but him, an' he hed what he hed his own self."

"I wouldn't let *my* darter marry no man ez plays kyerds," said a very young fellow, with great decision of manner, "no matter what he hed, nor how he hed it."

As the lady referred to was only two weeks old, and this solicitude concerning her matrimonial disposition was somewhat premature, there was a good-natured guffaw at the young fellow's expense.

"An' now," Tobe Rains resumed, "ef Josiah keeps on the way ez he hev started, he hain't a-goin' ter hev no more 'n the t'other boys round the mounting,—mebbe not ez much,—an' Melindy Price hed better hev a-tuken somebody what owned less but hed a harder grip."

A long silence fell upon the party. Three of the twenty men assembled, in dearth of anything else to do, took heart of grace and fell to work; fifteen leaned upon their hoes in a variety of postures, all equally expressive of sloth, and with slow eyes followed the graceful sweep of a hawk, drifting on the wind, without a motion of its wings, across the blue sky to the opposite range. Two, one of whom was the overseer, searched their pockets for a plug of tobacco, and when it was found its possessor gave to him that lacked. At length, Abner Blake, who furnished all the items of news, and led

56

the conversation, removed his eyes from the flight of the hawk, as the bird was absorbed in the variegated October foliage of the opposite mountain, and reopened the discussion. At the first word the three who were working paused in attentive quietude; the fifteen changed their position to one still more restful; the overseer sat down on a bowlder by the roadside, and placed his contemplative elbows on his knees and his chin in his hands.

"I hev hearn tell," said Abner Blake, with the pleasing consciousness of absorbing the attention of the company, and being able to meet high expectations, "ez how Josiah hev los' that thar brindled heifer ter Budd Wray, an' the main heft of his crap of corn. But mebbe he'll take a turn now an' win 'em back agin."

"'Tain't likely," remarked Tobe Rains.

"No, 'tain't," coincided the virtuous fifteen.

The industrious three, who might have done better in better company, went to work again for the space of a few minutes; but the next inarticulate gurgle, preliminary always to Blake's speech,—a sort of rising-bell to ring up somnolent attention,—brought them once more to a stand-still.

"An' cornsiderin' ez how Budd Wray,—he it war ez won 'em; I seen the heifer along o' the cow ter his house yestiddy evenin', ez I war a-comin' from a-huntin' yander ter the sulphur spring,—an' cornsiderin' ez he is nuthin' but a single man, an' hain't got no wife, it do look mighty graspin' ter be a-takin' from a man ez hev got a wife an' a houseful of his wife's kinsfolks ter look arter. Mighty graspin', it 'pears like ter me."

"I s'pose," said one of the three workers suggestively,—"I s'pose ez how Budd won it fair. 'Twarn't no onderhand job, war it?"

There was a portentous silence. The flight of the hawk, again floating above the mountains, now in the shadow of the resting clouds, now in the still sunshine, was the only motion in the landscape. The sudden bark of a fox in the woods near at hand smote the air shrilly.

"That thar ain't fur me ter say," Blake replied at last, with significant emphasis.

The suspicion fell upon the party like a revelation, with an auxiliary sense of surprise that it had not been earlier presented, so patent was the possibility.

Still that instinct of justice latent in the human heart kept the pause unbroken for a while. Then Blake, whose information on most points at issue entitled him to special consideration, proceeded to give his opinion on the subject: "I'm a perfessin' member of the church, an' I dunno one o' them thar kyerds from the t'other; an' what is more, I ain't a-wantin' ter know. I hev seen 'em a-playin' wunst, an' I hearn 'em a-talkin' that thar foolishness 'bout 'n 'high' an' 'low,' an' sech,—they'll all be low enough 'fore long. But what I say is, I dunno how come Josiah Tait, what's always been a peart, smart boy, an' his dad afore him always war a thrivin' man, an' Budd Wray war never nobody nor nuthin',—he war always mighty no-'count, him an' all his folks,—an' what I dunno is, how come he kin git the upper hand of Josiah Tait at these hyar kyerds, an' can't git it no other way. Ef he keeps on a-playin' of Old Sledge hyar at the Settlemint, he'll be wuth ez much ez anybody on the mounting what's done been a-workin' all thar days, an' hed a toler'ble start ter begin with. It don't look fair an' sensible ter me."

"'Pears like ter me," said the very young fellow, father of the very young daughter, "ef a man is old enough ter git married, he is old enough to take keer of hisself. I kin make out no good reason why Josiah Tait oughter be pertected agin Budd Wray. 'Pears ter me ef one of 'em kin larn ter play Old

Sledge, the t'other kin. An' Josiah hev got toler'ble good sense."

"That's how come all ye young muskrats dunno nuthin'," retorted Blake in some heat. "Jes' let one of you-uns git turned twenty year old, an' ye think ye air ez wise an' ez settled as ef ye war sixty, an' ye can't l'arn nuthin' more."

"All the same, I don't see ez Josiah Tait needs a dry-nuss ter keep off Wray an' sech critters," was the response. And here this controversy ended.

"Somehow," said Tobe Rains, reflectively, "it don't look likely ter me ez he an' Josiah Tait hev enny call ter be sech frien'ly folks. I hev hearn ez how Budd Wray war a-follerin' round Melindy Price afore she war married, an' she liked him fust-rate till Josiah tuk ter comin' 'bout 'n the Scrub-Oak Ridge, whar she lived in them days. That thar ain't the stuff ter make frien's out'n. Thar is some sort 'n cur'ous doin's a-goin' on 'bout'n these hyar frien'ly kyerds."

"I knowed that thar 'bout'n his a-follerin' round Melindy afore she war married. I 'lowed one time ez Melindy hed a mind ter marry Wray stiddier Josiah," said the young father, shaken in his partisanship. "An' it always 'peared like ter me ez it war mighty comical ez he an' Josiah tuk ter playin' of Old Sledge an' sech tergether."

These questions were not easy of solution. Many speculations were preferred concerning the suspicious circumstance of Budd Wray's singular proficiency in playing Old Sledge; but beyond disparaging innuendo and covert insinuation conjecture could not go. Everything was left doubtful, and so was the road.

It was hardly four o'clock, but the languid work had ceased and the little band was dispersing. Some had far to go through the deep woods to their homes, and those who lived closer at hand were not disposed to atone for their comrades' defection by prolonging their stay. The echoes for a long time vibrated among the lonely heights with the metallic sound of their horses' hoofs, every moment becoming fainter, until at last all was hushed. Dusky shadows, which seemed to be exhaled from the ground, rose higher and higher up the mountain side from the reservoir of gloom that lay in the valley. The sky was a lustrous contrast to the darkling earth. The sun still lingered, large and red, above the western summits; the clouds about it were gorgeous in borrowed color; even those hovering in the east had caught the reflection of the sunset splendor, and among their gold and crimson flakes swung the silver globe of the hunter's moon. Now and then, at long intervals, the bark of the fox quivered on the air; once the laurel stirred with a faint rustle, and a deer stood in the midst of the ill-mended road, catching upon his spreading antlers the mingled light of sun and moon. For a moment he was motionless, his hoof uplifted; the next, with an elastic spring, as of a creature without weight, he was flying up the steep slope and disappearing amid the slumberous shades of the dark pines. A sudden sound comes from far along the curves of the road,—a sound foreign to woods and stream and sky; again, and yet again, growing constantly more distinct, the striking of iron against stone, the quick, regular beat of a horse's tread, and an equestrian figure, facing the moon and with the sun at his back, rides between the steep ascent and the precipice on his way to the Settlement and the enticements of Old Sledge.

He was not the conventional type of the roistering blade. There was an expression of settled melancholy on his face very usual with these mountaineers, reflected, perhaps, from the indefinable tinge of sadness that rests upon the Alleghany wilds, that hovers about the purpling mountain-tops, that broods over the silent woods, that sounds in the voice of the singing waters. Nor was he like the prosperous

60

"perfessin' member" of the card-playing *culte*. His listless manner was that of stolidity, not of a studied calm; his brown jeans suit was old and worn and patched; his hat, which had seen many a drenching winter rain and scorching summer sun, had acquired sundry drooping curves undreamed of in its maker's philosophy. He rode a wiry gray mare without a saddle, and carried a heavy rifle. He was perhaps twenty-three years of age, a man of great strength and stature, and there were lines about his lips and chin which indicated a corresponding development of a firm will and tenacity of purpose. His slow brown eyes were fixed upon the horizon as he went around the ledge, and notwithstanding the languid monotony of the expression of his face he seemed absorbed in some definite train of thought, rather than lost in the vague, hazy reverie which is the habitual mental atmosphere of the quiescent mountaineer. The mare, left to herself, traveled along the rocky way in a debonair fashion implying a familiarity with worse roads, and soon was around the curve and beginning the sharp ascent which led to the Settlement. There was a rickety bridge to cross, that spanned a deep, narrow stream, which caught among its dark pools now a long, slender, polished lance of sunlight, and now a dart from the moon. As the rider went on upward the woods were dense as ever; no glimpse yet of the signet of civilization set upon the wilderness and called the Settlement. By the time he had reached the summit the last red rays of the day were fading from the tops of the trees, but the moon, full and high in the eastern heavens, shed so refulgent a light that it might be questioned whether the sun rose on a brighter world than that which he had left. A short distance along level ground, a turn to the right, and here, on the highest elevation of the range, was perched the little town. There was a clearing of ten acres, a blacksmith's shop, four log huts facing indiscriminately in any direction, a small store of one story and one room, and a new frame court-house, whitewashed and inclosed by a plank fence. In the last session of the legislature, the Settlement had been made the county-seat of a new county; the additional honor of a name had been conferred upon it, but as yet it was known among the population of the mountain by its time-honored and accustomed title.

Wray dismounted in front of the store, hitched the mare to a laurel bush, and, entering, discovered his two boon companions drearily waiting, and shuffling the cards again and again to while away the time. An inverted splint-basket served as table; a tallow dip, a great extravagance in these parts, blinked on the head of a barrel near by, and gave a most flickering and ineffectual light, but the steady radiance of the moon poured in a wide, white flood through the open door, and kindly supplied all deficiencies. The two young mountaineers were of the usual sad-eyed type, and the impending festivities might have seemed to those of a wider range of experience than the Settlement could furnish to be clouded with a funereal aspect. Before the fire, burning low and sullenly in the deep chimney, were sitting two elderly men, who looked with disfavor upon Wray as he came in and placed his gun with a clatter in the corner.

"Ye war a long time a-gittin' hyar, Budd," said one of the card-shufflers in a gentle voice, with curiously low-spirited cadences. He spoke slowly, too, and with a slight difficulty, as if he seldom had occasion to express himself in words and his organs were out of practice. He was the proprietor of the store, one Tom Scruggs, and this speech was by way of doing the honors. The other looked up with recognizing eyes, but said nothing.

"I war hendered some," replied Wray, seating himself in a rush-bottomed chair, and drawing close to the inverted basket. "Ez I war a-comin' along, 'bout haffen mile an' better from our house,—'twar nigh on ter three o'clock, I reckon,—I seen the bigges', fattes' buck I hev seen this year a-bouncin' through the laurel, an' I shot him. An' I hed to kerry him 'long home, 'kase suthin' mought hev got him ef I hed a-left him thar. An' it hendered me some."

"An' we hev ter sit hyar a-wastin' away an' a-waitin' while ye goes a-huntin' of deer," said Josiah Tait, angrily, and speaking for the first time. "I could hev gone an' shot twenty deer ef I would hev tuk the time. Ye said ez how ye war a-goin' ter be hyar an hour by sun, an' jes' look a-yander," pointing to the lustrous disc of the moon.

"That thar moon war high enough 'fore the sun war a-settin'," returned Wray. "Ef ye air in sech a hurry, whyn't yer cut them thar kyerds fur deal, an' stop that thar jowin' o' yourn. I hev hed ez much of that ez I am a-goin' ter swallow."

"I'll put it down ye with the ramrod o' that thar gun o' mine, ef ye don't take keer how ye talk," retorted the choleric Tait; "an' ef that don't set easy on yer stomach, I'll see how ye'll digest a bullet."

"I'm a-waitin' fur yer ramrod," said Wray. "Jes' try that fust, an' see how it works."

The melancholy-voiced store-keeper interrupted these amenities, not for the sake of peace,—white-winged angel,—but in the interests of Old Sledge. "Ef I hed a-knowed ez how ye two boys war a-goin' ter take ter quarrelin' an' a-fightin' round hyar, a-stiddier playin' of kyerds sensible-like, I wouldn't hev shet up shop so quick. I hed a good many little turns of work ter do, what I hev lef' ter play kyerds. An' ye two mought jow tergether some other day, it 'pears like ter me. Ye air a-wastin' more time a-jowin', Josiah, than Budd tuk up in comin' an' deer-huntin' tergether. Ye hev cut the lowest in the pack, so deal the kyerds, or give 'em ter them ez will."

The suggestion to resign the deal touched Josiah in a tender spot. He protested that he was only too willing to play,— that was all he wanted. "But ter be kep' a-waitin' hyar while Budd comes a-snakin' through the woods, an' a-stoppin' ter shoot wild varmints an' sech, an' then a-goin' home ter kerry 'em, an' then a-snakin' agin through the woods, an' a-gittin' hyar nigh on ter night-time,—that's what riles me."

"Waal, go 'long, now!" exclaimed Wray, fairly roused out of his imperturbability. "Deal them kyerds, an' stop a-talkin'. That thar tongue o' yourn will git cut out some o' these hyar days. It jes' goes like a grist-mill, an' it's enough ter make a man deef fur life."

Thus exhorted, Josiah dealt. In receiving their hands the players looked searchingly at every card, as if in doubtful recognition of an old acquaintance; but before the game was fairly begun another interruption occurred. One of the elderly men beside the fire rose and advanced upon the party.

"Thar is a word ez we hev laid off ter ax ye, Budd Wray, which will be axed twict,—wunst right hyar, an' wunst at the Jedgmint Day. War it ye ez interjuced this hyar coal o' fire from hell, that ye call Old Sledge, up hyar ter the Settlemint?"

The querist was a gaunt, forlorn-looking man, stoop-shouldered, and slow in his movements. There was, however, a distinct intimation of power in his lean, sinewy figure, and his face bore the scarlet scar of a wound torn by a furious fang, which, though healed long ago, was an ever-present reminder of a fierce encounter with a wild beast, in which he had come off victorious. The tones of his voice and the drift and rhetoric of his speech bespoke the loan of the circuit-rider.

The card-players looked up, less in surprise than exasperation, and Josiah Tait, fretfully anticipating Wray, spoke in reply: "No, he never. I fotched this hyar coal o' fire myself, an' ef ye don't look out an' stand back out'n the way it'll flare up an' singe ye. I larnt how ter play when I went down yander ter the Cross-Roads, an' I brung it ter the Settlemint myself."

There was a mingled glow of the pride of the innovator and the disdainful superiority of the iconoclast kindling within Josiah Tait as he claimed the patent for Old Sledge. The catechistic terrors of the Last Day had less reality for him than the present honor and glory appertaining to the traveled importer of a new game. The Judgment Day seemed imminent over his dodging head only when beholding the masterly scene-painting of the circuit-rider, and the fire and brimstone out of sight were out of mind.

"But ef ye air a-thinkin' of callin' me ter 'count fur sech," said Wray, nodding at the cards, "I'll hev ye ter know ez I kin stand up ter anything I does. I hev got no call ter be ashamed ov myself, an' I ain't afeard o' nuthin' an' nobody."

"Ye gin me ter onderstand, then, ez Josiah l'arned ye ter play?" asked the self-constituted grand inquisitor. "How come, then, Budd Wray, ez ye wins all the truck from Josiah, ef ye air jes' a-l'arnin'?"

There was an angry exclamation from Josiah, and Wray laughed out triumphantly. The walls caught the infrequent mirthful sound, and reverberated with a hollow repetition. From the dark forest just beyond the moon-flooded clearing the echo rang out. There was a subtle, weird influence in those exultant tones, rising and falling by fitful starts in that tangled, wooded desert; now loud and close at hand, now the faintest whisper of a sound. The men all turned their slow eyes toward the sombre shadows, so black beneath the silver moon, and then looked at each other.

"It's 'bout time fur me ter be a-startin'," said the old hunter. "Whenever I hear them critters a-laffin' that thar way in them woods I puts out fur home an' bars up the door, fur I hev hearn tell ez how the sperits air a-prowlin' round then, an' some mischief is a-happenin'."

"'T ain't nuthin' but Budd Wray a-laffin'," said the store-keeper reassuringly. "I hev hearn them thar rocks an' things a-answerin' back every minute in the day, when anybody hollers right loud."

"They don't laff, though, like they war a-laffin' jes' a while ago."

"No, they don't," admitted the store-keeper reluctantly; "but mebbe it air 'kase thar is nobody round hyar ez hev got much call ter laff."

He was unaware of the lurking melancholy in this speech, and it passed unnoticed by the others.

"It's this hyar a-foolin' along of Old Sledge an' sech ez calls the sperits up," said the old hunter. "An' ef ye knows what air good fur ye, ye'll light out from hyar an' go home. They air a-laffin' yit"—He interrupted himself, and glanced out of the door.

The faintest staccato laugh thrilled from among the leaves. And then all was silent, not even the bark of a dog nor a tremulous whisper of the night-wind.

The other elderly man, who had not yet spoken, rose from his seat by the fire. "I'm a-goin', too," he said. "I kem hyar ter the Settlemint," he added, turning upon the gamblers, "'kase I hev been called ter warn ye o' the wickedness o' yer

66

ways, ez Jonah afore me war tole ter go up ter Nineveh ter warn the folks thar."

"Things turns out powerful cur'ous wunst in a while," retorted Wray. "He war swallowed by a whale arterward."

"'Kase he wouldn't do ez he war tole; but even thar Providence perfected him. He kem out'n the whale agin, what nobody kin do ez gits swallowed in the pit. They hev ter stay."

"It hain't me ez keeps up this hyar game," said Wray sullenly, but stung to a slight repentance by this allusion to the pit. "It air Josiah hyar ez is a-aimin' ter win back the truck he hev los'; an' so air Tom, hyar. I hev hed toler'ble luck along o' this Old Sledge, but they know, an' they hev got ter stand up ter it, ez I never axed none of 'em ter play. Ef they scorches tharselves with this hyar coal o' fire from hell, ez ye calls it, Josiah brung it, an' it air Tom an' him a-blowin' on it ez hev kep' it a-light."

"I ain't a-goin' ter quit," said Josiah Tait angrily, the loser's desperate eagerness pulsing hot and quick through his veins,—"I ain't a-goin' ter quit till I gits back that thar brindled heifer an' that thar gray mare out yander, what Budd air a-ridin', an' them thar two wagon-loads o' corn."

"We hev said our say, an' we air a-goin'," remarked one of the unheeded counselors.

"An' play on of yer kyerds!" cried Josiah to the others, in a louder, shriller voice than was his wont, as the two elderly men stepped out of the door. The woods caught the sound and gave it back in a higher key.

"S'pose we stops fur ter-night," suggested the store-keeper; "them thar rocks do sound sort 'n cur'ous now."

"I ain't a-goin' ter stop fur nuthin' an' nobody!" exclaimed Josiah, in a tremor of keen anxiety to be at the sport. "Dad-burn the sperits! Let 'em come in, an' I 'll deal 'em a hand. Thar! that trick is mine. Play ter this hyar queen o' trumps."

The royal lady was recklessly thrown upon the basket, with all her foes in ambush. Somehow, they did not present themselves. Tom was destitute, and Budd followed with the seven. Josiah again pocketed the trick with unction. This trifling success went disproportionately far in calming his agitation, and for a time he played more needfully. Tom Scruggs's caution made ample amends for his lack of experience. So slow was he, and so much time did he require for consideration, that more than once he roused his companions to wrath. The anxieties with which he was beset preponderated over the pleasure afforded by the sport, and the winning back of a half-bushel measure, which he had placed in jeopardy and lost, so satisfied this prudent soul that he announced at the end of the game that he would play no more for this evening. The others were welcome, though, to continue if they liked, and he would sit by and look on. He snuffed the blinking tallow dip, and reseated himself, an eager spectator of the play that followed.

Wray was a cool hand. Despite the awkward, unaccustomed clutch upon the cards and the doubtful recognition he bestowed on each as it fell upon the basket, he displayed an imperturbability and nerve that usually come only of long practice, and a singular pertinacity in pursuing the line of tactics he had marked out,—lying in wait and pouncing unerringly upon his prey in the nick of time. The brindled heifer's mother followed her offspring into his ownership; a yoke of oxen, a clay-bank filly, ten hogs,—every moment he was growing richer. But his success did not for an instant shake his stolid calm, quicken his blood, nor relax his vigilant attention; his exultation was held well in hand under the domination of a strong will and a settled purpose. Josiah Tait became almost maddened by these heavy losses; his hands trembled, his eager exclamations were incoherent, his dull eyes blazed at fever heat, and ever and anon the echo of his shrill, raised voice rang back from the untiring rocks.

The single spectator of the game now and then, in the intervals of shuffling and dealing the cards, glanced over his shoulder at the dark trees whence the hidden mimic of the woods, with some strong suggestion of sinister intent, repeated the agitated tones. There was a silver line all along the summit of the foliage, along the roofs of the houses and the topmost rails of the fences; a sense of freshness and dew pervaded the air, and the grass was all a-sparkle. The shadows of the laurel about the door were beginning to fall on the step, every leaf distinctly defined in the moon's magical tracery. He knew without looking up that she had passed the meridian, and was swinging down the western sky.

"Boys," he said, in a husky under-tone,—he dared not speak aloud, for the mocker in the woods,—"boys, I reckon it's 'bout time we war a-quittin' o' this hyar a-playin' of Old Sledge; it's midnight an' past, an' Budd hev tolerable fur ter go."

The tallow dip, that had long been flickering near its end, suddenly went out, and the party suffered a partial eclipse. Josiah Tait dragged the inverted basket closer to the door and into the full brilliance of the moon, declaring that neither Wray nor he should leave the house till he had retrieved his misfortunes or lost every thing in the effort. The host, feeling that even hospitality has its limits, did not offer to light another expensive candle, but threw a quantity of pine-knots on the smouldering coals; presently a white blaze was streaming up the chimney, and in the mingled light of fire and moon the game went on.

"Ye oughter take keer, Josiah," remonstrated the sad-voiced store-keeper, as a deep groan and a deep curse emphasized the result of high, jack, and game for Wray, and low alone for Tait. "An' it's 'bout time ter quit."

"Dad-burn the luck!" exclaimed Josiah, in a hard, strained voice, "I ain't a-goin' ter leave this hyar spot till I hev won back them thar critters o' mine what he hev tuk. An' I kin do it,—I kin do it in one more game. I'll bet—I'll bet"—he paused in bewildered excitement; he had already lost to Wray everything available as a stake. There was a sudden unaccountable gleam of malice on the lucky winner's face; the quick glance flashed in the moonlight into the distended hot eyes of his antagonist. Wray laughed silently, and began to push his chair away from the basket.

"Stop! stop!" cried Josiah, hoarsely. "I hev got a house,—a house an' fifty acres, nigh about. I'll bet the house an' land agin what ye hev won from me,—them two cows, an' the brindled heifer, an' the gray mare, an' the clay-bank filly, an' them ten hogs, an' the yoke o' steers, an' the wagon, an' the corn,—them two loads o' corn: that will 'bout make it even, won't it?" He leaned forward eagerly as he asked the question.

"Look a-hyar, Josiah," exclaimed the store-keeper, aghast, "this hyar is a-goin' too fur! Hain't ye los' enough a'ready but ye must be a-puttin' up the house what shelters ye? Look at me, now: I ain't done los' nothin' but the half-bushel measure, an' I hev got it back agin. An' it air a blessin' that I *hev* got it agin, for 'twould hev been mighty ill-convenient round hyar 'thout it."

"Will ye take it?" said Josiah, almost pleadingly, persistently addressing himself to Wray, regardless of the remonstrant host. "Will ye put up the critters agin the house an' land?"

Wray made a feint of hesitating. Then he signified his willingness by seating himself and beginning to deal the

70

cards, saying before he looked at his hand, "That thar house an' land o' yourn agin the truck ez I hev won from ye?"

"Oh, Lord, boys, this *must* be sinful!" remonstrated the proprietor of the cherished half-bushel measure, appalled by the magnitude of the interests involved.

"Hold yer jaw! hold yer jaw!" said Josiah Tait. "I kin hardly make out one kyerd from another while ye're a-preachin' away, same ez the rider! I done tole ye, Budd," turning again to Wray, "I'll put up the house an' land agin the truck. I'll git a deed writ fur ye in the mornin', ef ye win it," he added, hastily, thinking he detected uncertainty still lurking in the expression of Wray's face. "The court air a-goin' tar sit hyar ter-morrer, an' the lawyers from the valley towns will be hyar toler'ble soon, I reckon. An' I'll git ye a deed writ fust thing in the mornin'."

"Ye hearn him say it?" said Wray, turning to Tom Scruggs.

"I hearn him," was the reply.

And the game went on.

"I beg," said Josiah, piteously, after carefully surveying his hand.

"I ain't a-goin' ter deal ye nare 'nother kyerd," said Wray. "Ye kin take a pint fust."

The point was scored by the faithful looker-on in Josiah's favor. High, low, and game were made by Wray, jack being in the pack. Thus the score was three to one. In the next deal, the trump, a spade, was allowed by Wray to stand. He led the king. "I'm low, anyhow," said Josiah, in momentary exultation, as he played the deuce to it. Wray next led the ace whisking for the jack, and caught it.

"Dad-burn the rotten luck!" cried Josiah.

71

With the advantage of high and jack a foregone conclusion, Wray began to play warily for game. But despite his caution he lost the next trick. Josiah was in doubt how to follow up this advantage; after an anxious interval of cogitation he said, "I b'lieve I'll throw away fur a while," and laid that safe card, the five of diamonds, upon the basket. "Tom," he added, "put on some more o' them knots. I kin hardly tell what I'm a-doin' of. I hev got the shakes, an' somehow 'nother my eyes is cranky, and wobble so ez I can't see."

The white sheets of flame went whizzing merrily up the chimney, and the clear light fell full upon the basket as Wray laid upon the five the ten of diamonds.

"Lord! Josiah!" exclaimed Tom Scruggs, becoming wild, and even more ill judged than usual, beginning to feel as if he were assisting at his friend's obsequies, and to have a more decided conviction that this way of coming by house and land and cattle and goods was sinful. "Lord! Josiah! that thar kyerd he's done saved 'll count him ten fur game. Ye had better hev played that thar queen o' di'monds, an' dragged it out 'n him."

"Good Lord in heaven!" shrieked Josiah, in a frenzy at this unwarrantable disclosure.

"Lord in heaven!" rang loud from the depths of the dark woods. "Heaven!" softly vibrated the distant heights. The crags close at hand clanged back the sound, and the air was filled with repetitions of the word, growing fainter and fainter, till they might have seemed the echo of a whisper.

The men neither heard nor heeded. Tom Scruggs, although appreciating the depth of the infamy into which he had unwittingly plunged, was fully resolved to stand stoutly upon the defensive,—he even extended his hand to take down his gun, which was laid across a couple of nails on the wall.

"Hold on, Josiah,—hold on!" cried Wray, as Tait drew his knife. "Tom never went fur ter tell, an' I'll give ye a ten ter make it fair. Thar's the ten o' hearts; an' a ten is the mos' ez that thar critter of a queen could hev made out ter hev tuk, anyhow."

Josiah hesitated.

"That thar is the mos' ez she could hev done," said the store-keeper, smoothing over the results of his carelessness. "The jacks don't count but fur one apiece, so that thar ten is the mos' ez she could hev made out ter git, even ef I hedn't a-forgot an' tole Budd she war in yer hand."

Josiah was mollified by this very equitable proposal, and resuming his chair he went on with the play. The ten of hearts which he had thus secured was, however, of no great avail in counting for game. Wray had already high and jack, and game was added to these. The score therefore stood six to two in his favor.

The perennial faith of the gambler in the next turn of the wheel was strong in Josiah Tait. Despite his long run of bad luck, he was still animated by the feverish delusion that the gracious moment was surely close at hand when success would smile upon him. Wray, it was true, needed to score only one point to turn him out of house and land, homeless and penniless. He was confident it would never be scored. If he could make the four chances he would be even with his antagonist, and then he could win back in a single point all that he had lost. His face wore a haggard, eager expectation, and the agitation of the moment thrilled through every nerve. He watched with fiery eyes the dealing of the cards, and after hastily scrutinizing his hand he glanced with keen interest to see the trump turned. It was a knave, counting one for the dealer. There was a moment of intense silence; he seemed petrified as his eyes met the triumphant gaze of his opponent. The next instant he was at Wray's throat.

The shadows of the swaying figures reeled across the floor, marring the exquisite arabesque of moonshine and laurel leaves,—quick, hard panting, a deep oath, and spasmodic efforts on the part of each to draw a sharp knife prevented by the strong intertwining arms of the other.

The store-keeper, at a safe distance, remonstrated with both, to no purpose, and as the struggle could end only in freeing a murderous hand he rushed into the clearing, shouting the magical word "Fight!" with all the strength of his lungs. There was no immediate response, save that the affrighted rocks rang with the frenzied cry, and the motionless woods and the white moonlight seemed pervaded with myriads of strange, uncanny voices. Then a cautious shutter of a glassless window was opened, and through the narrow chink there fell a bar of red light, on which was clearly defined an inquiring head, like an inquisitively expressive silhouette. "They air a-fightin' yander ter the store, whar they air a-playin' of Old Sledge," said the master of the shanty, for the enlightenment of the curious within. And then he closed the shutter, and like the law-abiding citizen that he was betook himself to his broken rest. This was the only expression of interest elicited.

A dreadful anxiety was astir in the store-keeper's thoughts. One of the men would certainly be killed; but he cared not so much for the shedding of blood in the abstract as that the deed should be committed on his premises at the dead of night; and there might be such a concatenation of circumstances, through the malefactor's willful perversion of the facts, that suspicion would fall upon him. The first circuit court ever held in the new county would be in session to-morrow; and the terrors of the law, deadly to an unaccustomed mind, were close upon him. Finding no help from without, he rushed back into the store, determined to make one more appeal to the belligerents. "Budd," he cried, "I'll holp ye ter hold Josiah, ef ye'll promise ye won't tech him ter hurt. He air crazed, through a-losin' of his truck. Say ye won't tech him ter hurt, an' I'll holp ye ter hold him."

Josiah succumbed to their united efforts, and presently made no further show of resistance, but sank, still panting, into one of the chairs beside the inverted basket, and gazed blankly, with the eyes of a despairing, hunted creature, out at the sheen of the moonlight.

"I ain't a-wantin' ter hurt nobody," said Wray, in a surly tone. "I never axed him ter play kyerds, nor ter bet, nor nuthin'. He l'arned me hisself, an' ef I hed los' stiddier of him he would be a-thinkin' now ez it's all right."

"I'm a-goin' ter stand up ter what I done said, though," Josiah declared brokenly. "Ye needn't be afeard ez how I ain't a-goin' ter make my words true. Ef ye comes hyar at noon ter-morrer, ye'll git that thar deed, an' ye kin take the house an' land ez I an' my folks hev hed nigh on ter a hundred year. I ain't a-goin' ter fail o' my word, though."

He rose suddenly, and stepped out of the door. His footfalls sounded with a sullen thud in the utter quietude of the place; a long shadow thrown by the sinking moon dogged him noiselessly as he went, until he plunged into the depths of the woods, and their gloom absorbed both him and his silent pursuer.

A dank, sunless morning dawned upon the house in which Josiah Tait and his fathers had lived for nearly a hundred years: it was a humble log cabin nestled in the dense forest, about four miles from the Settlement. Fifty cleared acres, in an irregular shape, lay behind it; the cornstalks, sole remnant of the crop lost at Old Sledge, were still standing, their sickly yellow tint blanched by contrast with the dark brown of the tall weeds in a neighboring field, that had grown up after the harvested wheat, and flourished in the summer sun, and died under the first fall of the frost. A heavy moisture lay upon them at noon, this dreary autumnal day; a wet cloud hung in the tree-tops; here and there among its gray vapors, a scarlet bough flamed with sharply accented intensity. There was no far-reaching perspective in the long aisles of the woods; the all-pervading mist had enwrapped the world, and here, close at hand, were bronze-green trees, and there spectre-like outlines of boles and branches, dimly seen in the haze, and beyond an opaque, colorless curtain. From the chimney of the house the smoke rose slowly; the doors were closed, and not a creature was visible save ten hogs prowling about in front of the dwelling among the fallen acorns, pausing and looking up with that odd, porcine expression of mingled impudence and malignity as Budd Wray appeared suddenly in the mist and made his way to the cabin.

He knocked; there was a low-toned response. After hesitating a moment, he lifted the latch and went in. He was evidently unexpected; the two occupants of the room looked at him with startled eyes, in which, however, the momentary surprise was presently merged in an expression of bitter dislike. The elder, a faded, careworn woman of fifty, turned back without a word to her employment of washing clothes. The younger, a pretty girl of eighteen, looked hard at him with fast-filling blue eyes, and rising from her low chair beside the fire said, in a voice broken by grief and resentment, "Ef this hyar house air yourn, Budd Wray, I wants ter git out 'n it."

"I hev come hyar ter tell ye a word," said Budd Wray, meeting her tearful glance with a stern stolidity. He flung himself into a chair, and fixing his moody eyes on the fire went on: "A word ez I hev been a-aimin' an' a-contrivin' ter tell ye ever sence ye war married ter Josiah Tait, an' afore that,—ever sence ye tuk back the word ez ye hed gin me afore ye ever seen him, 'kase o' his hevin' a house, an' critters, an' sech like. He hain't got none now,—none of 'em. I hev been a-layin' off ter bring him ter this pass fur a long time, 'count of the scandalous way ye done treated me a year ago las' June. He hain't got no house, nor no critters, nor nuthin'. I done it, an' I come hyar with the deed in my pocket ter tell ye what I done it fur."

Her tears flowed afresh, and she looked appealingly at him. He did not remove his indignant eyes from the blaze, stealing timidly up the smoky chimney. "I never hed nuthin' much," he continued, "an' I never said I hed nuthin' much, like Josiah; but I thought ez how ye an' me might make out toler'ble well, bein' ez we sot consider'ble store by each other in them days, afore he ever tuk ter comin' a-huntin' yander ter Scrub-Oak Ridge, whar ye war a-livin' then. I don't keer nuthin' 'bout 'n it now, 'ceptin' it riles me, an' I war bound ter spite ye fur it. I don't keer nuthin' more 'bout *ye* now than fur one o' them thar dead leaves. I want ye ter know I jes' done it ter spite ye,—*ye* is the one. I hain't got no grudge agin Josiah ter talk about. He done like any other man would."

The color flared into the drooping face, and there was a flash in the weeping blue eyes.

"I s'pose I hed a right ter make a ch'ice," she said, angrily, stung by these taunts.

"Jes' so," responded Wray, coolly; "ye hed a right ter make a ch'ice a-twixt two men, but no gal hev got a right ter put a man on one eend o' the beam, an' a lot o' senseless critters an' house an' land on the t'other. Ye never keered nuthin' fur me nor Josiah nuther, ef the truth war knowed; ye war all tuk up with the house an' land an' critters. An' they hev done lef ye, what nare one o' the men would hev done."

77

The girl burst into convulsive sobs, but the sight of her distress had no softening influence upon Wray. "I hev done it ter pay ye back fur what ye hev done ter me, an' I reckon ye'll 'low now ez we air toler'ble even. Ye tuk all I keered fur away from me, an' now I hev tuk all ye keer fur away from ye. An' I'm a-goin' now yander ter the Settlemint ter hev this hyar deed recorded on the book ter the court-house, like Lawyer Green tole me ter do right straight. I laid off, though, ter come hyar fust, an' tell ye what I hev been aimin' ter be able ter tell ye fur a year an' better. An' now I'm a-goin' ter git this hyar deed recorded."

He replaced the sheet of scrawled legal-cap in his pocket, and rose to go; then turned, and, leaning heavily on the back of his chair, looked at her with lowering eyes.

"Ye're a pore little critter," he said, with scathing contempt. "I dunno what ails Josiah nor me nuther ter hev sot our hearts on sech a little stalk o' cheat."

He went out into the enveloping mountain mist with the sound of her weeping ringing in his ears. His eyes were hot, and his angry heart was heavy. He had schemed and waited for his revenge with persistent patience. Fortune had favored him, but now that it had fully come, strangely enough it failed to satisfy him. The deed in his breast-pocket weighed like a stone, and as he rode on through the clouds that lay upon the mountain top, the sense of its pressure became almost unendurable. And yet, with a perplexing contrariety of emotion, he felt more bitterly toward her than ever, and experienced a delight almost savage in holding the possessions for which she had been so willing to resign him. "Jes' kicked me out 'n the way like I war nuthin' more 'n that thar branch o' pisen-oak, fur a passel o' cattle an' sech like critters, an' a house an' land,—'kase I don't count Josiah in. 'Twar the house an' land an' sech she war a-studyin' 'bout." And every moment the weight of the deed grew heavier. He took scant notice of external objects as he went, keeping mechanically along the path, closed in twenty yards ahead of him by the opaque curtain of mist. The trees at the greatest distance visible stood shadow-like and colorless in their curious, unreal atmosphere; but now and then the faintest flake of a pale rose tint would appear in the pearly haze, deepening and deepening, till at the vanishing point of the perspective a gorgeous scarlet-oak tree would rise, red enough to make a respectable appearance on the planet Mars. There was an audible stir breaking upon the silence of the solemn woods, the leaves were rustling together, and drops of moisture began to patter down upon the ground. The perspective grew gradually longer and longer, as the rising wind cleared the forest aisles; and when he reached the road that ran between the precipice and the steep ascent above, the clouds were falling apart, the mist had broken into thousands of fleecy white wreaths, clinging to the fantastically tinted foliage, and the sunlight was striking deep into the valley. The woods about the Settlement were all aglow with color, and sparkling with the tremulous drops that shimmered in the sun.

There was an unwonted air of animation and activity pervading the place. To the court-house fence were hitched several lean, forlorn horses, with shabby old saddles, or sometimes merely blankets; two or three wagons were standing among the stumps in the clearing. The door of the store was occupied by a coterie of mountaineers, talking with unusual vivacity of the most startling event that had agitated the whole country-side for a score of years,—the winning of Josiah Tait's house and land at Old Sledge. The same subject was rife among the choice spirits congregated in the court-house yard and about the portal of that temple of justice, and Wray's approach was watched with the keenest interest.

He dismounted, and walked slowly to the door, paused, and turning as with a sudden thought threw himself hastily upon his horse; he dashed across the clearing, galloped heedlessly down the long, steep slope, and the astounded loiterers heard the thunder of the hoofs as they beat at a break-neck speed upon the frail, rotten timbers of the bridge below.

Josiah Tait had put his troubles in to soak at the still-house, and this circumstance did not tend to improve the cheerfulness of his little, home when he returned in the afternoon. The few necessities left to the victims of Old Sledge had been packed together, and were in readiness to be transported with him, his wife, and mother-in-law to Melinda's old home on Scrub-Oak Ridge, when her brother should drive his wagon over for them the next morning.

They never knew how to account for it. While the forlorn family were sitting before the smoking fire, as the day waned, the door was suddenly burst open, and Budd Wray strode in impetuously. A brilliant flame shot up the chimney, and the deed which Josiah Tait had that day executed was a cinder among the logs. He went as he came, and the mystery was never explained.

There was, however, "a sayin' goin' 'bout the mounting ez how Josiah an' Melindy jes' 'ticed him, somehow 'nother, ter thar house, an' held him, an' tuk the deed away from him tergether. An' they made him send back the critters an' the corn what he done won away from 'em." This version came to his ears, and was never denied. He was more ashamed of relenting in his vengeance than of the wild legend that he had been worsted in a tussle with Melinda and Josiah.

And since the night of Budd Wray's barren success the playing of Old Sledge has become a lost art at the Settlement.

THE STAR IN THE VALLEY.

He first saw it in the twilight of a clear October evening. As the earliest planet sprang into the sky, an answering gleam shone red amid the glooms in the valley. A star too it seemed. And later, when the myriads of the fairer, whiter lights of a moonless night were all athrob in the great concave vault bending to the hills, there was something very impressive in that solitary star of earth, changeless and motionless beneath the ever-changing skies.

Chevis never tired of looking at it. Somehow it broke the spell that draws all eyes heavenward on starry nights. He often strolled with his cigar at dusk down to the verge of the crag, and sat for hours gazing at it and vaguely speculating about it. That spark seemed to have kindled all the soul and imagination within him, although he knew well enough its prosaic source, for he had once questioned the gawky mountaineer whose services he had secured as guide through the forest solitudes during this hunting expedition.

"That thar spark in the valley?" Hi Bates had replied, removing the pipe from his lips and emitting a cloud of strong tobacco smoke. "'Tain't nuthin' but the light in Jerry Shaw's house, 'bout haffen mile from the foot of the mounting. Ye pass that thar house when ye goes on the Christel road, what leads down the mounting off the Backbone. That's Jerry Shaw's house,—that's what it is. He's a blacksmith, an' he kin shoe a horse toler'ble well when he ain't drunk, ez he mos'ly is."

"Perhaps that is the light from the forge," suggested Chevis.

"That thar forge ain't run more 'n half the day, let 'lone o' nights. I hev never hearn tell on Jerry Shaw a-workin' o' nights,—nor in the daytime nuther, ef he kin git shet of it. No sech no 'count critter 'twixt hyar an' the Settlemint."

So spake Chevis's astronomer. Seeing the star even through the prosaic lens of stern reality did not detract from its poetic aspect. Chevis never failed to watch for it. The first faint glinting in the azure evening sky sent his eyes to that red reflection suddenly aglow in the valley; even when the mists rose above it and hid it from him, he gazed at the spot where it had disappeared, feeling a calm satisfaction to know that it was still shining beneath the cloud-curtain. He encouraged himself in this bit of sentimentality. These unique eventide effects seemed a fitting sequel to the picturesque day, passed in hunting deer, with horn and hounds, through the gorgeous autumnal forest; or perchance in the more exciting sport in some rocky gorge with a bear at bay and the frenzied pack around him; or in the idyllic pleasures of bird-shooting with a thoroughly-trained dog; and coming back in the crimson sunset to a well-appointed tent and a smoking supper of venison or wild turkey,—the trophies of his skill. The vague dreaminess of his cigar and the charm of that bright bit of color in the night-shrouded valley added a sort of romantic zest to these primitive enjoyments, and ministered to that keen susceptibility of impressions which Reginald Chevis considered eminently characteristic of a highly wrought mind and nature.

He said nothing of his fancies, however, to his fellow sportsman, Ned Varney, nor to the mountaineer. Infinite as was the difference between these two in mind and cultivation, his observation of both had convinced him that they were alike incapable of appreciating and comprehending his delicate and dainty musings. Varney was essentially a man of this world; his mental and moral conclusions had been adopted in a calm, mercantile spirit, as giving the best return for the outlay, and the market was not liable to fluctuations. And the mountaineer could go no further than the prosaic fact of the light in Jerry Shaw's house. Thus Reginald Chevis was wont to sit in contemplative silence on the crag until his cigar was burnt out, and afterward to lie awake deep in the night, listening to the majestic lyric welling up from the thousand nocturnal voices of these mountain wilds.

During the day, in place of the red light a gauzy little curl of smoke was barely visible, the only sign or suggestion of human habitation to be seen from the crag in all the many miles of long, narrow valley and parallel tiers of ranges. Sometimes Chevis and Varney caught sight of it from lower down on the mountain side, whence was faintly distinguishable the little log-house and certain vague lines marking a rectangular inclosure; near at hand, too, the forge, silent and smokeless. But it did not immediately occur to either of them to theorize concerning its inmates and their lives in this lonely place; for a time, not even to the speculative Chevis. As to Varney, he gave his whole mind to the matter in hand,—his gun, his dog, his game,—and his note-book was as systematic and as romantic as the ledger at home.

It might be accounted an event in the history of that log-hut when Reginald Chevis, after riding past it eighty yards or so, chanced one day to meet a country girl walking toward the house. She did not look up, and he caught only an indistinct glimpse of her face. She spoke to him, however, as she went by, which is the invariable custom with the inhabitants of the sequestered nooks among the encompassing mountains, whether meeting stranger or acquaintance. He lifted his hat in return, with that punctilious courtesy which he made a point of according to persons of low degree. In another moment she had passed down the narrow sandy road, overhung with gigantic trees, and, at a deft, even pace, hardly

83

slackened as she traversed the great log extending across the rushing stream, she made her way up the opposite hill, and disappeared gradually over its brow.

The expression of her face, half-seen though it was, had attracted his attention. He rode slowly along, meditating. "Did she go into Shaw's house, just around the curve of the road?" he wondered. "Is she Shaw's daughter, or some visiting neighbor?"

That night he looked with a new interest at the red star, set like a jewel in the floating mists of the valley.

"Do you know," he asked of Hi Bates, when the three men were seated, after supper, around the camp-fire, which sent lurid tongues of flame and a thousand bright sparks leaping high in the darkness, and illumined the vistas of the woods on every side, save where the sudden crag jutted over the valley,—"Do you know whether Jerry Shaw has a daughter,—a young girl?"

"Ye-es," drawled Hi Bates, disparagingly, "he hev."

A pause ensued. The star in the valley was blotted from sight; the rising mists had crept to the verge of the crag; nay, in the undergrowth fringing the mountain's brink, there were softly clinging white wreaths.

"Is she pretty?" asked Chevis.

"Waal, no, she ain't," said Hi Bates, decisively. "She's a pore, no 'count critter." Then he added, as if he were afraid of being misapprehended, "Not ez thar is any harm in the gal, ye onderstand. She's a mighty good, saft-spoken, quiet sort o' gal, but she's a pore, white-faced, slim little critter. She looks like she hain't got no sort'n grit in her. She makes me think o' one o' them slim little slips o' willow every time nor I sees her. She hain't got long ter live, I reckon," he concluded, dismally.

84

Reginald Chevis asked him no more questions about Jerry Shaw's daughter.

Not long afterward, when Chevis was hunting through the deep woods about the base of the mountain near the Christel road, his horse happened to cast a shoe. He congratulated himself upon his proximity to the forge, for there was a possibility that the blacksmith might be at work; according to the account which Hi Bates had given of Jerry Shaw's habits, there were half a dozen chances against it. But the shop was at no great distance, and he set out to find his way back to the Christel road, guided by sundry well-known landmarks on the mountain side: certain great crags hanging above the tree-tops, showing in grander sublimity through the thinning foliage, or beetling bare and grim; a dismantled and deserted hovel, the red-berried vines twining amongst the rotting logs; the full flow of a tumultuous stream making its last leap down a precipice eighty feet high, with yeasty, maddening waves below and a rainbow-crowned crystal sheet above. And here again the curves of the woodland road. As the sound of the falling water grew softer and softer in the distance, till it was hardly more than a drowsy murmur, the faint vibrations of a far-off anvil rang upon the air. Welcome indeed to Chevis, for however enticing might be the long rambles through the redolent October woods with dog and gun, he had no mind to tramp up the mountain to his tent, five miles distant, leading the resisting horse all the way. The afternoon was so clear and so still that the metallic sound penetrated far through the quiet forest. At every curve of the road he expected to see the log-cabin with its rail fence, and beyond the low-hanging chestnut-tree, half its branches resting upon the roof of the little shanty of a blacksmith's shop. After many windings a sharp turn brought him full upon the humble dwelling, with its background of primeval woods and the purpling splendors of the western hills. The chickens were going to roost in a

85

stunted cedar-tree just without the door; an incredibly old man, feeble and bent, sat dozing in the lingering sunshine on the porch; a girl, with a pail on her head, was crossing the road and going down a declivity toward a spring which bubbled up in a cleft of the gigantic rocks that were piled one above another, rising to a great height. A mingled breath of cool, dripping water, sweet-scented fern, and pungent mint greeted him as he passed it. He did not see the girl's face, for she had left the road before he went by, but he recognized the slight figure, with that graceful poise acquired by the prosaic habit of carrying weights upon the head, and its lithe, swaying beauty reminded him of the mountaineer's comparison,—a slip of willow.

And now, under the chestnut-tree, in anxious converse with Jerry Shaw, who came out hammer in hand from the anvil, concerning the shoe to be put on Strathspey's left fore-foot, and the problematic damage sustained since the accident. Chevis's own theory occupied some minutes in expounding, and so absorbed his attention that he did not observe, until the horse was fairly under the blacksmith's hands, that, despite Jerry Shaw's unaccustomed industry, this was by no means a red-letter day in his habitual dissipation. He trembled for Strathspey, but it was too late now to interfere. Jerry Shaw was in that stage of drunkenness which is greatly accented by an elaborate affectation of sobriety. His desire that Chevis should consider him perfectly sober was abundantly manifest in his rigidly steady gait, the preternatural gravity in his bloodshot eyes, his sparingness of speech, and the earnestness with which he enunciated the acquiescent formulæ which had constituted his share of the conversation. Now and then, controlling his faculties by a great effort, he looked hard at Chevis to discover what doubts might be expressed in his face concerning the genuineness of this staid deportment; and Chevis presently found it best to affect too. Believing that the blacksmith's histrionic attempts in the *rôle* of sober artisan were occupying his attention more than the paring of Strathspey's hoof, which he held between his knees on his leather apron, while the horse danced an animated measure on the other three feet, Chevis assumed an appearance of indifference, and strolled away into the shop. He looked about him, carelessly, at the horseshoes hanging on a rod in the rude aperture that served as window, at the wagon-tires, the plowshares, the glowing fire of the forge. The air within was unpleasantly close, and he soon found himself again in the door-way.

"Can I get some water here?" he asked, as Jerry Shaw reëntered, and began hammering vigorously at the shoe destined for Strathspey.

The resonant music ceased for a moment. The solemn, drunken eyes were slowly turned upon the visitor, and the elaborate affectation of sobriety was again obtrusively apparent in the blacksmith's manner. He rolled up more closely the blue-checked homespun sleeve from his corded hammer-arm, twitched nervously at the single suspender that supported his copper-colored jeans trousers, readjusted his leather apron hanging about his neck, and, casting upon Chevis another glance, replete with a challenging gravity, fell to work upon the anvil, every heavy and well-directed blow telling with the precision of machinery.

The question had hardly been heard before forgotten. At the next interval, when he was going out to fit the horse, Chevis repeated his request.

"Water, did ye say?" asked Jerry Shaw, looking at him with narrowing eyelids, as if to shut out all other contemplation that he might grapple with this problem. "Thar's no fraish water hyar, but ye kin go yander ter the house and ax fur some; or," he added, shading his eyes from the sunlight with his broad, blackened hand, and looking at the huge wall of stone beyond the road, "ye kin go down yander ter the spring, an' ax that thar gal fur a drink."

Chevis took his way, in the last rays of sunshine, across the road and down the declivity in the direction indicated by the blacksmith. A cool gray shadow fell upon him from the heights of the great rocks, as he neared them; the narrow path leading from the road grew dank and moist, and presently his feet were sunk in the still green and odorous water-loving weeds, the clumps of fern, and the pungent mint. He did not notice the soft verdure; he did not even see the beautiful vines that hung from earth-filled niches among the rocks, and lent to their forbidding aspect something of a smiling grace; their picturesque grouping, where they had fallen apart to show this sparkling fountain of bright up-springing water, was all lost upon his artistic perceptions. His eyes were fixed on the girl standing beside the spring, her pail filled, but waiting, with a calm, expectant look on her face, as she saw him approaching.

No creature could have been more coarsely habited: a green cotton dress, faded to the faintest hue; rough shoes, just visible beneath her skirts; a dappled gray and brown calico sun-bonnet, thrown aside on a moss-grown bowlder near at hand. But it seemed as if the wild nature about her had been generous to this being toward whom life and fortune had played the niggard. There were opaline lights in her dreamy eyes which one sees nowhere save in sunset clouds that brood above dark hills; the golden sunbeams, all faded from the landscape, had left a perpetual reflection in her bronze hair; there was a subtle affinity between her and other pliant, swaying, graceful young things, waving in the mountain breezes, fed by the rain and the dew. She was hardly more human to Chevis than certain lissome little woodland flowers, the very names of which he did not know,—pure white, star-shaped, with a faint green line threading its way through each of the five delicate petals; he had seen them embellishing the banks of lonely pools, or growing in dank, marshy places in the middle of the unfrequented road, where perhaps it had been mended in a primitive way with a few rotting rails.

"May I trouble you to give me some water?" asked Chevis, prosaically enough. She neither smiled nor replied. She took the gourd from the pail, dipped it into the lucent depths of the spring, handed it to him, and stood awaiting its return when he should have finished. The cool, delicious water was drained, and he gave the gourd back. "I am much obliged," he said.

"Ye're welcome," she replied, in a slow, singing monotone. Had the autumn winds taught her voice that melancholy cadence?

Chevis would have liked to hear her speak again, but the gulf between his station and hers—so undreamed of by her (for the differences of caste are absolutely unknown to the independent mountaineers), so patent to him—could be bridged by few ideas. They had so little in common that for a moment he could think of nothing to say. His cogitation suggested only the inquiry, "Do you live here?" indicating the little house on the other side of the road.

"Yes," she chanted in the same monotone, "I lives hyar."

She turned to lift the brimming pail. Chevis spoke again: "Do you always stay at home? Do you never go anywhere?"

Her eyes rested upon him, with a slight surprise looking out from among their changing lights. "No," she said, after a pause; "I hev no call to go nowhar ez I knows on."

She placed the pail on her head, took the dappled sun-bonnet in her hand, and went along the path with the assured, steady gait and the graceful backward poise of the figure that precluded the possibility of spilling a drop from the vessel.

He had been touched in a highly romantic way by the sweet beauty of this little woodland flower. It seemed hard that so perfect a thing of its kind should be wasted here, unseen by more appreciative eyes than those of bird, or rabbit, or the equally uncultured human beings about her; and it gave him a baffling sense of the mysterious injustice of life to reflect upon the difference in her lot and that of others of her age in higher spheres. He went thoughtfully through the closing shadows to the shop, mounted the re-shod Strathspey, and rode along the rugged ascent of the mountain, gravely pondering on worldly inequalities.

He saw her often afterward, although he spoke to her again but once. He sometimes stopped as he came and went on the Christel road, and sat chatting with the old man, her grandfather, on the porch, sunshiny days, or lounged in the barn-like door of Jerry Shaw's shop talking to the half-drunken blacksmith. He piqued himself on the readiness with which he became interested in these people, entered into their thoughts and feelings, obtained a comprehensive idea of the machinery of life in this wilderness,—more complicated than one could readily believe, looking upon the changeless face of the wide, unpopulated expanse of mountain ranges stretching so far beneath that infinite sky. They appealed to him from the basis of their common humanity, he thought, and the pleasure of watching the development of the common human attributes in this peculiar and primitive state of society never palled upon him. He regarded with contempt Varney's frivolous displeasure and annoyance because of Hi Bates's utter insensibility to the difference in their social position, and the necessity of either acquiescing in the supposititious equality or dispensing with the invaluable services of the proud and independent mountaineer; because of the *patois* of the untutored people, to hear which, Varney was wont to declare, set his teeth on edge; because of their narrow prejudices, their mental poverty, their idle shiftlessness, their uncouth dress and appearance. Chevis flattered himself that he entertained a broader view. He had not even a subacute idea that he looked upon these people and their inner life only as picturesque bits of the mental and moral landscape; that it was an æsthetic and theoretical pleasure their contemplation afforded him; that he was as far as ever from the basis of common humanity.

Sometimes while he talked to the old man on the sunlit porch, the "slip o' willow" sat in the door-way, listening too, but never speaking. Sometimes he would find her with her father at the forge, her fair, ethereal face illumined with an alien and fluctuating brilliancy, shining and fading as the breath of the fire rose and fell. He came to remember that face so well that in a sorry sketch-book, where nothing else was finished, there were several laborious pages lighted up with a faint reflection of its beauty. But he was as much interested perhaps, though less poetically, in that massive figure, the idle blacksmith. He looked at it all from an ideal point of view. The star in the valley was only a brilliant, set in the night landscape, and suggested a unique and pleasing experience.

How should he imagine what luminous and wistful eyes were turned upward to where another star burned,—the light of his camp-fire on the crag; what pathetic, beautiful eyes had learned to watch and wait for that red gleam high on the mountain's brow,—hardly below the stars in heaven it seemed! How could he dream of the strange, vague, unreasoning trouble with which his idle comings and goings had clouded that young life, a trouble as strange, as vague, as vast, as the limitless sky above her.

She understood him as little. As she sat in the open doorway, with the flare of the fire behind her, and gazed at the red light shining on the crag, she had no idea of the heights of worldly differences that divided them, more insurmountable than precipices and flying chutes of mountain torrents, and chasms and fissures of the wild ravine: she knew nothing of the life he had left, and of its rigorous artificialities and gradations of wealth and estimation. And with a heart full of pitiable unrealities she looked up at the glittering simulacrum of a star on the crag, while he gazed down on the ideal star in the valley.

The weeks had worn deep into November. Chevis and Varney were thinking of going home; indeed, they talked of breaking camp day after to-morrow, and saying a long adieu to wood and mountain and stream. They had had an abundance of good sport and a surfeit of roughing it. They would go back to town and town avocations invigorated by their holiday, and taking with them a fresh and exhilarating recollection of the forest life left so far behind.

It was near dusk, on a dull, cold evening, when Chevis dismounted before the door of the blacksmith's little log-cabin. The chestnut-tree hung desolate and bare on the eaves of the forge; the stream rushed by in swift gray whirlpools under a sullen gray sky; the gigantic wall of broken rocks loomed gloomy and sinister on the opposite side of the road,—not so much as a withered leaf of all their vines clung to their rugged surfaces. The mountains had changed color: the nearest ranges were black with the myriads of the grim black branches of the denuded forest; far away they stretched in parallel lines, rising tier above tier, and showing numberless gradations of a dreary, neutral tint, which grew ever fainter in the distance, till merged in the uniform tone of the sombre sky.

Indoors it was certainly more cheerful. A hickory fire dispensed alike warmth and light. The musical whir of a spinning-wheel added its unique charm. From the rafters depended numberless strings of bright red pepper-pods and ears of pop-corn; hanks of woolen and cotton yarn; bunches of medicinal herbs; brown gourds and little bags of seeds. On rude shelves against the wall were ranged cooking utensils, drinking vessels, etc., all distinguished by that scrupulous cleanliness which is a marked feature of the poor hovels of these mountaineers, and in striking contrast to the poor hovels of lowlanders. The rush-bottomed chairs, drawn in a semicircle before the rough, ill-adjusted stones which did duty as hearth, were occupied by several men, who seemed to be making the blacksmith a prolonged visit; various members of the family were humbly seated on sundry inverted domestic articles, such as wash-tubs, and splint-baskets made of white oak. There was circulating among Jerry Shaw's friends a flat bottle, facetiously denominated "tickler," readily emptied, but as readily replenished from a keg in the corner. Like the widow's cruse of oil, that keg was miraculously never empty. The fact of a still near by in the wild ravine might suggest a reason for its perennial flow. It was a good strong article of apple-brandy, and its effects were beginning to be distinctly visible.

Truly the ethereal woodland flower seemed strangely incongruous with these brutal and uncouth conditions of her life, as she stood at a little distance from this group, spinning at her wheel. Chevis felt a sudden sharp pang of pity for her when he glanced toward her; the next instant he had forgotten it in his interest in her work. It was altogether at variance with the ideas which he had hitherto entertained concerning that humble handicraft. There came across him a vague recollection from his city life that the peasant girls of art galleries and of the lyric stage were wont to sit at the wheel. "But perhaps they were spinning flax," he reflected.

This spinning was a matter of walking back and forth with smooth, measured steps and graceful, undulatory motion; a matter, too, of much pretty gesticulation,—the thread in one hand, the other regulating the whirl of the wheel. He thought he had never seen attitudes so charming.

Jerry Shaw hastened to abdicate and offer one of the rush-bottomed chairs with the eager hospitality characteristic of these mountaineers,—a a hospitality that meets a stranger on the threshold of every hut, presses upon him, ungrudgingly, its best, and follows him on his departure with protestations of regret out to the rickety fence. Chevis was more or less known to all of the visitors, and after a little, under the sense of familiarity and the impetus of the apple-brandy, the talk flowed on as freely as before his entrance. It was wilder and more antagonistic to his principles and prejudices than anything he had hitherto heard among these people, and he looked on and listened, interested in this new development of a phase of life which he had thought he had sounded from its lowest note to the top of its compass. He was glad to remain; the scene had impressed his cultivated perceptions as an interior by Teniers might have done, and the vehemence and lawlessness of the conversation and the threats of violence had little reality for him; if he thought about the subject under discussion at all, it was with a reassuring conviction that before the plans could be carried out the already intoxicated mountaineers would he helplessly drunk. Nevertheless, he glanced ever and anon at the young girl, loath that she should hear it, lest its virulent, angry bitterness should startle her. She was evidently listening, too, but her fair face was as calm and untroubled as one of the pure white faces of those flower-stars of his early stay in the mountains.

"Them Peels oughtn't ter be let live!" exclaimed Elijah Burr, a gigantic fellow, arrayed in brown jeans, with the accompaniments of knife, powder-horn, etc., usual with the hunters of the range; his gun stood, with those of the other guests, against the wall in a corner of the room. "They oughtn't ter be let live, an' I'd top off all three of 'em fur the skin an' horns of a deer."

"That thar is a true word," assented Jerry Shaw. "They oughter be run down an' kilt,—all three o' them Peels."

Chevis could not forbear a question. Always on the alert to add to his stock of knowledge of men and minds, always analyzing his own inner life and the inner life of those about him, he said, turning to his intoxicated host, "Who are the Peels, Mr. Shaw,—if I may ask?"

"Who air the Peels?" repeated Jerry Shaw, making a point of seizing the question. "They air the meanest men in these hyar mountings. Ye might hunt from Copperhead Ridge ter Clinch River, an' the whole spread o' the valley, an' never hear tell o' no sech no 'count critters."

"They oughtn't ter be let live!" again urged Elijah Burr. "No man ez treats his wife like that dad-burned scoundrel Ike Peel do oughter be let live. That thar woman is my sister an' Jerry Shaw's cousin,—an' I shot him down in his own door year afore las'. I shot him ter kill; but somehow 'nother I war that shaky, an' the cussed gun hung fire a-fust, an' that thar pore wife o' his'n screamed an' hollered so, that I never done nuthin' arter all but lay him up for four month an' better for that thar pore critter ter nuss. He'll see a mighty differ nex' time I gits my chance. An' 'tain't fur off," he added threateningly.

"Wouldn't it be better to persuade her to leave him?" suggested Chevis pacifically, without, however, any wild idea of playing peace-maker between fire and tow.

Burr growled a fierce oath, and then was silent.

A slow fellow on the opposite side of the fire-place explained: "Thar's whar all the trouble kem from. She wouldn't leave him, fur all he treated her awful. She said ez how he war mighty good ter her when he warn't drunk. So 'Lijah shot him."

This way of cutting the Gordian knot of domestic difficulties might have proved efficacious but for the shakiness induced by the thrill of fraternal sentiment, the infusion of apple-brandy, the protest of the bone of contention, and the hanging fire of the treacherous gun. Elijah Burr could remember no other failure of aim for twenty years.

"He won't git shet of me that easy agin!" Burr declared, with another pull at the flat tickler. "But ef it hedn't hev been fur what happened las' week, I mought hev let him off fur awhile," he continued, evidently actuated by some curiously distorted sense of duty in the premises. "I oughter hev kilt him afore. But now the cussed critter is a gone coon. Dad-burn the whole tribe!"

Chevis was desirous of knowing what had happened last week. He did not, however, feel justified in asking more questions. But apple-brandy is a potent tongue-loosener, and the unwonted communicativeness of the stolid and silent mountaineers attested its strength in this regard. Jerry Shaw, without inquiry, enlightened him.

"Ye see," he said, turning to Chevis, "'Lijah he thought ez how ef he could git that fool woman ter come ter his house, he could shoot Ike fur his meanness 'thout botherin' of her, an' things would all git easy agin. Waal, he went thar one day when all them Peels, the whole lay-out, war gone down ter the Settlemint ter hear the rider preach, an' he jes' run away with two of the brats,—the littlest ones, ye onderstand,—a-thinkin' he mought tole her off from Ike that thar way. We hearn ez how the pore critter war nigh onter distracted 'bout 'em, but Ike never let her come arter 'em. Leastways, she never kem. Las' week Ike kem fur 'em hisself,—him an' them two cussed brothers o' his'n. All 'Lijah's folks war out'n the way; him an' his boys war off a-huntin', an' his wife hed gone down ter the spring, a haffen mile an' better, a-washin' clothes; nobody war ter the house 'ceptin' them two chillen o' Ike's. An' Ike and his brothers jes' tuk the chillen away, an' set fire ter the house; an' time 'Lijah's wife got thar, 'twar nuthin' but a pile o' ashes. So we've determinated ter go up yander ter Laurel Notch, twenty mile along the ridge of the mounting, ter-night, an' wipe out them Peels,—'kase they air a-goin' ter move away. That thar wife o' Ike's, what made all the trouble, hev fretted an' fretted at Ike till he hev determinated ter break up an' wagon across the range ter Kaintucky, whar his uncle lives in the hills thar. Ike hev gin his cornsent ter go jes' ter pleasure her, 'kase she air mos' crazed ter git Ike away whar 'Lijah can't kill him. Ike's brothers is a-goin', too. I hearn ez how they'll make a start at noon ter-morrer."

"They'll never start ter Kaintucky ter-morrer," said Burr, grimly. "They'll git off, afore that, fur hell, stiddier Kaintucky. I hev been a-tryin' ter make out ter shoot that thar man ever sence that thar gal war married ter him, seven year ago,—seven year an' better. But what with her a-foolin' round, an' a-talkin', an' a-goin' on like she war distracted— she run right 'twixt him an' the muzzle of my gun wunst, or I would hev hed him that time fur sure—an' somehow 'nother that critter makes me so shaky with her ways of goin' on that I feel like I hain't got good sense, an' can't git no good aim at nuthin'. Nex' time, though, thar'll be a differ. She ain't a-goin' ter Kaintucky along of him ter be beat fur nuthin' when he's drunk."

It was a pitiable picture presented to Chevis's open-eyed imagination,—this woman standing for years between the two men she loved: holding back her brother from his vengeance of her wrongs by that subtle influence that shook his aim; and going into exile with her brute of a husband when that influence had waned and failed, and her wrongs were supplemented by deep and irreparable injuries to her brother. And the curious moral attitude of the man: the strong fraternal feeling that alternately nerved and weakened his revengeful hand.

"We air goin' thar 'bout two o'clock ter-night," said Jerry Shaw, "and wipe out all three o' them Peels,—Ike an' his two brothers."

"They oughtn't ter be let live," reiterated Elijah Burr, moodily. Did he speak to his faintly stirring conscience, or to a woful premonition of his sister's grief?

"They'll all three be stiff an' stark afore daybreak," resumed Jerry Shaw. "We air all kin ter 'Lijah, an' we air goin' ter holp him top off them Peels. Thar's ten of us an' three o' them, an' we won't hev no trouble 'bout it. An' we'll bring that pore critter, Ike's wife, an' her chillen hyar ter stay. She's welcome ter live along of us till 'Lijah kin fix some sort'n place fur her an' the little chillen. Thar won't be no trouble a-gittin' rid of the men folks, ez thar is ten of us an' three o' them, an' we air goin' ter take 'em in the night."

There was a protest from an unexpected quarter. The whir of the spinning-wheel was abruptly silenced. "I don't see no sense," said Celia Shaw, her singing monotone vibrating in the sudden lull,—"I don't see no sense in shootin' folks down like they war nuthin' better nor bear, nor deer, nor suthin' wild. I don't see no sense in it. An' I never did see none."

There was an astonished pause.

"Shet up, Cely! Shet up!" exclaimed Jerry Shaw, in mingled anger and surprise. "Them folks ain't no better nor bear, nor sech. They hain't got no right ter live,—them Peels."

"No, that they hain't!" said Burr.

"They is powerful no 'count critters, I know," replied the little woodland flower, the firelight bright in her opaline eyes and on the flakes of burnished gold gleaming in the dark masses of her hair. "They is always a-hangin' round the still an' a-gittin' drunk; but I don't see no sense in a-huntin' 'em down an' a-killin' 'em off. 'Pears ter me like they air better nor the dumb ones. I don't see no sense in shootin' 'em."

"Shet up, Cely! Shet up!" reiterated Shaw.

Celia said no more. Reginald Chevis was pleased with this indication of her sensibility; the other women—her mother and grandmother—had heard the whole recital with the utmost indifference, as they sat by the fire monotonously carding cotton. She was beyond her station in sentiment, he thought. However, he was disposed to recant this favorable estimate of her higher nature when, twice afterward, she stopped her work, and, filling the bottle from the keg, pressed it upon her father, despite her unfavorable criticism of the hangers-on of stills. Nay, she insisted. "Drink some more," she said. "Ye hain't got half enough yit." Had the girl no pity for the already drunken creature? She seemed systematically trying to make him even more helpless than he was.

He had fallen into a deep sleep before Chevis left the house, and the bottle was circulating among the other men with a rapidity that boded little harm to the unconscious Ike Peel and his brothers at Laurel Notch, twenty miles away. As Chevis mounted Strathspey he saw the horses of Jerry Shaw's friends standing partly within and partly without the blacksmith's shop They would stand there all night, he thought It was darker when he commenced the ascent of the mountain than he had anticipated. And what was this driving against his face,—rain? No, it was snow. He had not started a moment too soon. But Strathspey, by reason of frequent travel, knew every foot of the way, and perhaps there would only be a flurry. And so he went on steadily up and up the wild, winding road among the great, bare, black trees and the grim heights and chasms. The snow fell fast,—so fast and so silently, before he was half-way to the summit he had lost the vague companionship of the sound of his horse's hoofs, now muffled in the thick carpet so suddenly flung upon the ground. Still the snow fell, and when he had reached the mountain's brow the ground was deeply covered, and the whole aspect of the scene was strange. But though obscured by the fast-flying flakes, he knew that down in the bosom of the white valley there glittered still that changeless star.

"Still spinning, I suppose," he said to himself, as he looked toward it and thought of the interior of the log-cabin below. And then he turned into the tent to enjoy his cigar, his æsthetic reveries, and a bottle of wine.

But the wheel was no longer awhirl. Both music and musician were gone. Toiling along the snow-filled mountain ways; struggling with the fierce gusts of wind as they buffeted and hindered her, and fluttered derisively among her thin, worn, old garments; shivering as the driving flakes came full into the pale, calm face, and fell in heavier and heavier wreaths upon the dappled calico sun-bonnet; threading her way through unfrequented woodland paths, that she might shorten the distance; now deftly on the verge of a precipice, whence a false step of those coarse, rough shoes would fling her into unimaginable abysses below; now on the sides of steep ravines, falling sometimes with the treacherous, sliding snow, but never faltering; tearing her hands on the shrubs and vines she clutched to help her forward, and bruised and bleeding, but still going on; trembling more than with the cold, but never turning back, when a sudden noise in the terrible loneliness of the sheeted woods suggested the close proximity of a wild beast, or perhaps, to her ignorant, superstitious mind, a supernatural presence,—thus she journeyed on her errand of deliverance.

Her fluttering breath came and went in quick gasps; her failing limbs wearily dragged through the deep drifts; the cruel winds untiringly lashed her; the snow soaked through the faded green cotton dress to the chilled white skin,—it seemed even to the dull blood coursing feebly through her freezing veins. But she had small thought for herself during those long, slow hours of endurance and painful effort. Her pale lips moved now and then with muttered speculations: how the time went by; whether they had discovered her absence at home; and whether the fleeter horsemen were even now ploughing their way through the longer, winding mountain road. Her only hope was to outstrip their speed. Her prayer—this untaught being!—she had no prayer, except perhaps her life, the life she was so ready to imperil. She had no high, cultured sensibilities to sustain her. There was no instinct stirring within her that might have nerved her to save her father's, or her brother's, or a benefactor's life. She held the creatures that she would have died to warn in low estimation, and spoke of them with reprobation and contempt. She had known no religious training, holding up forever the sublimest ideal. The measureless mountain wilds were not more infinite to her than that great mystery. Perhaps, without any philosophy, she stood upon the basis of a common humanity.

When the silent horsemen, sobered by the chill night air and the cold snow, made their cautious approach to the little porch of Ike Peel's log-hut at Laurel Notch, there was a thrill of dismayed surprise among them to discover the door standing half open, the house empty of its scanty furniture and goods, its owners fled, and the very dogs disappeared; only, on the rough stones before the dying fire, Celia Shaw, falling asleep and waking by fitful starts.

"Jerry Shaw swore ez how he would hev shot that thar gal o' his'n,—that thar Cely," Hi Bates said to Chevis and Varney the next day, when he recounted the incident, "only he didn't think she hed her right mind; a-walkin' through this hyar deep snow full fifteen mile,—it's fifteen mile by the short cut ter Laurel Notch,—ter git Ike Peel's folks off 'fore Lijah an' her dad could come up an' settle Ike an' his brothers. Leastways, 'Lijah an' the t'others, fur Jerry hed got so drunk he couldn't go; he war dead asleep till ter-day, when they kem back a-fotchin' the gal with 'em. That thar Cely Shaw never did look ter me like she hed good sense, nohow. Always looked like she war queer an' teched in the head."

There was a furtive gleam of speculation on the dull face of the mountaineer when his two listeners broke into enthusiastic commendation of the girl's high heroism and courage. The man of ledgers swore that he had never heard of anything so fine, and that he himself would walk through fifteen miles of snow and midnight wilderness for the honor of shaking hands with her. There was that keen thrill about their hearts sometimes felt in crowded theatres, responsive to the cleverly simulated heroism of the boards; or in listening to a poet's mid-air song; or in looking upon some grand and ennobling phase of life translated on a great painter's canvas.

Hi Bates thought that perhaps they too were a little "teched in the head."

There had fallen upon Chevis a sense of deep humiliation. Celia Shaw had heard no more of that momentous conversation than he; a wide contrast was suggested. He began to have a glimmering perception that despite all his culture, his sensibility, his yearnings toward humanity, he was not so high a thing in the scale of being; that he had placed a false estimate upon himself. He had looked down on her with a mingled pity for her dense ignorance, her

102

coarse surroundings, her low station, and a dilettante's delight in picturesque effects, and with no recognition of the moral splendors of that star in the valley. A realization, too, was upon him that fine feelings are of most avail as the motive power of fine deeds.

He and his friend went down together to the little log-cabin. There had been only jeers and taunts and reproaches for Celia Shaw from her own people. These she had expected, and she had stolidly borne them. But she listened to the fine speeches of the city-bred men with a vague wonderment on her flower-like face,—whiter than ever to-day.

"It was a splendid—a noble thing to do," said Varney, warmly.

"I shall never forget it," said Chevis, "it will always be like a sermon to me."

There was something more that Reginald Chevis never forgot: the look on her face as he turned and left her forever; for he was on his way back to his former life, so far removed from her and all her ideas and imaginings. He pondered long upon that look in her inscrutable eyes,—was it suffering, some keen pang of despair?—as he rode down and down the valley, all unconscious of the heart-break he left behind him. He thought of it often afterward; he never penetrated its mystery.

He heard of her only once again. On the eve of a famous day, when visiting the outposts of a gallant corps, Reginald Chevis happened to recognize in one of the pickets the gawky mountaineer who had been his guide through those autumnal woods so far away. Hi Bates was afterward sought out and honored with an interview in the general's tent; for the accidental encounter had evoked many pleasant reminiscences in Chevis's mind, and among other questions he wished to ask was what had become of Jerry Shaw's daughter.

"She's dead,—long ago," answered Hi Bates. "She died afore the winter war over the year ez ye war a-huntin' thar. She never hed good sense ter my way o' thinkin', nohow, an' one night she run away, an' walked 'bout fifteen mile through a big snow-storm. Some say it settled on her chist. Anyhow, she jes' sorter fell away like afterward, an' never held up her head good no more. She always war a slim little critter, an' looked like she war teched in the head."

There are many things that suffer unheeded in those mountains: the birds that freeze on the trees; the wounded deer that leaves its cruel kind to die alone; the despairing, flying fox with its pursuing train of savage dogs and men. And the jutting crag whence had shone the camp-fire she had so often watched—her star, set forever—looked far over the valley beneath, where in one of those sad little rural graveyards she had been laid so long ago.

But Reginald Chevis has never forgotten her. Whenever he sees the earliest star spring into the evening sky, he remembers the answering red gleam of that star in the valley.

ELECTIONEERIN' ON BIG INJUN MOUNTING.

"An' ef ye'll believe me, he hev hed the face an' grace ter come a-prowlin' up hyar on Big Injun Mounting, electioneerin' fur votes, an' a-shakin' hands with every darned critter on it."

To a superficial survey the idea of a constituency might have seemed incongruous enough with these rugged wilds. The

104

July sunshine rested on stupendous crags; the torrent was bridged only by a rainbow hovering above the cataract; in all the wide prospect of valley and far-stretching Alleghany ranges the wilderness was broken by no field or clearing. But over this gloomy primeval magnificence of nature universal suffrage brooded like a benison, and candidates munificently endowed with "face an' grace" were wont to thread the tangled mazes of Big Injun Mounting.

The presence of voters in this lonely region was further attested by a group of teamsters, who had stopped at the wayside spring that the oxen might drink, and in the interval of waiting had given themselves over to the interest of local politics and the fervor of controversy.

"Waal, they tells me ez he made a powerful good 'torney-gineral las' time. An' it 'pears ter me ez the mounting folks oughter vote fur him agin them town cusses, 'kase he war born an' raised right down hyar on the slope of Big Injun Mounting. He never lef' thar till he war twenty year old, when he went ter live yander at Carrick Court House, an' arter a while tuk ter studyin' of law."

The last speaker was the most uncouth of the rough party, and poverty-stricken as to this world's goods. Instead of a wagon, he had only a rude "slide;" his lean oxen were thrust from the water by the stronger and better fed teams; and his argument in favor of the reëlection of the attorney for the State in this judicial circuit—called in the vernacular "the 'torney-gineral"—was received with scant courtesy.

"Ye're a darned fool ter be braggin' that Rufus Chadd air a mounting boy!" exclaimed Abel Stubbs, scornfully. "He hev hed the insurance ter git ez thick ez he kin with them town folks down thar at Ephesus, an' he hev made ez hard speeches agin everybody that war tuk ter jail from Big Injun ez ef he hed never laid eyes on 'em till that minit; an' arter all that the mounting folks hev done fur him, too! 'Twar thar vote that elected him the fust time he run, 'kase the convention put up that thar Taylor man, what nobody knowed nuthin' about an' jes' *de*spised; an' the t'other candidates wouldn't agree ter the convention, but jes' went before the people ennyhow, an' the vote war so split that Big Injun kerried Rufe Chadd in. An' what do he do? Ef it hedn't hev been fur his term a-givin' out he would hev jailed the whole mounting arter a while!"

The dwellers on Big Injun Mounting are not the first rural community that have aided in the election of a prosecuting officer, and afterward have become wroth with a fiery wrath because he prosecutes.

"An' them town folks," Abel Stubbs continued, after a pause,—"at fust they war mightily interrupted 'bout the way that the election hed turned out, an' they promised the Lord that they would never butt agin a convention no more while they lived in this life. Hevin' a mounting lawyer over them town folks in Colbury an' Ephesus war mighty humbling ter thar pride, I reckon; nobody hed never hearn tell o' sech a thing afore. But when these hyar horse-thieves an' mounting fellers ginerally got ter goin' in sech a constancy ter the pen'tiary, them town folks changed thar tune 'bout Rufe Chadd. They 'lowed ez they hed never hed sech a good 'torney-gineral afore. An' now they air goin' ter hev a new election, an' hyar is Rufe a-leadin' off at the head of the convention ez graceful ez ef he hed never butted agin it in his life."

"Waal," drawled a heavy fellow, speaking for the first time,—a rigid soul, who would fain vote the straight ticket,—"I won't support Rufe Chadd; an' yit I dunno how I kin git my cornsent ter vote agin the nominee."

"Rufe Chadd air goin' ter be beat like hell broke loose," said Abel Stubbs, hopefully.

"He will ef Big Injun hev enny say so 'bout 'n it," rejoined the rigid voter. "I hev never seen a man ez onpopular ez he is nowadays on this mounting."

"I hev hearn tell that the kin-folks of some of them convicts, what he made sech hard speeches agin, hev swore ter git even with him yit," said Abel Stubbs. "Rufe Chadd hev been shot at twice in the woods sence he kem up on Big Injun Mounting. I seen him yestiddy, an' he tole me so; an' he showed me his hat whar a rifle ball hed done gone through. An' I axed him ef he warn't afeard of all them men what hed sech a grudge agin him. 'Mister Stubbs,' he say, sorter saft,— ye know them's the ways he hev l'arned in Ephesus an' Colbury an' sech, an' he hed, afore he ever left Big Injun Mounting, the sassiest tongue that ever wagged,—'Mister Stubbs,' Rufe say, mighty perlite, 'foolin' with me is like makin' faces at a rattlesnake: it may be satisfying to the feelin's, but 't ain't safe.' That's what Rufe tole ter me."

"'T would pleasure me some ter see Rufe Chadd agin," said the driver of the slide. "Me an' him air jes' the same age,— thirty-three year. We used ter go huntin' tergether some. They tells me ez he hev app'inted ter speak termo-rrer at the Settlemint along of them t'other five candidates what air a-runnin' agin him. I likes ter hear him speak; he knocks things up somehow."

"He did talk mighty sharp an' stingin' the fust time he war electioneerin' on Big Injun Mounting," the rigid voter reluctantly admitted; "but mebbe he hev furgot how sence he hev done been livin' with them town folks."

"Ef ye wants ter know whether Rufe Chadd hev furgot how ter talk, jes' take ter thievin' of horses an' sech, will ye!" exclaimed Abel Stubbs, with an emphatic nod. "Ye oughter hev hearn the tale my brother brung from the court-house at Ephesus when Josh Green war tried. He said Rufe jes' tuk that jury out 'n tharselves; an' he gits jes' sech a purchase on

107

every jury he speaks afore. My brother says he believes that ef Rufe hed gin the word, that jury would hev got out 'n thar cheers an' throttled Josh. It's a mighty evil sort 'n gift,—this hyar way that Rufe talks."

"Waal, his tongue can't keep the party from bein' beat. I hates ter see it disgraced agin," said the rigid voter. "But law, I can't stand hyar all day jowin' 'bout Rufus Chadd! I hev got my wheat ter thrash this week, though I don't expec' ter make more 'n enough fur seed fur nex' year,—ef that. I must be joltin' along."

The ox-carts rumbled slowly down the steep hill, the slide continued its laborious ascent, and the forest was left once more to the fitful stir of the wind and the ceaseless pulsations of the falling torrent. The shadows of the oak leaves moved to and fro with dazzling effects of interfulgent sunbeams. Afar off the blue mountains shimmered through the heated air; but how cool was this clear rush of emerald water and the bounding white spray of the cataract! The sudden flight of a bird cleft the rainbow; there was a flash of moisture on his swift wings, and he left his wild, sweet cry echoing far behind him. Beetling high above the stream, the crags seemed to touch the sky. One glance up and up those towering, majestic steeps,—how it lifted the soul! The Settlement, perched upon the apparently inaccessible heights, was not visible from the road below. It cowered back affrighted from the verge of the great cliff and the grimly yawning abysses. The huts, three or four in number, were all silent, and might have been all tenantless, so lonely was their aspect. Behind them rose the dense forest, filling the background. In a rush-bottomed chair before the little store was the only human creature to be seen in the hamlet,—a man whose appearance was strangely at variance with his surroundings. He had the long, lank frame of the mountaineer; but instead of the customary brown jeans clothes, he wore a suit of blue flannel, and a dark straw hat was drawn over his brow. This simple attire and the cigar that he smoked had given great offense to the already prejudiced dwellers on Big Injun Mounting. It was not deemed meet that Rufe Chadd should "git tuk up with them town ways, an' sot hisself ter wearin' of store-clothes." His face was a great contrast to the faces of the stolid mountaineers. It was keenly chiseled; the constant friction of thought had worn away the grosser lines, leaving sharply defined features with abrupt turns of expression. The process might be likened to the gradual denudation of those storied strata of his mountains by the momentum of their torrents.

And here was no quiet spirit. It could brook neither defeat nor control; conventional barriers went down before it; and thus some years ago it had come to pass that a raw fellow from the unknown wildernesses of the circuit was precipitated upon it as the attorney for the State. A startling sensation had awaited the dull court-rooms of the villages. The mountaineer seemed to have brought from his rugged heights certain subtle native instincts, and the wily doublings of the fox, the sudden savage spring of the catamount, the deadly sinuous approach of the copperhead, were displayed with a frightful effect translated into human antagonism. There was a great awakening of the somnolent bar; counsel for the defense became eager, active, zealous, but the juries fell under his domination, as the weak always submit to the strong. Those long-drawn cases that hang on from term to term because of faint-hearted tribunals, too merciful to convict, too just to acquit, vanished as if by magic from the docket. The besom of the law swept the country, and his name was a terror and a threat.

His brethren of the bar held him in somewhat critical estimation. It was said that his talents were not of a high order; that he knew no law; that he possessed only a remarkable dexterity with the few broad principles familiar to him, and a certain swift suppleness in their application, alike effectual and imposing. He was a natural orator, they admitted. His success lay in his influence on a jury, and his influence on a jury was due to a magnetic earnestness and so strong a belief in his own powers that every word carried conviction with it. But he did not see in its entirety the massive grandeur of that greatest monument of human intellect known as the common law of England.

In the face of all detraction, however, there were the self-evident facts of his success and the improvement in the moral atmosphere wrought during his term of office. He was thinking of these things as he sat with his absorbed eyes fastened upon the horizon, and of the change in himself since he had left his humble home on the slope of Big Injun Mounting. There he had lived seventeen years in ignorance of the alphabet; he was the first of his name who could write it. From an almost primitive state he had overtaken the civilization of Ephesus and Colbury,—no great achievement, it might seem to a sophisticated imagination; but the mountains were a hundred years behind the progress of those centres. His talents had burst through the stony crust of circumstance, like the latent fires of a volcano. And he had plans for the future. Only a short while ago he had been confident when he thought of them; now they were hampered by the great jeopardy of his reëlection, because of the egregious blindness that could not distinguish duty from malice, justice from persecution. He had felt the strength of education and civilization; he was beginning to feel the terrible strength of ignorance. His faith in his own powers was on the wane. He had experienced a suffocating sense of impotence when, in stumping Big Injun Mounting, he had been called upon by the meagre but vociferous crowd to justify the hard bearing of the prosecution upon Josh Green "fur stealin' of Squire Bibb's old gray mare, that ye knows, Rufe,—fur ye hev plowed with her,—warn't wuth more 'n ten dollars. Ef Josh hedn't been in the dark, he wouldn't hev teched sech a pore old critter. Tell us 'bout 'n seven year in the pen'tiary fur a mare wuth ten dollars." What possibility— even with Chadd's wordy dexterity—of satisfying such demands as this! He found that the strength of ignorance lies in its blundering brutality. And he found, too, that mental supremacy does not of its inherent nature always aspire, but can be bent downward to low ends. The opposing candidates made capital of these illogical attacks; they charged him with his most brilliant exploits as ingenious perversions of the law and attempts upon the liberties of the people. Chadd began to despair of dissipating the prejudice and ignorance so readily crystallized by his opponents, and the only savage instinct left to him was to die game. He justified his past conduct by the curt declaration that he had done his duty according to the law, and he asked the votes of his fellow-citizens with an arrogant *hauteur* worthy of Coriolanus.

The afternoon was wearing away; the lengthening shadows were shifting; the solitary figure that had been motionless in the shade was now motionless in the golden sunshine. A sound broke upon the air other than the muffled thunder of the falls and the droning reiteration of the katydid. There came from the rocky path threading the forest the regular beat of horses' hoofs, and in a few moments three men rode into the clearing that sloped to the verge of the cliff. The first faint footfall was a spell to wake the Settlement to sudden life: sundry feminine faces were thrust out of the rude windows; bevies of lean-limbed, tow-headed, unkempt children started up from unexpected nooks; the store-keeper strolled to the door, and stood with his pipe in his mouth, leaning heavily against the frame; and Rufus Chadd changed

111

his position with a slow, lounging motion, and turned his eyes upon the road.

"Waal," said the store-keeper, with frank criticism, as the trio came in sight, "Isaac Boker's drunk agin. It's the natur' of the critter, I'm a-thinkin'. He hev been ter the still, ez sure ez ye air born. I hopes 't ain't a dancin'-drunk he hev got. The las' time he hed a dancin'-drunk, he jes' bounced up an' down the floor, an' hollered an' sung an' sech, an' made sech a disturbament that the Settle*mint* war kep' awake till daybreak, mighty nigh. 'T war mighty pore enjoymint for the Settle*mint*. 'T war like sittin' up with the sick an' dead, stiddier along of a happy critter like him. I'm powerful sorry fur his wife, 'kase he air mighty rough ter her when he air drunk; he cut her once a toler'ble bad slash. She hev hed ter do all the work fur four year,—plowin', an' choppin' wood, an cookin', an' washin', an' sech. It hev aged her some. An' all her chillen is gals,—little gals. Boys, now, mought grow some help, but gals is more no 'count the bigger they gits. She air a tried woman, surely. Isaac is drunk ez a constancy,—dancin'-drunk, mos'ly. Nuthin' kin stop him."

"A good thrashing would help him a little, I'm thinking," drawled the lawyer. "And if I lived here as a constancy I'd give it to him the first sober spell he had." His speech was slow; his voice was spiritless and languid; he still possessed the tone and idiom of the mountaineer, but he had lost the characteristic pronunciation, more probably from the influence of other associations than an appreciation of its incorrectness.

"That ain't the right sort o' sawder fur a candidate, Rufe," the store-keeper admonished him. "An' 'tain't safe no how fur sech a slim, stringy boy ez ye air ter talk that way 'bout'n Isaac Boker. He air a tremenjous man, an' ez strong ez an ox."

"I can thrash any man who beats his wife," protested the officer of the law. "I don't see how the Settlement gets its own consent to let that sort of thing go on."

"She air his wife," said the store-keeper, who was evidently of conservative tendencies. "An' she air powerful tuk up with him. I hev hearn her 'low ez he air better dancin'-drunk than other men sober. She could hev married other men; she didn't suffer with hevin' no ch'ice."

"He ought to be put under lock and key," said Chadd. "That would sober him. I wish these dancin'-drunk fellows could be sent to the state-prison. I could make a jury think ten years was almost too good for that wife-beating chap. I'd like to see him get away from me."

There was a certain calculating cruelty in his face as he said this. He was animated by no chivalric impulse to protect the weak and helpless; the spirit roused within him was rather the instinct of the beast of prey. The store-keeper looked askance at him. In his mental review of the changes wrought in the past few years there was one that had escaped Rufus Chadd's attention. The process was insinuating and gradual, but the result was bold and obvious. In the constant opposition in which he was placed to criminals, in the constant contemplation of the worst phases of human nature, in the active effort which his duty required to bring the perpetrators of all foul deeds to justice, he had grown singularly callous and pitiless. The individual criminal had been merged in the abstract idea of crime. After the first few cases he had been able to banish the visions of the horrors brought upon other lives than that of the prisoner by the verdict of guilty. Mother, wife, children,—these pale, pursuing phantoms were exorcised by prosaic custom, and his steely insensibility made him the master of many a harrowing court-room scene.

"That would be a mighty pore favor ter his wife," said the store-keeper, after a pause. "She hed ruther be beat."

The three men had dismounted, hitched their horses, and were now approaching the store. Rufus Chadd rose to shake hands with the foremost of the party. The quick fellow was easily schooled, and the store-keeper's comment upon his lack of policy induced him to greet the new-comers with a greater show of cordiality than he had lately practiced toward his constituents.

"I never looked ter find ye hyar this soon, Rufe," said one of the arrivals. "What hev ye done with the t'other candidates?"

"I left them behind, as I always do," said Chadd, laughing, "and as I expect to do again next Thursday week, if I can get you to promise to vote for me."

"I ain't a-goin' ter vote fur ye,—nary time," interpolated Boker, as he reeled heavily forward.

"Well, I'm sorry for that," said Chadd, with the candidate's long-suffering patience. "Why?"

Isaac Boker felt hardly equal to argument, but he steadied himself as well as he could, and looked vacantly into the eyes of his interlocutor for some pointed inspiration; perhaps he caught there an intimation of the contempt in which he was held. He still hesitated, but with a sudden anger inflaming his bloated face. Chadd waited a moment for a reply; then he turned carelessly away, saying that he would stroll about a little, as sitting still so long was fatiguing.

"Ef ye war whar ye oughter be, a-follerin' of the plow," said Isaac Boker, "ye wouldn't git a chance ter tire yerself a-sittin' in a cheer."

"I don't hold myself too high for plowing," replied Chadd, in a conciliatory manner. "Plowing is likely work for any able-bodied man." This speech was unlucky. There was in it

114

an undercurrent of suggestion to Isaac Boker's suspicious conscience. He thought Chadd intended a covert allusion to his own indolence in the field, and his wife's activity as a substitute. "It was only an accident that took me out of the furrow," Chadd continued.

"'Twar a killin' accident ter the country," said Isaac Boker. "Fur they tells me that ye don't know no more law than a mounting fox." Chadd laughed, but he sneered too. His patience was evaporating. Still he restrained his irritation by an effort, and Boker went on: "Folks ez is bred ter the plow ain't got the sense an' the showin' ter make peart lawyers. An' that's why I ain't a-goin' ter vote fur ye."

This plain speaking was evidently relished by the others; they said nothing, but their low acquiescent chuckle demonstrated their opinion.

"I haven't asked you for your vote," said Chadd, sharply.

The burly fellow paused for a moment, in stupid surprise; then his drunken wrath rising, he exclaimed, "An' whyn't ye ax me fur my vote, then? Ye're the damnedest critter in this country, Rufe Chadd, ter come electioneerin' on Big Injun Mounting, an' a-makin' out ez I ain't good enough ter be axed ter vote fur ye! Ye hed better not be tryin' ter sot me down lower 'n other folks. I'll break that empty cymlin' of a head of yourn," and he raised his clenched fist.

"If you come a step nearer I'll throw you off the bluff," said Chadd.

"That'll be a powerful cur'ous tale ter go the rounds o' the mounting," remarked one of the disaffected by-standers. "Ye hev done all ye kin ter torment yer own folks up hyar on Big Injun Mounting what elected ye afore; an' then ye comes up hyar agin, an' the fust man that says he won't vote fur ye must be flunged off'n the bluff."

"'Pears ter me," said Isaac Boker, surlily, and still shaking his fist, "ez thar ain't all yit in the pen'tiary that desarves ter go thar. Better men than ye air, Rufe Chadd, hev been locked up, an' hung too, sence ye war elected ter office."

There was a sudden change in the lawyer's attitude; a strong tension of the muscles, as of a wild-cat ready to spring; the quickening of his blood showed in his scarlet face; there was a fiery spark in his darkening eyes.

"Oh, come now, Rufe," said one of the lookers-on hastily. "Ye oughtn't ter git ter fightin' with a drunken man. Jes' walk yerself off fur a while."

"Oh, he can *say* what he likes while he's drunk," replied Chadd, with a short, scornful laugh. "But I tell you, now, he had better keep his fists for his wife."

The others gathered about the great, massive fellow, who was violently gesticulating and incoherently asserting his offended dignity. Chadd strolled away toward the gloomy woods, his hands in his pockets, and his eyes bent upon the ground. Glances of undisguised aversion followed him,— from the group about the store, from the figures in the windows and doors of the poor dwellings, even from the half-clad children who paused in their spiritless play to gaze after him. He was vaguely conscious of these pursuing looks of hatred, but only once he saw the universal sentiment expressed in a face. As the long shadows of the forest fell upon his path, he chanced to raise his eyes, and encountered those of a woman, standing in Boker's cabin. He went on, feeling like a martyr. The thick foliage closed upon him; the sound of his languid footsteps died in the distance, and the figures on the cliff stood in the sunset glow, watching the spot where he had disappeared, as silent and as motionless as if they had fallen under some strange, uncanny spell.

The calm of the woodland, the refreshing aromatic odors, the rising wind after the heat of the sultry day, exerted a revivifying influence upon the lawyer's spirits, as he walked on into the illimitable solitudes of the forest. Night was falling before he turned to retrace his way; above the opaque, colorless leaves there was the lambent glinting of a star; the fitful plaint of a whip-poor-will jarred the dark stillness; grotesque black shadows had mustered strong among the huge boles of the trees. But he took no note of the gathering gloom; somehow, his heart had grown suddenly light. He had forgotten the drunken wrangler and all the fretting turmoils of the canvass; once he caught himself in making plans, with his almost impossible success in the election as a basis. And yet, inconsistently enough, he felt a dismayed astonishment at his unaccountable elation. The workings of his own mind and their unexpected developments were always to him strange phenomena. He was introspective enough to take heed of this inward tumult, and he had a shrewd suspicion that more activity was there than in all the mental exercitations of the combined bench and bar of the circuit. But he harbored a vague distrust of this uncontrollable power within, so much stronger than the untutored creature to whom it appertained. A harassing sense of doubleness often possessed him, and he was torn by conflicting counsels,—the inherent inertia and conservatism of the mountaineer, who would fain follow forever the traditional customs of his ancestry, and an alien overwhelming impetus, which carried him on in spite of himself, and bewildered him with his own exploits. He was helpless under this unreasonable expectation of success, and regarded the mental gymnastic of joyous anticipation with perplexed surprise. "I'm fixing a powerful disappointment for myself," he said.

He could now see, through the long vista of the road, the open space where the Settlement was perched upon the crag.

The black, jagged outline of the rock serrated the horizon, and was cut sharply into the delicate, indefinable tints of the sky. Above it a great red moon was rising. There was the gleam of the waterfall; how did it give the sense of its emerald green in the darkness? The red, rising moon showed, but did not illumine, the humble cluster of log huts upon the great cliff. Here and there a dim yet genial flare of firelight came broadly flickering out into the night. It was darker still in the dense woods from which the road showed this nocturnal picture framed in the oak leaves above his head. But was a sudden flash of lightning shooting across that clear, tenderly-tinted sky? He felt his warm blood gushing down his face; he had a dizzying sense of falling heavily; and he heard, strangely dulled, a hoarse, terrified cry, which he knew he did not utter. It echoed far through the quiet woods, startling the apathetic inhabitants of the Settlement, and waking all the weird spirits of the rocks. The men sitting in the store took their pipes from their mouths, and looked at each other in surprise.

"What's that?" asked one of the newly-arrived candidates, an Ephesus man, who held that the mountains were not over and above safe for civilized people, and was fain to investigate unaccustomed sounds.

"Jes' somebody a-hollerin' fur thar cow, mebbe," said the store-keeper. "Or mebbe it air Isaac Boker, ez gits dancin'-drunk wunst in a while."

The cry rose again, filling all the rocky abysses and mountain heights with a frenzied horror. From the woods a dark figure emerged upon the crag; it seemed to speed along the sky, blotting out, as it went, the moon and stars. The men at the store sprang to their feet, shaken by a speechless agitation, when Isaac Boker rushed in among them, suddenly sobered, and covered with blood.

118

"I hev done it!" he exclaimed, with a pallid anguish upon his bloated face. "I met him in the woods, an' slashed him ter pieces."

The red moon turned to gold in the sky, and the world was flooded with a gentle splendor; and as the hours went by no louder sound broke upon the gilded dusk than the throb of the cataract, pulsing like the heart of the mountains, and the stir of the wind about the rude hut where the wounded man had been carried.

When Rufus Chadd opened his eyes upon the awe-stricken faces that clustered about the bed, he had no need to be reminded of what had happened. The wave of life, which it seemed would have carried him so far, had left him stranded here in the ebb, while all the world sailed on.

"They hev got Isaac Boker tied hard an' fast, Rufe," said the store-keeper, in an attempt to reply to the complex changes of expression that flitted over the pale face.

Chadd did not answer. He was thinking that no adequate retribution could be inflicted upon Isaac Boker. The crime was not only the destruction of merely sensuous human life, but, alas, of that subtler entity of human schemes, and upward-reaching ambitions, and the immeasurable opportunity of achievement, which after all is the essence of the thing called life. He was to die at the outset of his career, which his own steadfast purpose and unaided talent had rendered honorable and brilliant, for the unreasoning fury of a drunken mountaineer. And this was an end for a man who had turned his ambitious eyes upon a chief-justice's chair,—an absurd ambition but for its splendid effrontery! In all this bitterness, however, it was some comfort to know that the criminal had not escaped.

"Are you able to tell how it happened, Chadd?" asked one of the lawyers.

As Chadd again opened his eyes, they fell upon the face of a woman standing just within the door,—so drawn and piteous a face, with such lines of patient endurance burnt into it, with such a woful prophecy in the sunken, horror-stricken eyes, he turned his head that he might see it no more. He remembered that face with another expression upon it. It had given him a look like a stab from the door of Boker's hut, when he had passed in the afternoon. He wished never to see it again, and yet he was constrained to glance back. There it was, with its quiver of a prescient heart-break. He felt a strange inward thrill, a bewildering rush of emotion. That sense of doubleness and development which so mystified him was upon him now. He was surprised at himself when he said, distinctly, so that all might hear, "If I die—don't let them prosecute Isaac Boker."

There was a sudden silence, so intense that it seemed as if the hush of death had already fallen, or that the primeval stillness of creation was never broken. Had his soul gone out into the night? Was there now in the boundless spaces of the moonlit air some mysterious presence, as incomprehensible to this little cluster of overawed humanity as to the rocks and woods of the mighty, encompassing wilderness? How did the time pass? It seemed hours before the stone-like figure stirred again, and yet the white radiance on the puncheon floor had not shifted. His consciousness was coming back from those vague border-lands of life and death. He was about to speak once more. "Nobody can know how it happened except me." And then again, as he drifted away, "Don't let them prosecute."

There was a fine subject of speculation at the Settlement the next morning, when the country-side gathered to hear the candidates speak. The story of Isaac Boker's attack upon Rufus Chadd was repeated to every new-comer, and the astonishment created by the victim's uncharacteristic request when he had thought he was dying revived with each consecutive recital. It presently became known that no fatal result was to be anticipated. The doctor, who lived twenty miles distant, and who had just arrived, said that the wounds, though painful, were not dangerous, and his opinion added another element of interest to the eager discussion of the incident.

Thus relieved of the shadow of an impending tragedy, the knots of men congregated on the great cliff gradually gave themselves up to the object of their meeting. Candidates of smiling mien circulated among the saturnine, grave-faced mountaineers. In circulation, too, were other genial spirits, familiarly known as "apple-jack." It was a great occasion for the store-keeper; so pressing and absorbing were his duties that he had not a moment's respite, until Mr. Slade, the first speaker of the day, mounted a stump in front of the store and began to address his fellow-citizens. He was a large, florid man, with a rotund voice and a smooth manner, and he was considered Chadd's most formidable competitor. The mountaineers hastily concentrated in a semicircle about him, listening with the close attention singularly characteristic of rural audiences. Behind the crowd was the immensity of the unpeopled forests; below, the mad fret of the cataract; above, the vast hemisphere of the lonely skies; and far, far away was the infinite stretching of those blue ranges that the Indians called The Endless.

Chadd had lain in a sort of stupor all the morning, vaguely conscious of the distant mountains visible through the open window,—vaguely conscious of numbers of curious faces that came to the door and gazed in upon him,—vaguely conscious of the candidate's voice beginning to resound in the noontide stillness. Then he roused himself.

The sensation of the first speech came at its close. As Chadd lay in expectation of the stentorian "Hurrah for Slade!"

which should greet his opponent's peroration, his face flushed, his hands trembled; he lifted himself on his elbow, and listened again. He could hardly trust his senses, yet there it was once more,—his own name, vibrating in a prolonged cheer among the mountain heights, and echoing far down the narrow valley.

That sympathetic heart of the multitude, so quick to respond to a noble impulse, had caught the true interpretation of last night's scene, and to-day all the barriers of ignorance and misunderstanding were down.

The heaviest majority ever polled on Big Injun Mounting was in the reëlection of the attorney for the State. And the other candidates thought it a fine electioneering trick to get one's self artistically slashed; they became misanthropic in their views of the inconstancy of the people, and lost faith in saving grace and an overruling Providence.

This uncharacteristic episode in the life of Rufus Chadd was always incomprehensible to his associates. He hardly understood it himself. He had made a keen and subtle distinction in a high moral principle. As Abel Stubbs said, in extenuation of the inconsistency of voting for him, "I knows that this hyar Rufe Chadd air a powerful hard man, an' evil-doers ez offends agin the law ain't got no mercy ter expect from him. But then he don't hold no grudge agin them ez hev done *him* harm. An' that's what I'm a-lookin' at."

THE ROMANCE OF SUNRISE ROCK.

I.

What momentous morning arose with so resplendent a glory that it should have imprinted its indelible reflection on the face of this great Cumberland cliff; what eloquence of dawn so splendid that the dumb, insensate stone should catch its spirit and retain its expression forever and forever? A deep, narrow stream flowed around the base of the "paint-rock." Immense fissures separated it from its fellows. And charged with its subtler meaning it towered above them in isolated majesty. Moons waxed and waned; nations rose and fell; centuries came and went. And still it faced the east, and still, undimmed by storm and time, it reiterated the miracle and the prophecy of the rising sun.

"'Twar painted by the Injuns,—that's what I hev always hearn tell. Them folks war mos'ly leagued with the Evil One. That's how it kem they war gin the grasp ter scuffle up that thar bluff, ez air four hunderd feet high an' ez sheer ez a wall; it ain't got foothold fur a cockle-burr. I hev hearn tell that when they got ez high ez the pictur' they war 'lowed by the devil ter stand on air. An' I believes it. Else how'd they make out ter do that thar job?"

The hairy animal, whose jeans suit proclaimed him man, propounded this inquiry with a triumphant air. There was a sarcastic curve on the lips of his interlocutor. Clearly it was not worth his while to enlighten the mountaineer,—to talk of the unknown races whose work so long survives their names, to speculate upon the extent of their civilization and the mechanical contrivances that reached those dizzy heights, to confide his nebulous fancies clustering about the artist-poet who painted this grand, rude lyric upon the immortal rock. He turned from the strange picture, suspended between heaven and earth, and looked over the

123

rickety palings into the dismal little graveyard of the mountaineers. Nowhere, he thought, was the mystery of life and death so gloomily suggested. Humanity seemed so small, so transitory a thing, expressed in these few mounds in the midst of the undying grandeur of the mountains. Material nature conquers; man and mind are as naught. Only a reiteration of a well-conned lesson, for so far this fine young fellow of thirty had made a failure of life; the material considerations with which he had wrestled had got the better of him, and a place within the palings seemed rather preferable to his place without.

It was still strange to John Cleaver that his lines should have fallen in this wilderness; that the door of that house on the slope of the Backbone should be the only door upon earth open to him; that such men as this mountaineer were his neighbors and associates. The fact seemed a grotesque libel on likelihood. As he rode away he was thinking of his costly education, the sacrifices his father had made to secure it, his dying conviction, which was such a comfort to him, that in it he had left his penniless son a better thing than wealth,— with such training and such abilities what might he not reach? When John Cleaver returned from his medical studies in Paris to the Western city of his birth, to scores of charity patients, and to a fine social position by virtue of the prestige of a good family, there seemed only a little waiting needed. But the old physicians held on to life and the paying practice with the grip of the immortals. And he found it difficult to sustain existence while he waited.

At the lowest ebb of his fortunes there came to him a letter from a young lawyer, much in his own professional position, but who had confessed himself beaten and turned sheep-farmer. Here, among the mountains of East Tennessee, said the letter, he had bought a farm for a song; the land was the poorest he ever saw, but served his purposes, and the house was a phenomenal structure for these parts,—a six-room brick, built fifty years ago by a city man with a bucolic craze and consumptive tendencies. The people were terribly poor; still, if his friend would come he might manage to pick up something, for there was not a physician in a circuit of sixty miles.

So Cleaver had turned his face to the mountains. But unlike the sheep-farmer he did not meet his reverses lightly. The man was at bay. And like a savage thing he took his ill-fortune by the throat. Success had seemed so near that there was something like the pain of death in giving up the life to which he had looked forward with such certainty. He could not console himself with this comatose state, and call it life. He often told himself that there was nothing left but to think of what he might have done, and eat out his heart. His ambition died hard.

As his horse ambled along, a gruff voice broke his reverie, "'Light an' hitch," called out the master of a wayside hovel.

A man of different temperament might have found in Cleaver's uncouth surroundings some points of palliation. His heart might have warmed to the ignorant mountaineers' high and tender virtue of hospitality. A responsive respect might have been induced by the contemplation of their pride, so intense that it recognizes no superior, so inordinate that one is tempted to cry out, Here are the true republicans! or, indeed, Here are the only aristocrats! The rough fellow was shambling out to stop him with cordial insistence. An old crone, leaning on a stick in the door-way, called after her son, "Tell him ter 'light an' hitch, Peter, an' eat his supper along of we-uns." A young girl sitting on the rude porch, reeling yarn preparatory to weaving, glanced up, her sedate face suddenly illumined. Even the bare-footed, tow-headed children stood still in pleased expectation. Certainly John Cleaver's position in life was as false as it was painful. But

125

the great human heart was here, untutored though it was, and roughly accoutred. And he himself had found that Greek and Latin do not altogether avail.

The little log-house was encompassed by the splendor of autumnal foliage. A purple haze clung to the distant mountains; every range and every remove had a new tone and a new delight. The gray crags, near at hand, stood out sharply against the crimson sky. And high above them all in its impressive isolation loomed Sunrise Rock, heedless of the transitory dying day and the ineffective coming night.

The girl's reel was still whirling; at regular intervals it ticked and told off another cut. Cleaver's eyes were fixed upon her as he declined Peter Teake's invitation. He had seen her often before, but he did not know as yet that that face would play a strange part in the little mental drama that was to lead to the making of his fortune. Her cheek was flushed; her delicate crimson lips were slightly parted; the live gold of the sunbeams touched the dead-yellow, lustreless masses of her hair. Here and there the clustering tendrils separated, as they hung about her shoulders, and disclosed bright glimpses of a red cotton kerchief knotted around her throat; she wore a dark blue homespun dress, and despite the coarse texture of her attire there was something of the mingled brilliance and softness of the autumn tints in her humble presence. Her eyes reminded him of those deep, limpid mountain streams with golden-brown pebbles at the bottom. Scornful as he was, he was only a man—and a young man. With a sudden impulse he leaned forward and handed her a pretty cluster of ferns and berries which he had gathered in the forest.

The reel stopped, the thread broke. She looked up, as she received mechanically his woodland treasure, with so astonished a face that it induced in this man of the world a sense of embarrassment.

"Air they good yerbs fur somethin'?" she asked.

A quick comprehension of the ludicrous situation flashed through his mind. She evidently made no distinctions in the healing art as practiced by him and the "yerb-doctor," with whom he occasionally came into professional contact. And the presentation of the "yerbs" seemed a prescription instead of a compliment.

"No,—no," he said hastily, thinking of the possibility of a decoction. "They are not good for tea. They are of no use,—except to look at."

And he rode away, laughing softly.

Everything about the red brick house was disorganized and dilapidated; but the dining-room, which served the two young bachelors as a sitting-room also, was cheerful with the glow of a hickory fire and a kerosene lamp, and although the floor was bare and the tiny-paned windows curtained only with cobwebs, there was a suggestively comfortable array of pipes on the mantel-piece, and a bottle of gracious aspect. Sitting in front of the fire, the light full on his tawny beard and close-clipped blond hair, was a man of splendid proportions, a fine, frank, intellectual face, and a manner and accent that proclaimed him as distinctly exotic as his friend. He too had reared the great scaffolding of an elaborate education that he might erect the colossal edifice of his future. His hands beat the empty air and he had no materials wherewith to build. But there was the scaffolding, a fine thing in itself,—wasted, perhaps. For the sheep-farmer did not need it.

"Well, old sinner!" he exclaimed smilingly, as Cleaver entered. "Did you tell Tom to put up your 'beastis'? He is so 'brigaty' that he might not stand."

Were the two friends sojourning in the Cumberland Mountains on a camp-hunt, these excerpts from the prevalent dialect might have seemed to Cleaver a pleasantry of exquisite flavor. But they were no sojourners; they were permanently established here. And he felt that every concession to the customs of the region was a descent toward the level of its inhabitants. He thought Trelawney was already degenerating in this disheveled life,—mentally, in manner, even in speech. For with a philologist's zest Trelawney chased verbal monstrosities to their lair, and afterward displayed them in his daily conversation with as much pride as a connoisseur feels in exhibiting odd old china. As these reflections intruded themselves, Cleaver silently swore a mighty oath—an oath he had often sworn before—that he would not go down with him, he would not deteriorate too, he would hold hard to the traditions of a higher sphere.

But sins against convention could not detract from the impressiveness of the man lounging before the fire. If Trelawney only had money, how he would adorn the state of nabob!

"Brigaty!" he reiterated. "That's a funny word. It sounds as if it might be kin to the Italian *brigata*. Or, see here—*briga?*—eh?—*brigare*—*brigarsi?* I wonder how these people come by it."

A long pause ensued, broken only by the ticking of their watches: the waste of time asserted itself. All was silent without; no wind stirred; no leaf nor acorn fell; the mute mists pressed close to the window. Surely there were no other creatures in all the dreary world. And this, thought Cleaver, was what he had come to, after all his prestige, all his efforts!

"Trelawney," he said suddenly, "these are long evenings. Don't you think that with all this time on our hands—I don't know—but don't you think we might write something together?"

A frank surprise was in his friend's brown eyes. He replied doubtfully, "Write what?"

"I don't know," said Cleaver despondently.

"And suppose we had the talent to project 'something' and the energy to complete it, who would publish it?"

"I don't know," said the doctor, more hopelessly still.

Another pause. The foxes were barking in the moonlight, in the red autumn woods. That a man should feel less lonely for the sound of a wild thing's voice!

"My dear fellow," said John Cleaver, a certain passion of despair welling up in his tones,—he leaned forward and laid his hand on his friend's knee,—"it won't do for us to spend our lives here. We must turn about and get back into the world of men and action. Don't think I'm ungrateful for this haven,—you are the only one who held out a hand,—but we must get back, and go on with the rest. Help me, Trelawney,—help me think out some way. I'm losing faith in myself alone. Let us help each other. Many a man has made his pen his strongest friend; they were only men at last, just such as we are. Many of them were poor; the *best* of them were poor. We can try nothing else, Fred,—so little chance is left to us."

Trelawney laid his warm strong hand upon the cold nervous hand trembling on his knee. "Jack," he said, "I have given it all up. I am through forever with those cursed alternations of hope and despair. I don't believe we could write anything that would do—do any good, I mean. I wore out all energy and afflatus—the best part of me—waiting for the clients who never came. And all the time my appropriate sphere, my sheep-farm, was waiting for me here. I have found contentment, the manna from heaven, while you are still sighing for the flesh-pots of Egypt. Ambition has thrown me once; I sha'n't back the jade again. I am a shepherd, Jack, a shepherd.

'Pastorem, Tityre, pingues
Pascere oportet oves, deductum dicere carmen.'

That's it, my dear old boy. Sing a slender song! We've pitched our voices on too high a key for our style of vocalization. We must sing small, Jack,—sing a slender song!"

"I'll be damned if I do!" cried Cleaver, impetuously, springing to his feet and pacing the room with a quick stride.

But his friend's words dogged him deep into the night. They would not let him sleep. He lay staring blankly at the darkness, his thoughts busy with his forlorn position and his forlorn prospects, and that sense of helplessness, so terrible to a man, pressing heavily upon his heart. In the midst of the memories of his hopes, his ambitions, and his failures he was like a worm in the fire. The vague presence of the majestic company of mountains without preyed upon him; they seemed stolid, unmoved witnesses of his despair. The only human creature who might have understood him would not understand him. He knew that if he were writhing in pain with a broken limb, or the sentimental spurious anguish of a broken heart, Trelawney would resolve himself into every gracious phase of healing sympathy. But a broken life!—his friend would not make an effort. Yet why should he crave support? Was it true that he had pitched his voice too high? In this day of over-education, when every man is fitted for any noble sphere of intellectual achievement and only inborn talent survives, might it not be that he had mistaken a cultivated aspiration for latent power? And if indeed his purposes had outstripped his abilities, the result was tragic—tragic. He was as dead as if he were six feet deep in the ground. A bitter throe of shame came with these reflections. There is something so ludicrously contemptible

130

in a great personal ambition and a puny capacity. Ambition is the only grand passion that does not ennoble. We do not care that a low thing should lift its eyes. And if it does, we laugh.

There was a movement in the hall below. He had left Trelawney reading, but now his step was on the stairs, and with it rose the full mellow tones of his voice. He was singing of the spring-time in the autumn midnight. Poor Fred! It was always spring with him. He met his misfortunes with so cordial an outstretched hand that it might have seemed he disarmed them. It did not seem so to John Cleaver. He shifted his attitude with a groan. His friend's fatal apathy was an added pang to his own sorrows. And now the house was still, and he watched through all the long hours the western moonlight silently scale the gloomy pines, till on their plumy crests the yellow beams mingled with the red rays of the rising sun, and the empty, lonely day broke in its useless, wasted splendor upon the empty loneliness of the splendid night.

II.

Cleaver took little note, at this period, of those who came and went in his life; and he took little note of how he came and went in the lives of others. He had no idea of those inexplicable circles of thought and being that touch at a single point, and jar, perhaps. One day, while the Indian summer was still red on the hills,—he had reason to remember this day,—while the purple haze hovered over the landscape and mellowed to artistic delicacy the bold, bright colors of Sunrise Rock, he chanced to drive alone in his friend's rickety buggy along the road that passed on the opposite bank from the painted cliff and encircled the dreary little graveyard of the mountaineers. He became suddenly aware that there was a figure leaning against the palings; he recognized Selina Teake as he lifted his absorbed eyes. She held her sun-bonnet in her hand, and her yellow hair and fair face were unshaded; how little did he or she imagine what that face was to be to him afterward! He drew up his horse and spoke: "Well, this is the last place I should think you would want to come to."

She did not understand his dismal little joke at the graveyard. She silently fixed upon him those eyes, so suggestive of deep, clear waters in which some luminous planet has sunk a starry reflection.

"Did you intend to remain permanently?"

"I war restin' awhile," she softly replied.

He had a vague consciousness that she was the first of these proud mountaineers whom he had ever seen embarrassed or shy. She was indubitably blushing as he looked at her, and as she falteringly looked at him. How bright her eyes were, how red her delicate lips, what a faint fresh wild-rose was suddenly abloom on her cheek!

"Suppose you drive with me the remainder of the way," he suggested.

This was only the courtesy of the road in this region, and with her grave, decorous manner she stepped lightly into the vehicle, and they bowled away together. She was very mute and motionless as she sat beside him, her face eloquent with some untranslated emotion of mingled wonderment and pleasure and pain. Perhaps she drew in with the balsamic sunlit air the sweetest experience of her short life. He was silent too, his thoughts still hanging drearily about his blighted prospects and this fatal false step that had led him to the mountains; wondering whether he could have done better, whether he could have done otherwise at all, when it would end,—when, and how.

Trelawney was lounging against the rail fence in front of Teake's house, looking, in his negligent attire, like a prince in disguise, and talking to the mountaineers about a prospective deer-hunt. There was a surprised resentment on his face when Cleaver drove up, but the return of Selina with him made not a ripple among the Teakes. It would have been impossible to demonstrate to them that they stood on a lower social plane. Their standard of morality and respectability could not be questioned; there had never been a man or a woman of the humble name who had given the others cause for shame; they had lived in this house on their own land for a hundred years; they neither stole nor choused; they paid as they went, and asked no favors; they took no alms,—nay, they gave of their little! As to the artificial distinctions of money and education,—what do the ignorant mountaineers care about money and education!

Selina stood for a moment upon the cabin porch, her yellow hair gleaming like an aureola upon a background of crimson sumach leaves. A pet fawn came to the door and nibbled at her little sun-burned hands. As she turned to go in, Trelawney spoke to her. "Shall I bring you a fawn again? or will you have some venison from the hunt to-morrow?"

She fixed her luminous eyes upon him and laughed a little. There was no shyness in her face and manner now. Was Trelawney so accustomed a presence in her life, Cleaver wondered.

"Ah, I see," said Fred, laughing too. "I'll bring you some venison."

He was grave enough as he and his friend drove homeward together, and Cleaver was roused to the perception that there was a certain unwonted coldness slipping insidiously between them. It was not until they were seated before the fire that Trelawney again spoke. "How did it happen that you and she were together?" Evidently he had thought of nothing else since.

"Who?—the Lady Selina?" said Cleaver, mockingly. Trelawney's eyes warned him to forbear. "Oh, I met her walking, and I asked her to drive with me the rest of the way."

Nothing more was said for a time. Cleaver was thinking of the fawn which Fred had given her, of the patent fact that he was a familiar visitor at the Teake house. His question, and his long dwelling upon the subject before he asked it, seemed almost to indicate jealousy. Jealousy! Cleaver could hardly credit his own suspicion.

Trelawney broke the silence. "Education," he said abruptly, "what does education accomplish for women in our station of life? They learn to write a fashionable hand that nobody can decipher. They take a limited course of reading and remember nothing. Their study of foreign languages goes so far sometimes as to enable them to interject commonplace French phrases into their daily conversation, and render their prattle an affront to good taste as well an insult to the understanding. They have converted the piano into an instrument of torture throughout the length and breadth of the land. Sometimes they are learned; then they are given over to 'making an impression,' and are prone to discuss, with a fatal tendency to misapply terms, what they call 'philosophy.' As to their experience in society, no one will maintain that their flirtations and husband-hunting tend greatly to foster delicacy and refinement. What would that girl," nodding toward the log-cabin near Sunrise Rock, "think of the girls of our world who pursue 'society' as a man pursues a profession, who shove and jostle each other and pull caps for the great matches, and 'put up' with the others when no better may be had? She is my ideal of a modest, delicate young girl,—and she is the only sincere woman I ever saw. Upon my soul, I think the primitive woman holds her own very finely in comparison with the resultant of feminine culture."

Cleaver listened in stunned dismay. Could Trelawney have really fallen in love with the little mountaineer? He had adapted himself so readily to the habits of these people. He was so far from the world; he was dropping its chains. Many men under such circumstances, under far happier circumstances, had fallen into the fatal error of a *mésalliance*. Positively he might marry the girl. Cleaver felt it an imperative duty to make an effort to avert this almost grotesque catastrophe. In its very inception, however, he was hopeless. Trelawney had always been so intolerant of control, so tenacious of impressions and emotions, so careless of results and the opinion of society. These seemed only originalities of character when he was the leader of a clique of men of his own social position. Was Cleaver a snob because they seemed to him, now that his friend was brought low in the world, a bull-headed perversity, a ludicrous eccentricity, an unkempt republicanism, a raw incapacity to appreciate the right relations of things? In the delicately adjusted balance of life is that which is fine when a man is up, folly when a man is down?

"She is a pretty little thing," he said, slightingly, "and no doubt a good little thing. And, Trelawney, if I were in your place I wouldn't hang around her. Your feelings might become involved—she is so pretty—and she might fall in love with you, and"—

"You've said enough!" exclaimed Trelawney, fiercely.

It was monstrous! Trelawney would marry her. And he was as helpless to prevent it as if Fred intended to hang himself.

"Your railing at the women of society in that shallow fashion suggests the idea to me that you are trying to justify yourself in some tremendous folly. Do you contemplate marrying her?"

"That is exactly what I propose to do," said Trelawney.

"And you are mad enough to think you are really in love with her?"

"Why should I not be? If she were differently placed in point of wealth and station would there be any incongruity? I don't want to say anything hard of you, Cleaver, but you would be ready to congratulate me."

"I admit," retorted Cleaver, sharply, "that if she were your equal in station and appropriately educated I should not have a word of objection to say."

"And after all, is it the accident of position and fortune, or the human creature, that a man takes to his heart?"

"But her ignorance, Fred"—

"Great God! does a man fall in love with a society girl for the sake of what she calls her 'education?' Whatever attracts him, it is not that. They are all ignorant; this girl's ignorance is only relative."

"Ah,—you know all that is bosh, Fred."

"In point of manner you yourself must concede that she is in many respects superior to them. She has a certain repose and gravity and dignity difficult to find among young ladies of high degree whose education has not proved an antidote for flippancy. I won't be hard enough on them to compare the loveliness of her face or her fine, unspoiled nature. You don't want her to be learned any more than you want an azalea to be learned. An azalea in a green-house becomes showy and flaunting and has no fragrance, while here in the woods its exquisite sweetness fills the air for miles."

"Trelawney, you are fit for Bedlam."

136

"I knew you would say so. I thought so too at first. I tried to stamp it out, and put it down, and for a long time I fought all that is best in me."

"Does she know anything about your feelings?"

"Not one word, as yet."

"Then I hope something—anything—may happen to put a stop to it before she does."

This hasty wish seemed cruel to him afterward, and he regretted it.

"It would break my heart," said Trelawney, with an extreme earnestness. "I know you think I am talking wildly, but I tell you it would break my heart."

Cleaver fell to meditating ruefully upon the future in store for his friend in this desolate place. King Cophetua and the beggar-maid are a triumph of ideal contrast, eminently fascinating in an ideal point of view. But real life presents prosaic corollaries,—the Teakes, for example, on the familiar footing of Trelawney's brothers-in-law; the old crone with her pipe, his wife's grandmother; that ignorant girl, his wife—oh, these sublunary considerations are too inexorable. In his sluggish content he would never make another effort; he would always live here; he would sink, year by year, by virtue of his adaptability and uncouth associations nearer to the level of the mountaineers. This culminating folly seemed destined to complete the ruin of every prospect in a fine man's life.

Cleaver did not know what was to come, and he brooded upon these ideas.

III.

Those terrible problems of existence of which happier men at rare intervals catch a fleeting glimpse, and are struck

137

aghast for a moment, pursued John Cleaver relentlessly day by day. He could not understand this world; he could not understand the waste of himself and his friend in this useless, purposeless way; he could not even understand the magnificent waste of the nature about him. Sometimes he would look with haggard eyes on the late dawns and marvel that the sun should rise in such effulgence upon this sequestered spot; a perpetual twilight might have sufficed for the threnody, called life, here. He would gaze on Sunrise Rock, forever facing and reflecting the dawn, and wonder who and what was the man that in the forgotten past had stood on these red hills, and looked with his full heart in his eyes upon that sun, and smote the stone to sudden speech. Were his eyes haggard too? Was his life heavy? Were his fiery aspirations only a touch of the actual cautery to all that was sensitive within him? Did he know how his world was to pass away? Did he know how little he was in the world? Did he too wring his hands, and beat his breast, and sigh for the thing that was not?

Cleaver did the work that came to him conscientiously, although mechanically enough. But there was little work to do. Even the career of a humble country doctor seemed closed to him. He began to think he saw how it would end. He would be obliged to quit the profession; in sheer manliness he would be obliged to get to something at which he could work. A terrible pang here. He cared nothing for money,—this man, who was as poor as the very mountaineers. He was vowed to science as a monk is vowed to his order.

It was an unusual occurrence, therefore, when Trelawney came in one day and found that Cleaver had been called out professionally. He sat down to dine alone, but before he had finished carving, his friend entered.

138

"Well, doctor," said Trelawney cheerily, "how is your patient?"

Cleaver was evidently out of sorts and preoccupied. "These people are as uncivilized as the foxes that they live among," he exclaimed irrelevantly. "A case of malignant diphtheria, a physician their nearest neighbor, and they don't let him know till nearly the last gasp. Then they all go frantic together, and swear they had no idea it was serious. I could have brained that fool, Peter Teake. But it is a hopeless thing now."

A premonition thrilled through Trelawney. "Who is ill at Teake's?"

Cleaver was stricken dumb. His professional indignation had canceled all realization of the impending crisis. He remembered Fred's foolish fancy an instant too late. His silence answered for him. And Trelawney, a sudden blight upon his handsome face, rose and walked out heavily into the splendors of the autumn sunset. Cleaver was bitter with self-reproach. Still he felt an impotent anger that Fred should have persuaded himself that he was in love with this girl, and laid himself liable to this sentimental pain.

"A heart!" thought Cleaver, scornfully. "That a heart should trouble a man in a place like this!"

And yet his own well-schooled heart was all athrob with a keen, undreamed-of anguish when once more he had come back from the cabin in the gorge. As he entered, Trelawney, after one swift glance, turned his eyes away. He had learned from Cleaver's face all he feared to know. He might have learned more, a secret too subtly bitter for his friend to tell. King Cophetua was as naught to the beggar-maid. In her dying eyes John Cleaver had seen the fresh and pure affection that had followed him. In her tones he had heard it. Was she misled by that professional tenderness of manner which speaks so soothingly and touches so softly—as mechanical as the act of drawing off his gloves—that she should have been moved to cry out in her huskily pathetic voice, "How good—how good ye air!" and extend to him, amongst all her kindred who stood about, her little sun-burned hand?

And after that she was speechless, and when the little hand was unloosed it was cold.

She had loved him, and he had never known it until now. He felt like a traitor as he glanced at his friend's changed face, and he was crushed by a sense of the immense capacity of human nature for suffering. What a great heart-drama was this, with its incongruous and humble *dramatis personæ*: the little mountaineer, and these two poverty-stricken stragglers from the vast army of men of action,—deserters, even, it might seem. What chaotic sarcasm in this mysterious ordering of events,—Trelawney, with his grand sacrificial passion; the poor little girl, whose first fresh love had unsought followed another through these waste places; and he, all unconscious, absorbed in himself, his worldly considerations and the dying throes of his dear ambitions. And now, for him, who had felt least of all, was rising a great vicarious woe. If he had known this girl's heart-secret while she yet lived he might have thought scornfully of it, slightingly; who can say how? But now that she was dead it was as if he had been beloved by an angel, and was only too obtuse, too gross, too earthly-minded to hear the rustle of her wings. How pitiable was the thought of her misplaced affection; how hard it was for his friend; how hard it was for him that he had ever discovered it. Did she know that he cared nothing? Were the last days of her short life embittered with the pangs of a consciously unrequited love? Or did she tremble, and hope, and tremble again? Ah, poor, poor, pretty thing!

He had no name for a certain vague, mysterious thrill which quivered through every fibre whenever he thought of that humble, tender love that had followed him so long, unasked and unheeded. It began to hang about him now like a dimly-realized presence. Occasionally it occurred to him that his nerves were disordered, his health giving way, and he would commence a course of medicine, to forget it in his preoccupation, and discontinue it almost as soon as begun. What happened afterward was a natural sequence enough, although at the time it seemed wonderful indeed.

One misty midnight, when these strong feelings were upon him, it so chanced that he was driving from a patient's house on the summit of the ridge, and his way lay beneath Sunrise Rock along the road which encircled the little graveyard of the mountaineers. The moon was bright; so bright that the wreaths of vapor, hanging motionless among the pines, glistened like etherealized silver; so bright that the mounds within the inclosure—Was it the mist? Was it the moonbeam? Was it the glimmer of yellow hair? Did he see, leaning on the palings, "restin' awhile," the graceful figure he remembered so well? He was dreaming, surely; or were those deep, instarred eyes really fixed upon him with that wistful gaze which he had seen only twice before?—once here, where he had met her, and once when she died. She was approaching him; she was so close he might have touched her hand. Was it cold, he wondered; cold as it was when he held it last? He hardly knew,—but she was seated beside him, as in that crimson sunset-tide, and they were driving together at a frenzied speed through the broken shadows of the wintry woods. He did not turn his head, and yet he saw her face, drawn in lines of pallid light and eloquent with some untranslated emotion of mingled wonderment and pleasure and pain. Like the wind they sped together through the mist and the moonbeam, over the wild mountain road, through the flashing mountain waters, down, down the

141

steep slope toward the red brick house, where a light still burned, and his friend was waiting. He did not know when she slipped from his side. He did not know when this mad pace was checked. He only regained his faculties after he had burst into the warm home atmosphere, a ghastly horror in his face and his frantic fright upon his lips.

Trelawney stood breathless.

"Oh, forgive me," cried Cleaver. "I have spoken sacrilege. It was only hallucination; I know it now."

Trelawney was shaken. "Hallucination?" he faltered, with quivering lips.

"I did not reflect," said Cleaver. "I would not have jarred your feelings. I am ill and nervous."

Trelawney was too broken to resent, to heed, or to answer. He sat cold and shivering, unconscious of the changed eyes watching him, unconscious of a new idea kindling there,— beginning to flicker, to burn, to blaze,—unconscious of the motive with which his friend after a time drew close to the table and fell to writing with furious energy, unconscious that in this moment Cleaver's fortune was made.

And thus he wrote on day after day. So cleverly did he analyze his own mental and nervous condition, so unsparing and insidious was this curious introversion, that when his treatise on the "Derangement of the Nervous Functions" was given to the world it was in no degree remarkable that it should have attracted the favorable attention of the medical profession; that the portion devoted to hallucinations should have met with high praise in high quarters; that the young physician's successful work should have brought him suddenly to the remembrance of many people who had almost forgotten poor John Cleaver. No one knew, no one ever knew, its romantic inspiration. No one ever knew the strange source whence he had this keen

142

insight; how his imperious will had held his shaken, distraught nerves for the calm scrutiny of science; how his senses had played him false, and that stronger, subtler critical entity, his intellect, had marked the antics of its double self and noted them down.

Among the men to whom his treatise brought John Cleaver to sudden remembrance was a certain notable physician. He was growing infirm now, his health was failing, his heavy practice was too heavy for his weakening hands. He gave to the young fellow's work the meed of his rare approval, cleverly gauged the cleverness behind it, and wrote to Cleaver to come.

And so he returned to his accustomed and appropriate sphere. In his absence his world had flattened, narrowed, dulled strangely. People were sordid, and petty, and coarse-minded; and society—his little clique that he called society—possessed a painfully predominating element of snobs; men who had given him no notice before were pleased to be noticed now, and yet the lucky partnership was covertly commented upon as the freak of an old man in his dotage. He was suddenly successful, he had suddenly a certain prospect of wealth, he was suddenly bitter. He thought much in these days of his friend Trelawney and the independent, money-scorning aristocrats of the mountains, of the red hills of the Indian summer, and the towering splendors of Sunrise Rock. That high air was perhaps too rare for his lungs, but he was sensible of the density of the denser medium.

As to that vague and tender mystery, the ghost that he saw, it had been exorcised by prosaic science. But it made his fortune, it crowned his life, it bestowed upon him all he craved. Perhaps if she could know the wonderful work she had wrought in his future, the mountain girl, who had given her heart unasked, might rest more easily in her grave than on that night when she had come from among the moonlit mounds beneath Sunrise Rock, and once more sat beside him as he drove through shadow and sheen. For whether it was the pallid mist, whether it was the silver moon, whether it was the fantasy of an overwrought brain, or whether that mysterious presence was of an essence more ethereal than any, who can know?

In these days he carried his friend's interest close to his heart. He opened a way in the crowd, but Trelawney held back from the hands stretched out. He had become wedded to the place. The years since have brought him a quiet, uneventful, not unhappy existence. After a time he grew more cheerful, but not less gentle, and none the less beloved of his simple neighbors. They feel vaguely sometimes that since he first came among them he is a saddened man, and are moved to ask with sympathetic solicitude concerning the news from his supposititious folks "down thar in the valley whar ye hails from." The fortune in sheep-farming still eludes his languid pursuit. The red brick house is disorganized and dilapidated as of yore; a sense of loneliness broods upon it, hardly less intense than the loneliness of the mighty encompassing forest. Deep in these solitudes he often strolls for hours, most often in the crimson and purple eventides along the road that passes beneath Sunrise Rock and encircles the little graveyard of the mountaineers. Here Trelawney leans on the palings while the sun goes down, and looks, with his sore heart bleeding anew, upon one grassy mound till the shadows and the tears together blot it from his sight. Sometimes his heart is not sore, only sad. Sometimes it is tender and resigned, and he turns to the sunrise emblazoned on the rock and thinks of the rising Sun of Righteousness with healing in his wings. For the skepticism of his college days has fallen from him somehow, and his views have become primitive, like those of his primitive neighbors. There is a certain calm and strength in

144

the old theories. With the dawn of a gentle and hopeful peace in his heart, very like the comfort of religion, he goes his way in the misty moon-rise.

And sometimes John Cleaver, so far away, as with a second sight becomes subtly aware of these things. He remembers how Trelawney is deceived, and a remorse falls on him in the still darkness, and tears and mangles him. And yet there are no words for confession,—there is nothing to confess. Would his conjecture, his unsupported conviction, avail aught; would it not be cruel to re-open old wounds with the sharp torture of a doubt? And the daybreak finds him with these questions unsolved, and his heart turning wistfully to that true and loyal friend, with his faithful, unrequited love still lingering about the grave of the girl who died with her love unrequited.

THE DANCIN' PARTY AT HARRISON'S COVE.

"Fur ye see, Mis' Darley, them Harrison folks over yander ter the Cove hev determined on a dancin' party."

The drawling tones fell unheeded on old Mr. Kenyon's ear, as he sat on the broad hotel piazza of the New Helvetia Springs, and gazed with meditative eyes at the fair August sky. An early moon was riding, clear and full, over this wild spur of the Alleghanies; the stars were few and very faint; even the great Scorpio lurked, vaguely outlined, above the wooded ranges; and the white mist, that filled the long, deep, narrow valley between the parallel lines of mountains, shimmered with opalescent gleams.

All the world of the watering-place had converged to that focus, the ball-room, and the cool, moonlit piazzas were nearly deserted. The fell determination of the "Harrison folks" to give a dancing party made no impression on the preoccupied old gentleman. Another voice broke his reverie,—a soft, clear, well-modulated voice,—and he started and turned his head as his own name was called, and his niece, Mrs. Darley, came to the window.

"Uncle Ambrose,—are you there? So glad! I was afraid you were down at the summer-house, where I hear the children singing. Do come here a moment, please. This is Mrs. Johns, who brings the Indian peaches to sell,—you know the Indian peaches?"

Mr. Kenyon knew the Indian peaches, the dark crimson fruit streaked with still darker lines, and full of blood-red juice, which he had meditatively munched that very afternoon. Mr. Kenyon knew the Indian peaches right well. He wondered, however, what had brought Mrs. Johns back in so short a time, for although the principal industry of the mountain people about the New Helvetia Springs is selling fruit to the summer sojourners, it is not customary to come twice on the same day, nor to appear at all after night-fall.

Mrs. Darley proceeded to explain.

"Mrs. Johns's husband is ill and wants us to send him some medicine."

Mr. Kenyon rose, threw away the stump of his cigar, and entered the room. "How long has he been ill, Mrs. Johns?" he asked, dismally.

Mr. Kenyon always spoke lugubriously, and he was a dismal-looking old man. Not more cheerful was Mrs. Johns; she was tall and lank, and with such a face as one never sees except in these mountains,—elongated, sallow, thin, with pathetic, deeply sunken eyes, and high cheek-bones, and so settled an expression of hopeless melancholy that it must be that naught but care and suffering had been her lot; holding

146

out wasted hands to the years as they pass,—holding them out always, and always empty. She wore a shabby, faded calico, and spoke with the peculiar expressionless drawl of the mountaineer. She was a wonderful contrast to Mrs. Darley, all furbelows and flounces, with her fresh, smooth face and soft hair, and plump, round arms half-revealed by the flowing sleeves of her thin, black dress. Mrs. Darley was in mourning, and therefore did not affect the ball-room. At this moment, on benevolent thoughts intent, she was engaged in uncorking sundry small phials, gazing inquiringly at their labels, and shaking their contents.

In reply to Mr. Kenyon's question, Mrs. Johns, sitting on the extreme edge of a chair and fanning herself with a pink calico sun-bonnet, talked about her husband, and a misery in his side and in his back, and how he felt it "a-comin' on nigh on ter a week ago." Mr. Kenyon expressed sympathy, and was surprised by the announcement that Mrs. Johns considered her husband's illness "a blessin', 'kase ef he war able ter git out'n his bed, he 'lowed ter go down ter Harrison's Cove ter the dancin' party, 'kase Rick Pearson war a-goin' ter be thar, an' hed said ez how none o' the Johnses should come."

"What, Rick Pearson, that terrible outlaw!" exclaimed Mrs. Darley, with wide open blue eyes. She had read in the newspapers sundry thrilling accounts of a noted horse thief and outlaw, who with a gang of kindred spirits defied justice and roamed certain sparsely-populated mountainous counties at his own wild will, and she was not altogether without a feeling of fear as she heard of his proximity to the New Helvetia Springs,—not fear for life or limb, because she was practical-minded enough to reflect that the sojourners and employés of the watering-place would far outnumber the outlaw's troop, but fear that a pair of shiny bay ponies, Castor and Pollux, would fall victims to the crafty wiles of the expert horse thief.

"I think I have heard something of a difficulty between your people and Rick Pearson," said old Mr. Kenyon. "Has a peace never been patched up between them?"

"No-o," drawled Mrs. Johns; "same as it always war. My old man'll never believe but what Rick Pearson stole that thar bay filly we lost 'bout five year ago. But I don't believe he done it; plenty other folks around is ez mean ez Rick, leastways mos' ez mean; plenty mean enough ter steal a horse, ennyhow. Rick *say* he never tuk the filly; say he war a-goin' ter shoot off the nex' man's head ez say so. Rick say he'd ruther give two bay fillies than hev a man say he tuk a horse ez he never tuk. Rick say ez how he kin stand up ter what he does do, but it's these hyar lies on him what kills him out. But ye know, Mis' Darley, ye know yerself, he never give nobody two bay fillies in this world, an' what's more he's never goin' ter. My old man an' my boy Kossute talks on 'bout that thar bay filly like she war stole yestiddy, an' 't war five year ago an' better; an' when they hearn ez how Rick Pearson hed showed that red head o' his'n on this hyar mounting las' week, they war fightin' mad, an' would hev lit out fur the gang sure, 'ceptin' they hed been gone down the mounting fur two days. An' my son Kossute, he sent Rick word that he had better keep out 'n gunshot o' these hyar woods; that he didn't want no better mark than that red head o' his'n, an' he could hit it two mile off. An' Rick Pearson, he sent Kossute word that he would kill him fur his sass the very nex' time he see him, an' ef he don't want a bullet in that pumpkin head o' his'n he hed better keep away from that dancin' party what the Harrisons hev laid off ter give, 'kase Rick say he's a-goin' ter it hisself, an' is a-goin' ter dance too; he ain't been invited, Mis' Darley, but Rick don't keer fur that. He is a-goin' ennyhow, an' he say ez how he ain't a-

148

goin' ter let Kossute come, 'count o' Kossute's sass an' the fuss they've all made 'bout that bay filly that war stole five year ago,—'t war five year an' better. But Rick say ez how he is goin', fur all he ain't got no invite, an' is a-goin' ter dance too, 'kase you know, Mis' Darley, it's a-goin' ter be a dancin' party; the Harrisons hev determined on that. Them gals of theirn air mos' crazed 'bout a dancin' party. They ain't been a bit of account sence they went ter Cheatham's Cross-Roads ter see thar gran'mother, an' picked up all them queer new notions. So the Harrisons hev determined on a dancin' party; an' Rick say ez how he is goin' ter dance too; but Jule, *she* say ez how she know thar ain't a gal on the mounting ez would dance with him; but I ain't so sure 'bout that, Mis' Darley; gals air cur'ous critters, ye know yerself; thar's no sort o' countin' on 'em; they'll do one thing one time, an' another thing nex' time; ye can't put no dependence in 'em. But Jule say ef he kin git Mandy Tyler ter dance with him, it's the mos' he kin do, an' the gang'll be no whar. Mebbe he kin git Mandy ter dance with him, 'kase the other boys say ez how none o' them is a-goin' ter ax her ter dance, 'count of the trick she played on 'em down ter the Wilkins settlemint—las' month, war it? no, 't war two month ago, an' better; but the boys ain't forgot how scandalous she done 'em, an' none of 'em is a-goin' ter ax her ter dance."

"Why, what did she do?" exclaimed Mrs. Darley, surprised. "She came here to sell peaches one day, and I thought her such a nice, pretty, well-behaved girl."

"Waal, she hev got mighty quiet say-nuthin' sort'n ways, Mis' Darley, but that thar gal do behave *re*diculous. Down thar ter the Wilkins settlemint,—ye know it's 'bout two mile or two mile'n a half from hyar,—waal, all the gals walked down thar ter the party an hour by sun, but when the boys went down they tuk thar horses, ter give the gals a ride home behind 'em. Waal, every boy axed his gal ter ride while the party war goin' on, an' when 't war all over they all set out fur ter come home. Waal, this hyar Mandy Tyler is a mighty favorite 'mongst the boys,—they ain't got no sense, ye know, Mis' Darley,—an' stiddier one of 'em axin' her ter ride home, thar war five of 'em axed her ter ride, ef ye'll believe me, an' what do ye think she done, Mis' Darley? She tole all five of 'em yes; an' when the party war over, she war the last ter go, an' when she started out'n the door, thar war all five of them boys a-standin' thar waitin' fur her, an' every one a-holdin' his horse by the bridle, an' none of 'em knowed who the others war a-waitin' fur. An' this hyar Mandy Tyler, when she got ter the door an' seen 'em all a-standin' thar, never said one word, jest walked right through 'mongst 'em, an' set out fur the mounting on foot with all them five boys a-followin' an' a-leadin' thar horses an' a-quarrelin' enough ter take off each others' heads 'bout which one war a-goin' ter ride with her; which none of 'em did, Mis' Darley, fur I hearn ez how the whole lay-out footed it all the way ter New Helveshy. An' thar would hev been a fight 'mongst 'em, 'ceptin' her brother, Jacob Tyler, went along with 'em, an' tried ter keep the peace a-twixt 'em. An' Mis' Darley, all them married folks down thar at the party—them folks in the Wilkins settlemint is the biggest fools, sure—when all them married folks come out ter the door, an' see the way Mandy Tyler hed treated them boys, they jest hollered and laffed an' thought it war mighty smart an' funny in Mandy; but she never say a word till she kem up the mounting, an' I never hearn ez how she say ennything then. An' now the boys all say none of 'em is a-goin' ter ax her ter dance, ter pay her back fur them fool airs of hern. But Kossute say he'll dance with her ef none the rest will. Kossute he thought 't war all mighty funny too,—he's sech a fool 'bout gals, Kossute is,— but Jule, she thought ez how 't war scandalous."

Mrs. Darley listened in amused surprise; that these mountain wilds could sustain a first-class coquette was an idea that had not hitherto entered her mind; however, "that thar Mandy" seemed, in Mrs. Johns's opinion at least, to merit the unenviable distinction, and the party at Wilkins settlement and the prospective gayety of Harrison's Cove awakened the same sentiments in her heart and mind as do the more ambitious germans and kettledrums of the lowland cities in the heart and mind of Mrs. Grundy. Human nature is the same everywhere, and the Wilkins settlement is a microcosm. The metropolitan centres, stripped of the civilization of wealth, fashion, and culture, would present only the bare skeleton of humanity outlined in Mrs. Johns's talk of Harrison's Cove, the Wilkins settlement, the enmities and scandals and sorrows and misfortunes of the mountain ridge. As the absurd resemblance developed, Mrs. Darley could not forbear a smile. Mrs. Johns looked up with a momentary expression of surprise; the story presented no humorous phase to her perceptions, but she too smiled a little as she repeated, "Scandalous, ain't it?" and proceeded in the same lack-lustre tone as before.

"Yes,—Kossute say ez how he'll dance with her ef none the rest will, fur Kossute say ez how he hev laid off ter dance, Mis' Darley; an' when I ax him what he thinks will become of his soul ef he dances, he say the devil may crack away at it, an' ef he kin hit it he's welcome. Fur soul or no soul he's a-goin' ter dance. Kossute is a-fixin' of hisself this very minit ter go; but I am verily afeard the boy'll be slaughtered, Mis' Darley, 'kase thar is goin' ter be a fight, an' ye never in all yer life hearn sech sass ez Kossute and Rick Pearson done sent word ter each other."

Mr. Kenyon expressed some surprise that she should fear for so young a fellow as Kossuth. "Surely," he said, "the man is not brute enough to injure a mere boy; your son is a mere boy."

"That's so," Mrs. Johns drawled. "Kossute ain't more 'n twenty year old, an' Rick Pearson is double that ef he is a day; but ye see it's the fire-arms ez makes Kossute more 'n a match fur him, 'kase Kossute is the best shot on the mounting, an' Rick knows that in a shootin' fight Kossute 's better able ter take keer of hisself an' hurt somebody else nor ennybody. Kossute 's more likely ter hurt Rick nor Rick is ter hurt him in a shootin' fight; but ef Rick did n't hurt him, an' he war ter shoot Rick, the gang would tear him ter pieces in a minit; and 'mongst 'em I'm actually afeard they 'll slaughter the boy."

Mr. Kenyon looked even graver than was his wont upon receiving this information, but said no more; and after giving Mrs. Johns the febrifuge she wished for her husband, he returned to his seat on the piazza.

Mrs. Darley watched him with some little indignation as he proceeded to light a fresh cigar. "How cold and unsympathetic uncle Ambrose is," she said to herself. And after condoling effusively with Mrs. Johns on her apprehensions for her son's safety, she returned to the gossips in the hotel parlor, and Mrs. Johns, with her pink calico sun-bonnet on her head, went her way in the brilliant summer moon light.

The clear lustre shone white upon all the dark woods and chasms and flashing waters that lay between the New Helvetia Springs and the wide, deep ravine called Harrison's Cove, where from a rude log hut the vibrations of a violin, and the quick throb of dancing feet, already mingled with the impetuous rush of a mountain stream close by and the weird night-sounds of the hills,—the cry of birds among the tall trees, the stir of the wind, the monotonous chanting of frogs at the water-side, the long, drowsy drone of the nocturnal insects, the sudden faint blast of a distant hunter's horn, and the far baying of hounds.

Mr. Harrison had four marriageable daughters, and had arrived at the conclusion that something must be done for the girls; for, strange as it may seem, the prudent father exists even among the "mounting folks." Men there realize the importance of providing suitable homes for their daughters as men do elsewhere, and the eligible youth is as highly esteemed in those wilds as is the much scarcer animal at a fashionable watering-place. Thus it was that Mr. Harrison had "determined on a dancin' party." True, he stood in bodily fear of the judgment day and the circuit-rider; but the dancing party was a rarity eminently calculated to please the young hunters of the settlements round about, so he swallowed his qualms, to be indulged at a more convenient season, and threw himself into the vortex of preparation with an ardor very gratifying to the four young ladies, who had become imbued with sophistication at Cheatham's Cross-Roads.

Not so Mrs. Harrison; she almost expected the house to fall and crush them, as a judgment on the wickedness of a dancing party; for so heinous a sin, in the estimation of the greater part of the mountain people, had not been committed among them for many a day. Such trifles as killing a man in a quarrel, or on suspicion of stealing a horse, or wash-tub, or anything that came handy, of course, does not count; but a dancing party! Mrs. Harrison could only hold her idle hands, and dread the heavy penalty that must surely follow so terrible a crime.

It certainly had not the gay and lightsome aspect supposed to be characteristic of such a scene of sin: the awkward young mountaineers clogged heavily about in their uncouth clothes and rough shoes, with the stolid-looking, lack-lustre maids of the hill, to the violin's monotonous iteration of The Chicken in the Bread-Trough, or The Rabbit in the Pea-Patch,—all their grave faces as grave as ever. The music now and then changed suddenly to one of those wild, melancholy strains sometimes heard in old-fashioned dancing tunes, and the strange pathetic cadences seemed more attuned to the rhythmical dash of the waters rushing over their stone barricades out in the moonlight yonder, or to the plaintive sighs of the winds among the great dark arches of the primeval forests, than to the movement of the heavy, coarse feet dancing a solemn measure in the little log cabin in Harrison's Cove. The elders, sitting in rush-bottomed chairs close to the walls, and looking on at the merriment, well-pleased despite their religious doubts, were somewhat more lively; every now and then a guffaw mingled with the violin's resonant strains and the dancers' well-marked pace; the women talked to each other with somewhat more animation than was their wont, under the stress of the unusual excitement of a dancing party, and from out the shed-room adjoining came an anticipative odor of more substantial sin than the fiddle or the grave jiggling up and down the rough floor. A little more cider too, and a very bad article of illegally-distilled whiskey, were ever and anon circulated among the pious abstainers from the dance; but the sinful votaries of Terpsichore could brook no pause nor delay, and jogged up and down quite intoxicated with the mirthfulness of the plaintive old airs and the pleasure of other motion than following the plow or hoeing the corn.

And the moon smiled right royally on her dominion: on the long, dark ranges of mountains and mist-filled valleys between; on the woods and streams, and on all the half-dormant creatures either amongst the shadow-flecked foliage or under the crystal waters; on the long, white, sandy road winding in and out through the forest; on the frowning crags of the wild ravine; on the little bridge at the entrance of the gorge, across which a party of eight men, heavily armed and gallantly mounted, rode swiftly and disappeared amid the gloom of the shadows.

154

The sound of the galloping of horses broke suddenly on the music and the noise of the dancing; a moment's interval, and the door gently opened and the gigantic form of Rick Pearson appeared in the aperture. He was dressed, like the other mountaineers, in a coarse suit of brown jeans somewhat the worse for wear, the trowsers stuffed in the legs of his heavy boots; he wore an old soft felt hat, which he did not remove immediately on entering, and a pair of formidable pistols at his belt conspicuously challenged attention. He had auburn hair, and a long full beard of a lighter tint reaching almost to his waist; his complexion was much tanned by the sun, and roughened by exposure to the inclement mountain weather; his eyes were brown, deep-set, and from under his heavy brows they looked out with quick, sharp glances, and occasionally with a roguish twinkle; the expression of his countenance was rather good-humored,— a sort of imperious good-humor, however,—the expression of a man accustomed to have his own way and not to be trifled with, but able to afford some amiability since his power is undisputed.

He stepped slowly into the apartment, placed his gun against the wall, turned, and solemnly gazed at the dancing, while his followers trooped in and obeyed his example. As the eight guns, one by one, rattled against the wall, there was a startled silence among the pious elders of the assemblage, and a sudden disappearance of the animation that had characterized their intercourse during the evening. Mrs. Harrison, who by reason of flurry and a housewifely pride in the still unrevealed treasures of the shed-room had well-nigh forgotten her fears, felt that the anticipated judgment had even now descended, and in what terrible and unexpected guise! The men turned the quids of tobacco in their cheeks and looked at each other in uncertainty; but the dancers bestowed not a glance upon the new-comers, and the musician in the corner, with his eyes half-closed, his head bent low upon the instrument, his hard, horny hand moving the bow back and forth over the strings of the crazy old fiddle, was utterly rapt by his own melody. At the supreme moment when the great red beard had appeared portentously in the door-way and fear had frozen the heart of Mrs. Harrison within her at the ill-omened apparition, the host was in the shed-room filling a broken-nosed pitcher from the cider-barrel. When he re-entered, and caught sight of the grave sun-burned face with its long red beard and sharp brown eyes, he too was dismayed for an instant, and stood silent at the opposite door with the pitcher in his hand. The pleasure and the possible profit of the dancing party, for which he had expended so much of his scanty store of this world's goods and risked the eternal treasures laid up in heaven, were a mere phantasm; for, with Rick Pearson among them, in an ill frame of mind and at odds with half the men in the room, there would certainly be a fight, and in all probability one would be killed, and the dancing party at Harrison's Cove would be a text for the bloody-minded sermons of the circuit-rider for all time to come. However, the father of four marriageable daughters is apt to become crafty and worldly-wise; only for a moment did he stand in indecision; then, catching suddenly the small brown eyes, he held up the pitcher with a grin of invitation. "Rick!" he called out above the scraping of the violin and the clatter of the dancing feet, "slip round hyar ef ye kin, I've got somethin' for ye;" and he shook the pitcher significantly.

Not that Mr. Harrison would for a moment have thought of Rick Pearson in a matrimonial point of view, for even the sophistication of the Cross-Roads had not yet brought him to the state of mind to consider such a half loaf as this better than no bread, but he felt it imperative from every point of view to keep that set of young mountaineers dancing in peace and quiet, and their guns idle and out of mischief against the wall. The great red beard disappeared and

156

reappeared at intervals, as Rick Pearson slipped along the gun-lined wall to join his host and the cider-pitcher, and after he had disposed of the refreshment, in which the gang shared, he relapsed into silently watching the dancing and meditating a participation in that festivity.

Now, it so happened that the only young girl unprovided with a partner was "that thar Mandy Tyler," of Wilkins settlement renown; the young men had rigidly adhered to their resolution to ignore her in their invitations to dance, and she had been sitting since the beginning of the festivities, quite neglected, among the married people, looking on at the amusement which she had been debarred sharing by that unpopular bit of coquetry at Wilkins settlement. Nothing of disappointment or mortification was expressed in her countenance; she felt the slight of course,— even a "mounting" woman is susceptible of the sting of wounded pride; all her long-anticipated enjoyment had come to naught by this infliction of penance for her ill-timed jest at the expense of those five young fellows dancing with their triumphant partners and bestowing upon her not even a glance; but she looked the express image of immobility as she sat in her clean pink calico, so carefully gotten up for the occasion, her short black hair curling about her ears, and watched the unending reel with slow, dark eyes. Rick's glance fell upon her, and without further hesitation he strode over to where she was sitting and proffered his hand for the dance. She did not reply immediately, but looked timidly about her at the shocked pious ones on either side, who were ready but for mortal fear to aver that "dancin' ennyhow air bad enough, the Lord knows, but dancin' with a horse thief air jest scandalous!" Then, for there is something of defiance to established law and prejudice in the born flirt everywhere, with a sudden daring spirit shining in her brightening eyes, she responded, "Don't keer ef I do," with a dimpling half-laugh; and the next minute the two outlaws were flying down the middle together.

While Rick was according grave attention to the intricacies of the mazy dance and keeping punctilious time to the scraping of the old fiddle, finding it all a much more difficult feat than galloping from the Cross Roads to the "Snake's Mouth" on some other man's horse with the sheriff hard at his heels, the solitary figure of a tall gaunt man had followed the long winding path leading deep into the woods, and now began the steep descent to Harrison's Cove. Of what was old Mr. Kenyon thinking, as he walked on in the mingled shadow and sheen? Of St. Augustin and his Forty Monks, probably, and what they found in Britain. The young men of his acquaintance would gladly have laid you any odds that he could think of nothing but his antique hobby, the ancient church. Mr. Kenyon was the most prominent man in St. Martin's church in the city of B——, not excepting the rector. He was a lay-reader, and officiated upon occasions of "clerical sore-throat," as the profane denominate the ministerial summer exodus from heated cities. This summer, however, Mr. Kenyon's own health had succumbed, and he was having a little "sore-throat" in the mountains on his own account. Very devout was Mr. Kenyon. Many people wondered that he had never taken orders. Many people warmly congratulated themselves that he never had; for drier sermons than those he selected were surely never heard, and a shuddering imagination shrinks appalled from the problematic mental drought of his ideal original discourse. But he was an integrant part of St. Martin's; much of his piety, materialized into contributions, was built up in its walls and shone before men in the costliness of its decorations. Indeed, the ancient name had been conferred upon the building as a sort of tribute to Mr. Kenyon's well-known enthusiasm concerning apostolic succession and kindred doctrines.

158

Dull and dismal was Mr. Kenyon, and therefore it may be considered a little strange that he should be a notable favorite with men. They were of many different types, but with one invariable bond of union: they had all at one time served as soldiers; for the war, now ten years passed by, its bitterness almost forgotten, had left some traces that time can never obliterate. What a friend was the droning old churchman in those days of battle and blood-shed and suffering and death! Not a man sat within the walls of St. Martin's who had not received some signal benefit from the hand stretched forth to impress the claims of certain ante-Augustin British clergy to consideration and credibility; not a man who did not remember stricken fields where a good Samaritan went about under shot and shell, succoring the wounded and comforting the dying; not a man who did not applaud the indomitable spirit and courage that cut his way from surrender and safety, through solid barriers of enemies, to deliver the orders on which the fate of an army depended; not a man whose memory did not harbor fatiguing recollections of long, dull sermons read for the souls' health of the soldiery. And through it all,—by the camp-fires at night, on the long white country-roads in the sunshiny mornings; in the mountains and the morasses; in hilarious advance and in cheerless retreat; in the heats of summer and by the side of frozen rivers, the ancient British clergy went through it all. And, whether the old churchman's premises and reasoning were false, whether his tracings of the succession were faulty, whether he dropped a link here or took in one there, he had caught the spirit of those staunch old martyrs, if not their falling churchly mantle.

The mountaineers about the New Helvetia Springs supposed that Mr. Kenyon was a regularly ordained preacher, and that the sermons which they had heard him read were, to use the vernacular, out of his own head. For many of them were accustomed on Sunday mornings to occupy humble back benches in the ball-room, where on week-day evenings the butterflies sojourning at New Helvetia danced, and on the Sabbath metaphorically beat their breasts, and literally avowed that they were "miserable sinners," following Mr. Kenyon's lugubrious lead.

The conclusion of the mountaineers was not unnatural, therefore, and when the door of Mr. Harrison's house opened and another uninvited guest entered, the music suddenly ceased. The half-closed eyes of the fiddler had fallen upon Mr. Kenyon at the threshold, and, supposing him a clergyman, he immediately imagined that the man of God had come all the way from New Helvetia Springs to stop the dancing and snatch the revelers from the jaws of hell. The rapturous bow paused shuddering on the string, the dancing feet were palsied, the pious about the walls were racking their slow brains to excuse their apparent conniving at sin and bargaining with Satan, and Mr. Harrison felt that this was indeed an unlucky party and it would undoubtedly be dispersed by the direct interposition of Providence before the shed-room was opened and the supper eaten. As to his soul—poor man! these constantly recurring social anxieties were making him callous to immortality; this life was about to prove too much for him, for the fortitude and tact even of a father of four marriageable young ladies has a limit. Mr. Kenyon, too, seemed dumb as he hesitated in the door-way, but when the host, partially recovering himself, came forward and offered a chair, he said with one of his dismal smiles that he hoped Mr. Harrison had no objection to his coming in and looking at the dancing for a while. "Don't let me interrupt the young people, I beg," he added, as he seated himself. The astounded silence was unbroken for a few moments. To be sure he was not a circuit-rider, but even the sophistication of Cheatham's Cross-Roads had never heard of a preacher who did not object to dancing. Mr. Harrison could not believe his ears, and asked for a more explicit expression of opinion.

"Ye say ye don't keer ef the boys an' gals dance?" he inquired. "Ye don't think it's sinful?"

And after Mr. Kenyon's reply, in which the astonished "mounting folks" caught only the surprising statement that dancing if properly conducted was an innocent, cheerful, and healthful amusement, supplemented by something about dancing in the fear of the Lord, and that in all charity he was disposed to consider objections to such harmless recreations a tithing of mint and anise and cummin, whereby might ensue a neglect of weightier matters of the law; that clean hands and clean hearts—hands clean of blood and ill-gotten goods, and hearts free from falsehood and cruel intention—these were the things well-pleasing to God,— after his somewhat prolix reply, the gayety recommenced. The fiddle quavered tremulously at first, but soon resounded with its former vigorous tones, and the joy of the dance was again exemplified in the grave joggling back and forth.

Meanwhile Mr. Harrison sat beside this strange new guest and asked him questions concerning his church, being instantly, it is needless to say, informed of its great antiquity, of the journeying of St. Augustin and his Forty Monks to Britain, of the church they found already planted there, of its retreat to the hills of Wales under its oppressors' tyranny, of many cognate themes, side issues of the main branch of the subject, into which the talk naturally drifted, the like of which Mr. Harrison had never heard in all his days. And as he watched the figures dancing to the violin's strains, and beheld as in a mental vision the solemn gyrations of those renowned Forty Monks to the monotone of old Mr. Kenyon's voice, he abstractedly hoped that the double dance would continue without interference till a peaceable dawn.

His hopes were vain. It so chanced that Kossuth Johns, who had by no means relinquished all idea of dancing at Harrison's Cove and defying Rick Pearson, had hitherto been detained by his mother's persistent entreaties, some necessary attentions to his father, and the many trials which beset a man dressing for a party who has very few clothes, and those very old and worn. Jule, his sister-in-law, had been most kind and complaisant, putting on a button here, sewing up a slit there, darning a refractory elbow, and lending him the one bright ribbon she possessed as a neck-tie. But all these things take time, and the moon did not light Kossuth down the gorge until she was shining almost vertically from the sky, and the Harrison Cove people and the Forty Monks were dancing together in high feather. The ecclesiastic dance halted suddenly, and a watchful light gleamed in old Mr. Kenyon's eyes as he became silent and the boy stepped into the room. The moonlight and the lamp-light fell mingled on the calm, inexpressive features and tall, slender form of the young mountaineer. "Hy're, Kossute!" A cheerful greeting from many voices met him. The next moment the music ceased once again, and the dancing came to a stand-still, for as the name fell on Pearson's ear he turned, glanced sharply toward the door, and drawing one of his pistols from his belt advanced to the middle of the room. The men fell back; so did the frightened women, without screaming, however, for that indication of feminine sensibility had not yet penetrated to Cheatham's Cross-Roads, to say nothing of the mountains.

"I told ye that ye warn't ter come hyar," said Rick Pearson imperiously, "and ye've got ter go home ter yer mammy, right off, or ye'll never git thar no more, youngster."

"I've come hyar ter put *you* out, ye cussed red-headed horse thief!" retorted Kossuth, angrily; "ye hed better tell me whar that thar bay filly is, or light out, one."

162

It is not the habit in the mountains to parley long on these occasions. Kossuth had raised his gun to his shoulder as Rick, with his pistol cocked, advanced a step nearer. The outlaw's weapon was struck upward by a quick, strong hand, the little log cabin was filled with flash, roar, and smoke, and the stars looked in through a hole in the roof from which Rick's bullet had sent the shingles flying. He turned in mortal terror and caught the hand that had struck his pistol,—in mortal terror, for Kossuth was the crack shot of the mountains and he felt he was a dead man. The room was somewhat obscured by smoke, but as he turned upon the man who had disarmed him, for the force of the blow had thrown the pistol to the floor, he saw that the other hand was over the muzzle of young Johns's gun, and Kossuth was swearing loudly that by the Lord Almighty if he didn't take it off he would shoot it off.

"My young friend," Mr. Kenyon began, with the calmness appropriate to a devout member of the one catholic and apostolic church; but then, the old Adam suddenly getting the upper-hand, he shouted out in irate tones, "If you don't stop that noise, I'll break your head! Well, Mr. Pearson," he continued, as he stood between the combatants, one hand still over the muzzle of young Johns's gun, the other, lean and sinewy, holding Pearson's powerful right arm with a vise-like grip, "well, Mr. Pearson, you are not so good a soldier as you used to be; you didn't fight boys in the old times."

Rick Pearson's enraged expression suddenly gave way to a surprised recognition. "Ye may drag me through hell an' beat me with a soot-bag ef hyar ain't the old fightin' preacher agin!" he cried.

"I have only one thing to say to you," said Mr. Kenyon. "You must go. I will not have you here shooting boys and breaking up a party."

Rick demurred. "See hyar, now," he said, "ye've got no business meddlin'."

"You must go," Mr. Kenyon reiterated.

"Preachin's yer business," Rick continued; "pears like ye don't 'tend to it, though."

"You must go."

"S'pose I say I won't," said Rick, good-humoredly; "I s'pose ye'd say ye'd make me."

"You must go," repeated Mr. Kenyon. "I am going to take the boy home with me, but I intend to see you off first."

Mr. Kenyon had prevented the hot-headed Kossuth from firing by keeping his hand persistently over the muzzle of the gun; and young Johns had feared to try to wrench it away lest it should discharge in the effort. Had it done so, Mr. Kenyon would have been in sweet converse with the Forty Monks in about a minute and a quarter. Kossuth had finally let go the gun, and made frantic attempts to borrow a weapon from some of his friends, but the stern authoritative mandate of the belligerent peace-maker had prevented them from gratifying him, and he now stood empty-handed beside Mr. Kenyon, who had shouldered the old rifle in an absent-minded manner, although still retaining his powerful grasp on the arm of the outlaw.

"Waal, parson," said Rick at length, "I'll go, jest ter pleasure you-uns. Ye see, I ain't forgot Shiloh."

"I am not talking about Shiloh now," said the old man. "You must get off at once,—all of you," indicating the gang, who had been so whelmed in astonishment that they had not lifted a finger to aid their chief.

"Ye say ye'll take that—that"—Rick looked hard at Kossuth while he racked his brains for an injurious epithet—"that sassy child home ter his mammy?"

"Come, I am tired of this talk," said Mr. Kenyon; "you must go."

Rick walked heavily to the door and out into the moonlight. "Them was good old times," he said to Mr. Kenyon, with a regretful cadence in his peculiar drawl; "good old times, them War days. I wish they was back agin,—I wish they was back agin. I ain't forgot Shiloh yit, though, and I ain't a-goin' ter. But I'll tell ye one thing, parson," he added, his mind reverting from ten years ago to the scene just past, as he unhitched his horse and carefully examined the saddle-girth and stirrups, "ye're a mighty queer preacher, ye air, a-sittin' up an' lookin' at sinners dance an' then gittin' in a fight that don't consarn ye,—ye're a mighty queer preacher! Ye ought ter be in my gang, that's whar *ye* ought ter be," he exclaimed with a guffaw, as he put his foot in the stirrup; "ye've got a damned deal too much grit fur a preacher. But I ain't forgot Shiloh yit, an' I don't mean ter, nuther."

A shout of laughter from the gang, an oath or two, the quick tread of horses' hoofs pressing into a gallop, and the outlaw's troop were speeding along the narrow paths that led deep into the vistas of the moonlit summer woods.

As the old churchman, with the boy at his side and the gun still on his shoulder, ascended the rocky, precipitous slope on the opposite side of the ravine above the foaming waters of the wild mountain stream, he said but little of admonition to his companion; with the disappearance of the flame and smoke and the dangerous ruffian his martial spirit had cooled; the last words of the outlaw, the highest praise Rick Pearson could accord to the highest qualities Rick Pearson could imagine—he had grit enough to belong to the gang— had smitten a tender conscience. He, at his age, using none of the means rightfully at his command, the gentle suasion of religion, must needs rush between armed men, wrench their weapons from their hands, threatening with such violence that an outlaw and desperado, recognizing a parallel of his own belligerent and lawless spirit, should say that he ought to belong to the gang! And the heaviest scourge of the sin-laden conscience was the perception that, so far as the unsubdued old Adam went, he ought indeed.

He was not so tortured, though, that he did not think of others. He paused on reaching the summit of the ascent, and looked back at the little house nestling in the ravine, the lamp-light streaming through its open doors and windows across the path among the laurel bushes, where Rick's gang had hitched their horses.

"I wonder," said the old man, "if they are quiet and peaceable again; can you hear the music and dancing?"

"Not now," said Kossuth. Then, after a moment, "Now, I kin," he added, as the wind brought to their ears the oft-told tale of the rabbit's gallopade in the pea-patch. "They're a-dancin' now, and all right agin."

As they walked along, Mr. Kenyon's racked conscience might have been in a slight degree comforted had he known that he was in some sort a revelation to the impressible lad at his side, that Kossuth had begun dimly to comprehend that a Christian may be a man of spirit also, and that bravado does not constitute bravery. Now that the heat of anger was over, the young fellow was glad that the fearless interposition of the warlike peace-maker had prevented any killing, "'kase ef the old man hedn't hung on ter my gun like he done, I'd have been a murderer like he said, an' Rick would hev been dead. An' the bay filly ain't sech a killin' matter nohow; ef it war the roan three-year-old now, 'twould be different."

OVER ON THE T'OTHER MOUNTING.

Stretching out laterally from a long oblique line of the Southern Alleghanies are two parallel ranges, following the same course through several leagues, and separated by a narrow strip of valley hardly half a mile in width. As they fare along arm in arm, so to speak, sundry differences between the close companions are distinctly apparent. One is much the higher, and leads the way; it strikes out all the bold curves and angles of the course, meekly attended by the lesser ridge; its shadowy coves and sharp ravines are repeated in miniature as its comrade falls into the line of march; it seems to have its companion in charge, and to conduct it away from the majestic procession of mountains that traverses the State.

But, despite its more imposing appearance, all the tangible advantages are possessed by its humble neighbor. When Old Rocky-Top, as the lower range is called, is fresh and green with the tender verdure of spring, the snow still lies on the summit of the T'other Mounting, and drifts deep into treacherous rifts and chasms, and muffles the voice of the singing pines; and all the crags are hung with gigantic glittering icicles, and the woods are gloomy and bleak. When the sun shines bright on Old Rocky-Top, clouds often hover about the loftier mountain, and storms brew in that higher atmosphere; the all-pervading winter winds surge wildly among the groaning forests, and wrench the limbs from the trees, and dash huge fragments of cliffs down deep gorges, and spend their fury before they reach the sheltered lower spur. When the kindly shades of evening slip softly down on drowsy Rocky-Top, and the work is laid by in the rough little houses, and the simple home-folks draw around the hearth, day still lingers in a weird, paralytic life among the tree-tops of the T'other Mounting; and the only remnant of the world visible is that stark black line of its summit, stiff and hard against the faint green and saffron tints of the sky. Before the birds are well awake on Old Rocky-Top, and while the shadows are still thick, the T'other Mounting has been called up to a new day. Lonely dawns these: the pale gleam strikes along the October woods, bringing first into uncertain twilight the dead yellow and red of the foliage, presently heightened into royal gold and crimson by the first ray of sunshine; it rouses the timid wild-fowl; it drives home the plundering fox; it meets, perhaps, some lumbering bear or skulking mountain wolf; it flecks with light and shade the deer, all gray and antlered; it falls upon no human habitation, for the few settlers of the region have a persistent predilection for Old Rocky-Top. Somehow, the T'other Mounting is vaguely in ill repute among its neighbors,—it has a bad name.

"It's the onluckiest place ennywhar nigh about," said Nathan White, as he sat one afternoon upon the porch of his log-cabin, on the summit of Old Rocky-Top, and gazed up at the heights of the T'other Mounting across the narrow valley. "I hev hearn tell all my days ez how, ef ye go up thar on the T'other Mounting, suthin' will happen ter ye afore ye kin git away. An' I knows myself ez how—'twar ten year ago an' better—I went up thar, one Jan'ry day, a-lookin' fur my cow, ez hed strayed off through not hevin' enny calf ter our house; an' I fund the cow, but jes' tuk an' slipped on a icy rock, an' bruk my ankle-bone. 'Twar sech a job a-gittin' off'n that thar T'other Mounting an' back over hyar, it hev l'arned me ter stay away from thar."

"Thar war a man," piped out a shrill, quavering voice from within the door,—the voice of Nathan White's father, the oldest inhabitant of Rocky-Top,—"thar war a man hyar,

168

nigh on ter fifty year ago,—he war mightily gin ter thievin' horses; an' one time, while he war a-runnin' away with Pete Dilks's dapple-gray mare,—they called her Luce, five year old she war,—Pete, he war a-ridin' a-hint him on his old sorrel mare,—*her* name 'twar Jane, an'—the Jeemes boys, they war a-ridin' arter the horse-thief too. Thar, now! I clar forgits what horses them Jeemes boys war a-ridin' of." He paused for an instant in anxious reflection. "Waal, sir! it do beat all that I can't remember them Jeemes boys' horses! Anyways, they got ter that thar tricky ford through Wild-Duck River, thar on the side o' the T'other Mounting, an' the horse-thief war ahead, an' he hed ter take it fust. An' that thar river,—it rises yander in them pines, nigh about," pointing with a shaking fore-finger,—"an' that thar river jes' spun him out 'n the saddle like a top, an' he warn't seen no more till he hed floated nigh ter Colbury, ez dead ez a door-nail, nor Pete's dapple-gray mare nuther; she bruk her knees agin them high stone banks. But he war a good swimmer, an' he war drowned. He war witched with the place, ez sure ez ye air born."

A long silence ensued. Then Nathan White raised his pondering eyes with a look of slow curiosity. "What did Tony Britt say he war a-doin' of, when ye kem on him suddint in the woods on the T'other Mounting?" he asked, addressing his son, a stalwart youth, who was sitting upon the step, his hat on the back of his head, and his hands in the pockets of his jeans trousers.

"He said he war a-huntin', but he hedn't hed no sort'n luck. It 'pears ter me ez all the game thar is witched somehow, an' ye can't git no good shot at nuthin'. Tony tole me to-day that he got up three deer, an' hed toler'ble aim; an' he missed two, an' the t'other jes' trotted off with a rifle-ball in his flank, ez onconsarned ez ef he hed hit him with an acorn."

169

"I hev always hearn ez everything that belongs on that thar T'other Mounting air witched, an' ef ye brings away so much ez a leaf, or a stone, or a stick, ye fotches a curse with it," chimed in the old man, "'kase thar hev been sech a many folks killed on the T'other Mounting."

"I tole Tony Britt that thar word," said the young fellow, "an' 'lowed ter him ez how he hed tuk a mighty bad spot ter go a-huntin'."

"What did he say?" demanded Nathan White.

"He say he never knowed ez thar war murders commit on T'other Mounting, an' ef that war he 'spects 'twar nuthin' but Injuns, long time ago. But he 'lowed the place war powerful onlucky, an' he believed the mounting war witched."

"Ef Tony Britt's arter enny harm," said the octogenarian, "he'll never come off 'n that thar T'other Mounting. It's a mighty place fur bad folks ter make thar eend. Thar's that thar horse thief I war a-tellin' 'bout, an' that dapple-gray mare,—her name 'twar Luce. An' folks ez is a-runnin' from the sheriff jes' takes ter the T'other Mounting ez nateral ez ef it war home; an' ef they don't git cotched, they is never hearn on no more." He paused impressively. "The rocks falls on 'em, an' kills 'em; an' I'll tell ye jes' how I knows," he resumed, oracularly. "'Twar sixty year ago, nigh about, an' me an' them Jeemes boys war a-burnin' of lime tergether over on the T'other Mounting. We hed a lime-kiln over thar, jes' under Piney Notch, an' never hed no luck, but jes' stuck ter it like fools, till Hiram Jeemes got one of his eyes put out. So we quit burnin' of lime on the T'other Mounting, 'count of the place bein' witched, an' kem over hyar ter Old Rocky-Top, an' got along toler'ble well, cornsiderin'. But one day, whilst we war a-workin on the T'other Mounting, what d' ye think I fund in the rock? The print of a bare foot in the solid stone, ez plain an' ez nateral ez ef the track hed been lef' in the clay yestiddy. Waal, I knowed it war the track o' Jeremiah

Stubbs, what shot his step-brother, an' gin the sheriff the slip, an' war las' seen on the T'other Mounting, 'kase his old shoe jes' fit the track, fur we tried it. An' a good while arterward I fund on that same T'other Mounting—in the solid stone, mind ye—a fish, what he had done br'iled fur supper, jes' turned ter a stone."

"So thar's the Bible made true," said an elderly woman, who had come to the door to hear this reminiscence, and stood mechanically stirring a hoe-cake batter in a shallow wooden bowl. "Ax fur a fish, an' ye 'll git a stone."

The secret history of the hills among which they lived was indeed as a sealed book to these simple mountaineers.

"The las' time I war ter Colbury," said Nathan White, "I hearn the sheriff a-talkin' 'bout how them evil-doers an' sech runs fur the T'other Mounting fust thing; though he 'lowed ez it war powerful foxy in 'em ter try ter hide thar, kase he said, ef they wunst reaches it, he mought ez well look fur a needle in a hay-stack. He 'lowed ef he hed a posse a thousand men strong he couldn't git 'em out."

"He can't find 'em, 'kase the rocks falls on 'em, or swallers 'em in," said the old man. "Ef Tony Britt is up ter mischief he'll never come back no more. He'll git into worser trouble than ever he see afore."

"He hev done seen a powerful lot of trouble, fust one way an' another, 'thout foolin' round the T'other Mounting," said Nathan White. "They tells me ez he got hisself indicted, I believes they calls it, or suthin', down yander ter the court at Colbury,—that war year afore las',—an' he hed ter pay twenty dollars fine; 'kase when he war overseer of the road he jes' war constant in lettin' his friends, an' folks ginerally, off 'thout hevin' 'em fined, when they didn't come an' work on the road,—though that air the way ez the overseers hev always done, without nobody a-tellin' on 'em an' sech. But

171

them ez warn't Tony Britt's friends seen a mighty differ. He war dead sure ter fine Caleb Hoxie seventy-five cents, 'cordin' ter the law, fur every day that he war summonsed ter work an' never come; 'kase Tony an' Caleb hed some sort 'n grudge agin one another 'count of a spavined horse what Caleb sold ter Tony, makin' him out to be a sound critter,— though Caleb swears he never knowed the horse war spavined when he sold him ter Tony, no more 'n nuthin'. Caleb war mightily worked up 'bout this hyar finin' business, an' him an' Tony hed a tussle 'bout it every time they kem tergether. But Caleb war always sure ter git the worst of it, 'kase Tony, though he air toler'ble spindling sort o' build, he air somehow or other sorter stringy an' tough, an' makes a right smart show in a reg'lar knock-down an' drag-out fight. So Caleb he war beat every time, an' fined too. An' he tried wunst ter shoot Tony Britt, but he missed his aim. An' when he war a-layin' off how ter fix Tony, fur treatin' him that way, he war a-stoppin', one day, at Jacob Green's blacksmith's shop, yander, a mile down the valley, an' he war a-talkin' 'bout it ter a passel o' folks thar. An' Lawyer Rood from Colbury war thar, an' Jacob war a-shoein' of his mare; an' he heard the tale, an' axed Caleb whyn't he report Tony ter the court, an' git him fined fur neglect of his duty, bein' overseer of the road. An' Caleb never knowed before that it war the law that everybody what war summonsed an' didn't come must be fined, or the overseer must be fined hisself; but he knowed that Tony hed been a-lettin' of his friends off, an' folks ginerally, an' he jes' 'greed fur Lawyer Rood ter stir up trouble fur Tony. An' he done it. An' the court fined Tony twenty dollars fur them ways o' his'n. An' it kept him so busy a-scufflin' ter raise the twenty dollars that he never hed a chance ter give Caleb Hoxie more'n one or two beatin's the whole time he war a-scrapin' up the money."

This story was by no means unknown to the little circle, nor did its narrator labor under the delusion that he was telling a new thing. It was merely a verbal act of recollection, and an attentive silence reigned as he related the familiar facts. To people who live in lonely regions this habit of retrospection (especially noticeable in them) and an enduring interest in the past may be something of a compensation for the scanty happenings of the present. When the recital was concluded, the hush for a time was unbroken, save by the rush of the winds, bringing upon their breath the fragrant woodland odors of balsams and pungent herbs, and a fresh and exhilarating suggestion of sweeping over a volume of falling water. They stirred the fringed shadow of a great pine that stood, like a sentinel, before Nathan White's door and threw its colorless simulacrum, a boastful lie twice its size, far down the sunset road. Now and then the faint clangor of a cow-bell came from out the tangled woods about the little hut, and the low of homeward-bound cattle sounded upon the air, mellowed and softened by the distance. The haze that rested above the long, narrow valley was hardly visible, save in the illusive beauty with which it invested the scene,—the tender azure of the far-away ranges; the exquisite tones of the gray and purple shadows that hovered about the darkening coves and along the deep lines marking the gorges; the burnished brilliance of the sunlight, which, despite its splendor, seemed lonely enough, lying motionless upon the lonely landscape and on the still figures clustered about the porch. Their eyes were turned toward the opposite steeps, gorgeous with scarlet oak and sumac, all in autumnal array, and their thoughts were busy with the hunter on the T'other Mounting and vague speculations concerning his evil intent.

"It 'pears ter me powerful strange ez Tony goes a-foolin' round that thar T'other Mounting, cornsiderin' what happened yander in its shadow," said the woman, coming again to the door, and leaning idly against the frame; the bread was baking over the coals. "That thar wife o' his'n, afore she died, war always frettin' 'kase way down thar on the backbone, whar her house war, the shadow o' the T'other Mounting laid on it fur an hour an' better every day of the worl'. She 'lowed ez it always put her in mind o' the shadow o' death. An' I thought 'bout that thar sayin' o' hern the day when I see her a-lyin' stiff an' cold on the bed, an' the shadow of the T'other Mounting drapping in at the open door, an' a-creepin' an' a-creepin' over her face. An' I war plumb glad when they got that woman under ground, whar, ef the sunshine can't git ter her, neither kin the shadow. Ef ever thar war a murdered woman, she war one. Arter all that hed come an' gone with Caleb Hoxie, fur Tony Britt ter go arter him, 'kase he war a yerb-doctor, ter git him ter physic his wife, who war nigh about dead with the lung fever, an' gin up by old Dr. Marsh!—it looks ter me like he war plumb crazy,—though him an' Caleb hed sorter made friends 'bout the spavined horse an' sech afore then. Jes' ez soon ez she drunk the stuff that Caleb fixed fur her she laid her head back an' shet her eyes, an' never opened 'em no more in this worl'. She war a murdered woman, an' Caleb Hoxie done it through the yerbs he fixed fur her."

A subtile amethystine mist had gradually overlaid the slopes of the T'other Mounting, mellowing the brilliant tints of the variegated foliage to a delicious hazy sheen of mosaics; but about the base the air seemed dun-colored, though transparent; seen through it, even the red of the crowded trees was but a sombre sort of magnificence, and the great masses of gray rocks, jutting out among them here and there, wore a darkly frowning aspect. Along the summit there was a blaze of scarlet and gold in the full glory of the sunshine; the topmost cliffs caught its rays, and gave them back in unexpected gleams of green or grayish-yellow, as of mosses, or vines, or huckleberry bushes, nourished in the heart of the deep fissures.

174

"Waal," said Nathan White, "I never did believe ez Caleb gin her ennythink ter hurt,—though I knows thar is them ez does. Caleb is the bes' yerb-doctor I ever see. The rheumatiz would nigh on ter hev killed me, ef it warn't fur him, that spell I hed las' winter. An' Dr. Marsh, what they hed up afore the gran' jury, swore that the yerbs what Caleb gin her war nuthin' ter hurt; *he* said, though, they couldn't holp nor hender. An' but fur Dr. Marsh they would hev jailed Caleb ter stand his trial, like Tony wanted 'em ter do. But Dr. Marsh said she died with the consumption, jes' the same, an' Caleb's yerbs war wholesome, though they warn't no 'count at all."

"I knows I ain't a-goin' never ter tech nuthin' he fixes fur me no more," said his wife, "an' I'll be bound nobody else in these hyar mountings will, nuther."

"Waal," drawled her son, "I knows fur true ez he air tendin' now on old Gideon Croft, what lives over yander in the valley on the t'other side of the T'other Mounting, an' is down with the fever. He went over thar yestiddy evening, late; I met him when he war goin', an' he tole me."

"He hed better look out how he comes across Tony Britt," said Nathan White; "fur I hearn, the las' time I war ter the Settlemint, how Tony hev swore ter kill him the nex' time he see him, fur a-givin' of pizenous yerbs ter his wife. Tony air mightily outdone 'kase the gran' jury let him off. Caleb hed better be sorter keerful how he goes a-foolin' round these hyar dark woods."

The sun had sunk, and the night, long held in abeyance, was coming fast. The glooms gathered in the valley; a soft gray shadow hung over the landscape, making familiar things strange. The T'other Mounting was all a dusky, sad purple under the faintly pulsating stars, save that high along the horizontal line of its summit gleamed the strange red radiance of the dead and gone sunset. The outline of the foliage was clearly drawn against the pure lapis lazuli tint of the sky behind it; here and there the uncanny light streamed through the bare limbs of an early leafless tree, which looked in the distance like some bony hand beckoning, or warning, or raised in horror.

"*Anythink* mought happen thar!" said the woman, as she stood on night-wrapped Rocky-Top and gazed up at the alien light, so red in the midst of the dark landscape. When she turned back to the door of the little hut, the meagre comforts within seemed almost luxury, in their cordial contrast to the desolate, dreary mountain yonder and the thought of the forlorn, wandering hunter. A genial glow from the hearth diffused itself over the puncheon floor; the savory odor of broiling venison filled the room as a tall, slim girl knelt before the fire and placed the meat upon the gridiron, her pale cheeks flushing with the heat; there was a happy suggestion of peace and unity when the four generations trooped in to their supper, grandfather on his grandson's arm, and a sedate two-year-old bringing up the rear. Nathan White's wife paused behind the others to bar the door, and once more, as she looked up at the T'other Mounting, the thought of the lonely wanderer smote her heart. The red sunset light had died out at last, but a golden aureola heralded the moon-rise, and a gleaming thread edged the masses of foliage; there was no faint suggestion now of mist in the valley, and myriads of stars filled a cloudless sky. "He hev done gone home by this time," she said to her daughter-in-law, as she closed the door, "an' ef he ain't, he'll hev a moon ter light him."

"Air ye a-studyin' 'bout Tony Britt yit?" asked Nathan White. "He hev done gone home a good hour by sun, I'll be bound. Jes' ketch Tony Britt a-huntin' till sundown, will ye! He air a mighty pore hand ter work. 'Stonishes me ter hear he air even a-huntin' on the T'other Mounting."

176

"I don't believe he's up ter enny harm," said the woman; "he hev jes' tuk ter the woods with grief."

"'Pears ter me," said the daughter-in-law, rising from her kneeling posture before the fire, and glancing reproachfully at her husband,—"'pears ter me ez ye mought hev brought him hyar ter eat his supper along of we-uns, stiddier a-leavin' him a-grievin' over his dead wife in them witched woods on the T'other Mounting."

The young fellow looked a trifle abashed at this suggestion. "I never wunst thought of it," he said. "Tony never stopped ter talk more'n a minit, nohow."

The evening wore away; the octogenarian and the sedate two-year-old fell asleep in their chairs shortly after supper; Nathan White and his son smoked their cob-pipes, and talked fitfully of the few incidents of the day; the women sat in the firelight with their knitting, silent and absorbed, except that now and then the elder, breaking from her reverie, declared, "I can't git Tony Britt out'n my head nohow in the worl'."

The moon had come grandly up over the T'other Mounting, casting long silver lights and deep black shadows through all the tangled recesses and yawning chasms of the woods and rocks. In the vast wilderness the bright rays met only one human creature, the belated hunter making his way homeward through the dense forest with an experienced woodman's craft. For no evil intent had brought Tony Britt to the T'other Mounting; he had spent the day in hunting, urged by that strong necessity without which the mountaineer seldom makes any exertion. Dr. Marsh's unavailing skill had cost him dear; his only cow was sold to make up the twenty dollars fine which his revenge on Caleb Hoxie had entailed upon him; without even so much as a spavined horse tillage was impossible, and the bounteous harvest left him empty-handed, for he had no crops to gather. The hardships of extreme poverty had reinforced the sorrows that came upon him in battalions, and had driven him far through long aisles of the woods, where the night fell upon him unaware. The foliage was all embossed with exquisite silver designs that seemed to stand out some little distance from the dark masses of leaves; now and then there came to his eyes that emerald gleam never seen upon verdure in the daytime,—only shown by some artificial light, or the moon's sweet uncertainty. The wind was strong and fresh, but not cold; here and there was a glimmer of dew. Once, and once only, he thought of the wild traditions which peopled the T'other Mounting with evil spirits. He paused with a sudden chill; he glanced nervously over his shoulder down the illimitable avenues of the lonely woods. The grape-vines, hanging in festoons from tree to tree, were slowly swinging back and forth, stirred by the wind. There was a dizzy dance of shadows whirling on every open space where the light lay on the ground. The roar and fret of Wild-Duck River, hidden there somewhere in the pines, came on the breeze like a strange, weird, fitful voice, crying out amid the haunted solitudes of the T'other Mounting. He turned abruptly, with his gun on his shoulder, and pursued his way through the trackless desert in the direction of his home. He had been absorbed in his quest and his gloomy thoughts, and did not realize the distance he had traversed until it lay before him to be retraced; but his superstitious terror urged him to renewed exertions. "Ef ever I gits off'n this hyar witched mounting," he said to himself, as he tore away the vines and brambles that beset his course, "I'll never come back agin while I lives." He grew calmer when he paused on a huge projecting crag, and looked across the narrow valley at the great black mass opposite, which he knew was Old Rocky-Top; its very presence gave him a sense of companionship and blunted his fear, and he sat down to rest for a few minutes, gazing at the outline of the range he knew so well, so unfamiliar from a new stand-point. How low it seemed from the heights of the T'other Mounting! Could that faint gleam be the light in Nathan White's house? Tony Britt glanced further down the indistinct slope, where he knew his own desolate, deserted hut was crouched. "Jes' whar the shadow o' the T'other Mounting can reach it," he thought, with a new infusion of bitterness. He averted his eyes; he would look no longer; he threw himself at full length among the ragged clumps of grass and fragments of rock, and turned his face to the stars. It all came back to him then. Sometimes, in his sordid cares and struggles for his scanty existence, his past troubles were dwarfed by the present. But here on the lonely cliff, with the infinite spaces above him and the boundless forest below, he felt anew his isolation. No light on earth save the far gleam from another man's home, and in heaven only the drowning face of the moon, drifting slowly through the blue floods of the skies. He was only twenty-five; he had youth and health and strength, but he felt that he had lived his life; it seemed long, marked as it was by cares and privation and persistent failure. Little as he knew of life, he knew how hard his had been, even meted by those of the poverty-stricken wretches among whom, his lot was cast. "An' sech luck!" he said, as his sad eyes followed the drifting dead face of the moon. "Along o' that thar step-mother o' mine till I war growed; an' then when I war married, an' we hed got the house put up, an' war beginnin' ter git along like other folks kin, an' Caroline's mother gin her that thar calf what growed ter a cow, an' through pinchin' an' savin' we made out ter buy that thar horse from Caleb Hoxie, jes' ez we war a-startin' ter work a crap he lays down an' dies; an' that cussed twenty dollars ez I hed ter pay ter the court; an' Car'line jes' a-gittin' sick, an' a-wastin' an' a-wastin' away, till I, like a fool, brung Caleb thar, an' he pizens her with his yerbs—God A'mighty! ef I could jes' lay my hands wunst on that scoundrel I wouldn't leave a mite of him, ef he war pertected by a hundred lyin', thievin' gran' juries! But he can't stay a-hidin' forevermo'. He's got ter 'count ter me, ef he ain't ter the law; an' he'll see a mighty differ a-twixt us. I swear he'll never draw another breath!"

He rose with a set, stern face, and struck a huge bowlder beside him with his hard clenched hand as he spoke. He had not even an ignorant idea of an impressive dramatic pose; but if the great gaunt cliff had been the stage of a theatre his attitude and manner at that instant would have won him applause. He was all alone with his poverty and his anguished memories, as men with such burdens are apt to be.

The bowlder on which, in his rude fashion, he had registered his oath was harder than his hard hand, and the vehemence of the blow brought blood; but he had scarcely time to think of it. His absorbed reverie was broken by a rustling other than that of the eddying wind. He raised his head and looked about him, half expecting to see the antlers of a deer. Then there came to his ears the echo of the tread of man. His eyes mechanically followed the sound. Forty feet down the face of the crag a broad ledge jutted out, and upon it ran a narrow path, made by stray cattle, or the feet of their searching owners; it was visible from the summit for a distance of a hundred yards or so, and the white glamour of the moonbeams fell full upon it. Before a speculation had suggested itself, a man walked slowly into view along the path, and with starting eyes the hunter recognized his dearest foe. Britt's hand lay upon the bowlder; his oath was in his mind; his unconscious enemy had come within his power. Swifter than a flash the temptation was presented. He remembered the warnings of his lawyer at Colbury last week, when the grand jury had failed to find a true bill against Caleb Hoxie,—that he was an innocent man, and must go unscathed, that any revenge for fancied wrongs would be

180

dearly rued; he remembered, too, the mountain traditions of the falling rocks burying evil-doers in the heart of the hills. Here was his opportunity. He would have a life for a life, and there would be one more legend of the very stones conspiring to punish malefactors escaped from men added to the terrible "sayin's" of the T'other Mounting. A strong belief in the supernatural influences of the place was rife within him; he knew nothing of Gideon Croft's fever and the errand that had brought the herb-doctor through the "witched mounting;" had he not been transported thither by some invisible agency, that the rocks might fall upon him and crush him?

The temptation and the resolve were simultaneous. With his hand upon the bowlder, his hot heart beating fast, his distended eyes burning upon the approaching figure, he waited for the moment to come. There lay the long, low, black mountain opposite, with only the moon beams upon it, for the lights in Nathan White's house were extinguished; there was the deep, dark gulf of the valley; there, forty feet below him, was the narrow, moon-flooded path on the ledge, and the man advancing carelessly. The bowlder fell with a frightful crash, the echoes rang with a scream of terror, and the two men—one fleeing from the dreadful danger he had barely escaped, the other from the hideous deed he thought he had done—ran wildly in opposite directions through the tangled autumnal woods.

Was every leaf of the forest endowed with a woful voice, that the echo of that shriek might never die from Tony Britt's ears? Did the storied, retributive rocks still vibrate with this new victim's frenzied cry? And what was this horror in his heart! Now,—so late,—was coming a terrible conviction of his enemy's innocence, and with it a fathomless remorse.

All through the interminable night he fled frantically along the mountain's summit, scarcely knowing whither, and caring for nothing except to multiply the miles between him and the frightful object that he believed lay under the bowlder which he had dashed down the precipice. The moon sank beneath the horizon; the fantastic shadows were merged in the darkest hour of the night; the winds died, and there was no voice in all the woods, save the wail o' Wild-Duck River and the forever-resounding screams in the flying wretch's ears. Sometimes he answered them in a wild, hoarse, inarticulate cry; sometimes he flung his hands above his head and wrung them in his agony; never once did he pause in his flight. Panting, breathless, exhausted, he eagerly sped through the darkness; tearing his face upon the brambles; plunging now and then into gullies and unseen quagmires; sometimes falling heavily, but recovering himself in an instant, and once more struggling on; striving to elude the pursuing voices, and to distance forever his conscience and his memory.

And then came that terrible early daylight that was wont to dawn upon the T'other Mounting when all the world besides was lost in slumber; the wan, melancholy light showed dimly the solemn trees and dense undergrowth; the precarious pitfalls about his path; the long deep gorges; the great crags and chasms; the cascades, steely gray, and white; the huge mass, all hung about with shadows, which he knew was Old Rocky-Top, rising from the impenetrably dark valley below. It seemed wonderful to him, somehow, that a new day should break at all. If, in a revulsion of nature, that utter blackness had continued forever and ever it would not have been strange, after what had happened. He could have borne it better than the sight of the familiar world gradually growing into day, all unconscious of his secret. He had begun the descent of the T'other Mounting, and he seemed to carry that pale dawn with him; day was breaking when he reached the foot of Old Rocky-Top, and as he climbed up to his own deserted, empty little shanty, it too stood plainly defined in the morning light. He dragged himself to the door, and impelled by some morbid fascination he glanced over his shoulder at the T'other Mounting. There it was, unchanged, with the golden largess of a gracious season blazing upon every autumnal leaf. He shuddered, and went into the fireless, comfortless house. And then he made an appalling discovery. As he mechanically divested himself of his shot-pouch and powder-horn he was stricken by a sudden consciousness that he did not have his gun! One doubtful moment, and he remembered that he had laid it upon the crag when he had thrown himself down to rest. Beyond question, it was there yet. His conscience was still now,—his remorse had fled. It was only a matter of time when his crime would be known. He recollected his meeting with young White while he was hunting, and then Britt cursed the gun which he had left on the cliff. The discovery of the weapon there would be strong evidence against him, taken in connection with all the other circumstances. True, he could even yet go back and recover it, but he was mastered by the fear of meeting some one on the unfrequented road, or even in the loneliness of the T'other Mounting, and strengthening the chain of evidence against him by the fact of being once more seen in the fateful neighborhood. He resolved that he would wait until night-fall, and then he would retrace his way, secure his gun, and all might yet be well with him. As to the bowlder,—were men never before buried under the falling rocks of the T'other Mounting?

Without food, without rest, without sleep, his limbs rigid with the strong tension of his nerves, his eyes bloodshot, haggard, and eager, his brain on fire, he sat through the long morning hours absently gazing across the narrow valley at the solemn, majestic mountain opposite, and that sinister

183

jutting crag with the indistinctly defined ledges of its rugged surface.

After a time, the scene began to grow dim; the sun was still shining, but through a haze becoming momently more dense. The brilliantly tinted foliage upon the T'other Mounting was fading; the cliffs showed strangely distorted faces through the semi-transparent blue vapor, and presently they seemed to recede altogether; the valley disappeared, and all the country was filled with the smoke of distant burning woods. He was gasping when he first became sensible of the smoke-laden haze, for he had seen nothing of the changing aspect of the landscape. Before his vision was the changeless picture of a night of mingled moonlight and shadow, the ill-defined black mass where Old Rocky-Top rose into the air, the impenetrable gloom of the valley, the ledge of the crag, and the unconscious figure slowly coming within the power of his murderous hand. His eyes would look on no other scene, no other face, so long as he should live.

He had a momentary sensation of stifling, and then a great weight was lifted. For he had begun to doubt whether the unlucky locality would account satisfactorily for the fall of that bowlder and the horrible object beneath it; a more reasonable conclusion might be deduced from the fact that he had been seen in the neighborhood, and the circumstance of the deadly feud. But what wonder would there be if the dry leaves on the T'other Mounting should be ignited and the woods burned! What explanations might not such a catastrophe suggest!—a frantic flight from the flames toward the cliff and an accidental fall. And so he waited throughout the long day, that was hardly day at all, but an opaque twilight, through which could be discerned only the stony path leading down the slope from his door, only the blurred outlines of the bushes close at hand, only the great gaunt limbs of a lightning-scathed tree, seeming entirely

184

severed from the unseen trunk, and swinging in the air sixty feet above the earth.

Toward night-fall the wind rose and the smoke-curtain lifted, once more revealing to the settlers upon Old Rocky-Top the sombre T'other Mounting, with the belated evening light still lurid upon the trees,—only a strange, faint resemblance of the sunset radiance, rather the ghost of a dead day. And presently this apparition was gone, and the deep purple line of the witched mountain's summit grew darker against the opaline skies, till it was merged in a dusky black, and the shades of the night fell thick on the landscape.

The scenic effects of the drama, that serve to widen the mental vision and cultivate the imagination of even the poor in cities, were denied these primitive, simple people; but that magnificent pageant of the four seasons, wherein was forever presented the imposing splendor of the T'other Mounting in an ever-changing grandeur of aspect, was a gracious recompense for the spectacular privileges of civilization. And this evening the humble family party on Nathan White's porch beheld a scene of unique impressiveness.

The moon had not yet risen; the winds were awhirl; the darkness draped the earth as with a pall. Out from the impenetrable gloom of the woods on the T'other Mounting there started, suddenly, a scarlet globe of fire; one long moment it was motionless, but near it the spectral outline of a hand appeared beckoning, or warning, or raised in horror,—only a leafless tree, catching in the distance a semblance of humanity. Then from the still ball of fire there streamed upward a long, slender plume of golden light, waving back and forth against the pale horizon. Across the dark slope of the mountain below, flashes of lightning were shooting in zigzag lines, and wherever they gleamed were seen those frantic skeleton hands raised and wrung in

185

anguish. It was cruel sport for the cruel winds; they maddened over gorge and cliff and along the wooded steeps, carrying far upon their wings the sparks of desolation. From the summit, myriads of jets of flame reached up to the placid stars; about the base of the mountain lurked a lake of liquid fire, with wreaths of blue smoke hovering over it; ever and anon, athwart the slope darted the sudden lightning, widening into sheets of flame as it conquered new ground.

The astonishment on the faces grouped about Nathan White's door was succeeded by a startled anxiety. After the first incoherent exclamations of surprise came the pertinent inquiry from his wife, "Ef Old Rocky-Top war ter ketch too, whar would we-uns run ter?"

Nathan White's countenance had in its expression more of astounded excitement than of bodily fear. "Why, bless my soul!" he said at length, "the woods away over yander, what hev been burnin' all day, ain't nigh enough ter the T'other Mounting ter ketch it,—nuthin' like it."

"The T'other Mounting would burn, though, ef fire war put ter it," said his son. The two men exchanged a glance of deep significance.

"Do ye mean ter say," exclaimed Mrs. White, her fire-lit face agitated by a sudden superstitious terror, "that that thar T'other Mounting is fired by witches an' sech?"

"Don't talk so loud, Matildy," said her husband. "Them knows best ez done it."

"Thar's one thing sure," quavered the old man: "that thar fire will never tech a leaf on Old Rocky-Top. Thar's a church on this hyar mounting,—bless the Lord fur it!—an' we lives in the fear o' God."

There was a pause, all watching with distended eyes the progress of the flames.

"It looks like it mought hev been kindled in torment," said the young daughter-in-law.

"It looks down thar," said her husband, pointing to the lake of fire, "like the pit itself."

The apathetic inhabitants of Old Rocky-Top were stirred into an activity very incongruous with their habits and the hour. During the conflagration they traversed long distances to reach each other's houses and confer concerning the danger and the questions of supernatural agency provoked by the mysterious firing of the woods. Nathan White had few neighbors, but above the crackling of the timber and the roar of the flames there rose the quick beat of running footsteps; the undergrowth of the forest near at hand was in strange commotion; and at last, the figure of a man burst forth, the light of the fire showing the startling pallor of his face as he staggered to the little porch and sank, exhausted, into a chair.

"Waal, Caleb Hoxie!" exclaimed Nathan White, in good-natured raillery; "ye're skeered, fur true! What ails ye, ter think Old Rocky-Top air a-goin' ter ketch too? 'Tain't nigh dry enough, I'm a-thinkin'."

"Fire kindled that thar way can't tech a leaf on Old Rocky-Top," sleepily piped out the old man, nodding in his chair, the glare of the flames which rioted over the T'other Mounting gilding his long white hair and peaceful, slumberous face. "Thar's a church on Old Rocky-Top,— bless the"—The sentence drifted away with his dreams.

"Does ye believe—them—them"—Caleb Hoxie's trembling white lips could not frame the word—"them—done it?"

"Like ez not," said Nathan White. "But that ain't a-troublin' of ye an' me. I ain't never hearn o' them witches a-tormentin' of honest folks what ain't done nuthin' hurtful ter nobody," he added, in cordial reassurance.

His son was half hidden behind one of the rough cedar posts, that his mirth at the guest's display of cowardice might not be observed. But the women, always quick to suspect, glanced meaningly at each other with widening eyes, as they stood together in the door-way.

"I dunno,—I dunno," Caleb Hoxie declared huskily. "I ain't never done nuthin' ter nobody, an' what do ye s'pose them witches an' sech done ter me las' night, on that T'other Mounting? I war a-goin' over yander to Gideon Croft's fur ter physic him, ez he air mortal low with the fever; an' ez I war a-comin' alongside o' that thar high bluff"—it was very distinct, with the flames wreathing fantastically about its gray, rigid features—"they throwed a bowlder ez big ez this hyar porch down on ter me. It jes' grazed me, an' knocked me down, an' kivered me with dirt. An' I run home a-hollerin'; an' it seemed ter me ter-day ez I war a-goin' ter screech an' screech all my life, like some onsettled crazy critter. It 'peared like 'twould take a bar'l o' hop tea ter git me quiet. An' now look yander!" and he pointed tremulously to the blazing mountain.

There was an expression of conviction on the women's faces. All their lives afterward it was there whenever Caleb Hoxie's name was mentioned; no more to be moved or changed than the stern, set faces of the crags among the fiery woods.

"Thar's a church on this hyar mounting," said the old man feebly, waking for a moment, and falling asleep the next.

Nathan White was perplexed and doubtful, and a superstitious awe had checked the laughing youngster behind the cedar post.

A great cloud of flame came rolling through the sky toward them, golden, pellucid, spangled through and through with fiery red stars; poising itself for one moment high above the valley, then breaking into myriads of sparks, and showering down upon the dark abysses below.

"Look-a-hyar!" said the elder woman in a frightened undertone to her daughter-in-law; "this hyar wicked critter air too onlucky ter be a-sittin' 'longside of us; we'll all be burnt up afore he gits hisself away from hyar. An' who is that a-comin' yander?" For from the encompassing woods another dark figure had emerged, and was slowly approaching the porch. The wary eyes near Caleb Hoxie saw that he fell to trembling, and that he clutched at a post for support. But the hand pointing at him was shaken as with a palsy, and the voice hardly seemed Tony Britt's as it cried out, in an agony of terror, "What air ye a-doin' hyar, a-sittin' 'longside o' livin' folks? Yer bones air under a bowlder on the T'other Mounting, an' ye air a dead man!"

They said ever afterward that Tony Britt had lost his mind "through goin' a-huntin' jes' one time on the T'other Mounting. His spirit air all broke, an' he's a mighty tame critter nowadays." Through his persistent endeavor he and Caleb Hoxie became quite friendly, and he was even reported to "'low that he war sati'fied that Caleb never gin his wife nuthin' ter hurt." "Though," said the gossips of Old Rocky-Top, "them women up ter White's will hev it no other way but that Caleb pizened her, an' they wouldn't take no yerbs from him no more 'n he war a rattlesnake. But Caleb always 'pears sorter skittish when he an' Tony air tergether, like he didn't know when Tony war a-goin' ter fotch him a lick. But law! Tony air that changed that ye can't make him mad 'thout ye mind him o' the time he called Caleb a ghost."

A dark, gloomy, deserted place was the charred T'other Mounting through all the long winter. And when spring came, and Old Rocky-Top was green with delicate fresh verdure, and melodious with singing birds and chorusing breezes, and bedecked as for some great festival with violets and azaleas and laurel-blooms, the T'other Mounting was stark and wintry and black with its desolate, leafless trees. But after a while the spring came for it, too: the buds swelled and burst; flowering vines festooned the grim gray crags; and the dainty freshness of the vernal season reigned upon its summit, while all the world below was growing into heat and dust. The circuit-rider said it reminded him of a tardy change in a sinner's heart: though it come at the eleventh hour, the glorious summer is before it, and a full fruition; though it work but an hour in the Lord's vineyard, it receives the same reward as those who labored through all the day.

"An' it always did 'pear ter me ez thar war mighty little jestice in that," was Mrs. White's comment.

But at the meeting when that sermon was preached Tony Britt told his "experience." It seemed a confession, for according to the gossips he "'lowed that he hed flung that bowlder down on Caleb Hoxie,—what the witches flung, ye know,—'kase he believed then that Caleb hed killed his wife with pizenous yerbs; an' he went back the nex' night an' fired the woods, ter make folks think when they fund Caleb's bones that he war a-runnin' from the blaze an' fell off'n the bluff." And everybody on Old Rocky-Top said incredulously, "Pore Tony Britt! He hev los' his mind through goin' a-huntin' jes' one time on the T'other Mounting."

THE "HARNT" THAT WALKS CHILHOWEE.

June had crossed the borders of Tennessee. Even on the summit of Chilhowee Mountain the apples in Peter Giles's orchard were beginning to redden, and his Indian corn, planted on so steep a declivity that the stalks seemed to have much ado to keep their footing, was crested with tassels and plumed with silk. Among the dense forests, seen by no man's eye, the elder was flying its creamy banners in honor of June's coming, and, heard by no man's ear, the pink and white bells of the azalea rang out melodies of welcome.

"An' it air a toler'ble for'ard season. Yer wheat looks likely; an' yer gyarden truck air thrivin' powerful. Even that cold spell we-uns hed about the full o' the moon in May ain't done sot it back none, it 'pears like ter me. But, 'cording ter my way o' thinkin', ye hev got chickens enough hyar ter eat off every pea-bloom ez soon ez it opens." And Simon Burney glanced with a gardener's disapproval at the numerous fowls, lifting their red combs and tufted top-knots here and there among the thick clover under the apple-trees.

"Them's Clarsie's chickens,—my darter, ye know," drawled Peter Giles, a pale, listless, and lank mountaineer. "An' she hev been gin ter onderstand ez they hev got ter be kep' out 'n the gyarden; 'thout," he added indulgently,—"'thout I'm a-plowin', when I lets 'em foller in the furrow ter pick up worms. But law! Clarsie is so spry that she don't ax no better 'n ter be let ter run them chickens off 'n the peas."

Then the two men tilted their chairs against the posts of the little porch in front of Peter Giles's log cabin, and puffed their pipes in silence. The panorama spread out before them showed misty and dreamy among the delicate spiral wreaths of smoke. But was that gossamer-like illusion, lying upon the far horizon, the magic of nicotian, or the vague presence of distant heights? As ridge after ridge came down from the sky

191

in ever-graduating shades of intenser blue, Peter Giles might have told you that this parallel system of enchantment was only "the mountings:" that here was Foxy, and there was Big Injun, and still beyond was another, which he had "hearn tell ran spang up into Virginny." The sky that bent to clasp this kindred blue was of varying moods. Floods of sunshine submerged Chilhowee in liquid gold, and revealed that dainty outline limned upon the northern horizon; but over the Great Smoky mountains clouds had gathered, and a gigantic rainbow bridged the valley.

Peter Giles's listless eyes were fixed upon a bit of red clay road, which was visible through a gap in the foliage far below. Even a tiny object, that ant-like crawled upon it, could be seen from the summit of Chilhowee. "I reckon that's my brother's wagon an' team," he said, as he watched the moving atom pass under the gorgeous triumphal arch. "He 'lowed he war goin' ter the Cross-Roads ter-day."

Simon Burney did not speak for a moment. When he did, his words seemed widely irrelevant. "That's a likely gal o' yourn," he drawled, with an odd constraint in his voice,—"a likely gal, that Clarsie."

There was a quick flash of surprise in Peter Giles's dull eyes. He covertly surveyed his guest, with an astounded curiosity rampant in his slow brains. Simon Burney had changed color; an expression of embarrassment lurked in every line of his honest, florid, hard-featured face. An alert imagination might have detected a deprecatory self-consciousness in every gray hair that striped the black beard raggedly fringing his chin.

"Yes," Peter Giles at length replied, "Clarsie air a likely enough gal. But she air mightily sot ter hevin' her own way. An' ef 't ain't give ter her peaceable-like, she jes' takes it, whether or no."

This statement, made by one presumably fully informed on the subject, might have damped the ardor of many a suitor,—for the monstrous truth was dawning on Peter Giles's mind that suitor was the position to which this slow, elderly widower aspired. But Simon Burney, with that odd, all-pervading constraint still prominently apparent, mildly observed, "Waal, ez much ez I hev seen of her goin's-on, it 'pears ter me ez her way air a mighty good way. An' it ain't comical that she likes it."

Urgent justice compelled Peter Giles to make some amends to the absent Clarissa. "That's a fac'," he admitted. "An' Clarsie ain't no hand ter jaw. She don't hev no words. But then," he qualified, truth and consistency alike constraining him, "she air a toler'ble hard-headed gal. That air a true word. Ye mought ez well try ter hender the sun from shining ez ter make that thar Clarsie Giles do what she don't want ter do."

To be sure, Peter Giles had a right to his opinion as to the hardness of his own daughter's head. The expression of his views, however, provoked Simon Burney to wrath; there was something astir within him that in a worthier subject might have been called a chivalric thrill, and it forbade him to hold his peace. He retorted: "Of course ye kin say that, ef so minded; but ennybody ez hev got eyes kin see the change ez hev been made in this hyar place sence that thar gal hev been growed. I ain't a-purtendin' ter know that thar Clarsie ez well ez you-uns knows her hyar at home, but I hev seen enough, an' a deal more'n enough, of her goin's-on, ter know that what she does ain't done fur *herself*. An' ef she will hev her way, it air fur the good of the whole tribe of ye. It 'pears ter me ez thar ain't many gals like that thar Clarsie. An' she air a merciful critter. She air mighty savin' of the feelin's of everything, from the cow an' the mare down ter the dogs, an' pigs, an' chickens; always a-feedin' of 'em jes' ter the time, an' never draggin', an' clawin', an' beatin' of 'em. Why, that thar Clarsie can't put her foot out'n the door, that every dumb beastis on this hyar place ain't a-runnin' ter git nigh her. I hev seen them pigs mos' climb the fence when she shows her face at the door. 'Pears ter me ez that thar Clarsie could tame a b'ar, ef she looked at him a time or two, she's so savin' o' the critter's feelin's! An' thar's that old yaller dog o' yourn," pointing to an ancient cur that was blinking in the sun, "he's older'n Clarsie, an' no 'count in the worl'. I hev hearn ye say forty times that ye would kill him, 'ceptin' that Clarsie purtected him, an' hed sot her heart on his a-livin' along. An' all the home-folks, an' everybody that kems hyar to sot an' talk awhile, never misses a chance ter kick that thar old dog, or poke him with a stick, or cuss him. But Clarsie!— I hev seen that gal take the bread an' meat off'n her plate, an' give it ter that old dog, ez 'pears ter me ter be the worst dispositionest dog I ever see, an' no thanks lef' in him. He hain't hed the grace ter wag his tail fur twenty year. That thar Clarsie air surely a merciful critter, an' a mighty spry, likely young gal, besides."

Peter Giles sat in stunned astonishment during this speech, which was delivered in a slow, drawling monotone, with frequent meditative pauses, but nevertheless emphatically. He made no reply, and as they were once more silent there rose suddenly the sound of melody upon the air. It came from beyond that tumultuous stream that raced with the wind down the mountain's side; a great log thrown from bank to bank served as bridge. The song grew momentarily more distinct; among the leaves there were fugitive glimpses of blue and white, and at last Clarsie appeared, walking lightly along the log, clad in her checked homespun dress, and with a pail upon her head.

She was a tall, lithe girl, with that delicately transparent complexion often seen among the women of these

194

mountains. Her lustreless black hair lay along her forehead without a ripple or wave; there was something in the expression of her large eyes that suggested those of a deer,—something free, untamable, and yet gentle. "'Tain't no wonder ter me ez Clarsie is all tuk up with the wild things, an' critters ginerally," her mother was wont to say. "She sorter looks like 'em, I'm a-thinkin'."

As she came in sight there was a renewal of that odd constraint in Simon Burney's face and manner, and he rose abruptly. "Waal," he said, hastily, going to his horse, a raw-boned sorrel, hitched to the fence, "it's about time I war a-startin' home, I reckons."

He nodded to his host, who silently nodded in return, and the old horse jogged off with him down the road, as Clarsie entered the house and placed the pail upon a shelf.

"Who d'ye think hev been hyar a-speakin' of compli*mints* on ye, Clarsie?" exclaimed Mrs. Giles, who had overheard through the open door every word of the loud, drawling voice on the porch.

Clarsie's liquid eyes widened with surprise, and a faint tinge of rose sprang into her pale face, as she looked an expectant inquiry at her mother.

Mrs. Giles was a slovenly, indolent woman, anxious, at the age of forty-five, to assume the prerogatives of advanced years. She had placed all her domestic cares upon the shapely shoulders of her willing daughter, and had betaken herself to the chimney-corner and a pipe.

"Yes, thar hev been somebody hyar a-speakin' of compli*mints* on ye, Clarsie," she reiterated, with chuckling amusement. "He war a mighty peart, likely boy,—that he war!"

Clarsie's color deepened.

"Old Simon Burney!" exclaimed her mother, in great glee at the incongruity of the idea. "*Old Simon Burney!*—jes' a-sittin' out thar, a-wastin' the time, an' a-burnin' of daylight—jes' ez perlite an' smilin' ez a basket of chips—a-speakin' of compli*mints* on ye!"

There was a flash of laughter among the sylvan suggestions of Clarsie's eyes,—a flash as of sudden sunlight upon water. But despite her mirth she seemed to be unaccountably disappointed. The change in her manner was not noticed by her mother, who continued banteringly,—

"Simon Burney air a mighty pore old man. Ye oughter be sorry fur him, Clarsie. Ye mustn't think less of folks than ye does of the dumb beastis,—that ain't religion. Ye knows ye air sorry fur mos' everything; why not fur this comical old consarn? Ye oughter marry him ter take keer of him. He said ye war a merciful critter; now is yer chance ter show it! Why, air ye a-goin' ter weavin', Clarsie, jes' when I wants ter talk ter ye 'bout'n old Simon Burney? But law! I knows ye kerry him with ye in yer heart."

The girl summarily closed the conversation by seating herself before a great hand-loom; presently the persistent thump, thump, of the batten and the noisy creak of the treadle filled the room, and through all the long, hot afternoon her deft, practiced hands lightly tossed the shuttle to and fro.

The breeze freshened, after the sun went down, and the hop and gourd vines were all astir as they clung about the little porch where Clarsie was sitting now, idle at last. The rain clouds had disappeared, and there bent over the dark, heavily wooded ridges a pale blue sky, with here and there the crystalline sparkle of a star. A halo was shimmering in the east, where the mists had gathered about the great white moon, hanging high above the mountains. Noiseless wings flitted through the dusk; now and then the bats swept by so close as to wave Clarsie's hair with the wind of their flight. What an airy, glittering, magical thing was that gigantic spider-web suspended between the silver moon and her shining eyes! Ever and anon there came from the woods a strange, weird, long-drawn sigh, unlike the stir of the wind in the trees, unlike the fret of the water on the rocks. Was it the voiceless sorrow of the sad earth? There were stars in the night besides those known to astronomers: the stellular fireflies gemmed the black shadows with a fluctuating brilliancy; they circled in and out of the porch, and touched the leaves above Clarsie's head with quivering points of light. A steadier and an intenser gleam was advancing along the road, and the sound of languid footsteps came with it; the aroma of tobacco graced the atmosphere, and a tall figure walked up to the gate.

"Come in, come in," said Peter Giles, rising, and tendering the guest a chair. "Ye air Tom Pratt, ez well ez I kin make out by this light. Waal, Tom, we hain't furgot ye sence ye done been hyar."

As Tom had been there on the previous evening, this might be considered a joke, or an equivocal compliment. The young fellow was restless and awkward under it, but Mrs. Giles chuckled with great merriment.

"An' how air ye a-comin' on, Mrs. Giles?" he asked propitiatorily.

"Jes' toler'ble, Tom. Air they all well ter yer house?"

"Yes, they're toler'ble well, too." He glanced at Clarsie, intending to address to her some polite greeting, but the expression of her shy, half-startled eyes, turned upon the far-away moon, warned him. "Thar never war a gal so skittish," he thought. "She'd run a mile, skeered ter death, ef I said a word ter her."

And he was prudently silent.

"Waal," said Peter Giles, "what's the news out yer way, Tom? Ennything a-goin' on?"

"Thar war a shower yander on the Backbone; it rained toler'ble hard fur a while, an' sot up the corn wonderful. Did ye git enny hyar?"

"Not a drap."

"'Pears ter me ez I kin see the clouds a-circlin' round Chilhowee, an' a-rainin' on everybody's corn-field 'ceptin' ourn," said Mrs. Giles. "Some folks is the favored of the Lord, an' t'others hev ter work fur everything an' git nuthin'. Waal, waal; we-uns will see our reward in the nex' worl'. Thar's a better worl' than this, Tom."

"That's a fac'," said Tom, in orthodox assent.

"An' when we leaves hyar once, we leaves all trouble an' care behind us, Tom; fur we don't come back no more." Mrs. Giles was drifting into one of her pious moods.

"I dunno," said Tom. "Thar hev been them ez hev."

"Hev what?" demanded Peter Giles, startled.

"Hev come back ter this hyar yearth. Thar's a harnt that walks Chilhowee every night o' the worl'. I know them ez hev seen him."

Clarsie's great dilated eyes were fastened on the speaker's face. There was a dead silence for a moment, more eloquent with these looks of amazement than any words could have been.

"I reckons ye remember a puny, shriveled little man, named Reuben Crabb, ez used ter live yander, eight mile along the ridge ter that thar big sulphur spring," Tom resumed, appealing to Peter Giles. "He war born with only one arm."

"I 'members him," interpolated Mrs. Giles, vivaciously. "He war a mighty porely, sickly little critter, all the days of his life.

'Twar a wonder he war ever raised ter be a man,—an' a pity, too. An' 'twar powerful comical, the way of his takin' off; a stunted, one-armed little critter a-ondertakin' ter fight folks an' shoot pistols. He hed the use o' his one arm, sure."

"Waal," said Tom, "his house ain't thar now, 'kase Sam Grim's brothers burned it ter the ground fur his a-killin' of Sam. That warn't all that war done ter Reuben fur killin' of Sam. The sheriff run Reuben Crabb down this hyar road 'bout a mile from hyar,—mebbe less,—an' shot him dead in the road, jes' whar it forks. Waal, Reuben war in company with another evil-doer,—*he* war from the Cross-Roads, an' I furgits what he hed done, but he war a-tryin' ter hide in the mountings, too; an' the sheriff lef' Reuben a-lying thar in the road, while he tries ter ketch up with the t'other; but his horse got a stone in his hoof, an' he los' time, an' hed ter gin it up. An' when he got back ter the forks o' the road whar he had lef' Reuben a-lyin' dead, thar war nuthin' thar 'ceptin' a pool o' blood. Waal, he went right on ter Reuben's house, an' them Grim boys hed burnt it ter the ground; but he seen Reuben's brother Joel. An' Joel, he tole the sheriff that late that evenin' he hed tuk Reuben's body out'n the road an' buried it, 'kase it hed been lyin' thar in the road ever sence early in the mornin', an' he couldn't leave it thar all night, an' he hedn't no shelter fur it, sence the Grim boys hed burnt down the house. So he war obleeged ter bury it. An' Joel showed the sheriff a new-made grave, an' Reuben's coat whar the sheriff's bullet hed gone in at the back an' kem out'n the breast. The sheriff 'lowed ez they'd fine Joel fifty dollars fur a-buryin' of Reuben afore the cor'ner kem; but they never done it, ez I knows on. The sheriff said that when the cor'ner kem the body would be tuk up fur a 'quest. But thar hed been a powerful big frishet, an' the river 'twixt the cor'ner's house an' Chilhowee couldn't be forded fur three weeks. The cor'ner never kem, an' so thar it all stayed. That war four year ago."

"Waal," said Peter Giles, dryly, "I ain't seen no harnt yit. I knowed all that afore."

Clarsie's wondering eyes upon the young man's moonlit face had elicited these facts, familiar to the elders, but strange, he knew, to her.

"I war jes' a-goin' on ter tell," said Tom, abashed. "Waal, ever sence his brother Joel died, this spring, Reuben's harnt walks Chilhowee. He war seen week afore las', 'bout daybreak, by Ephraim Blenkins, who hed been a-fishin', an' war a-goin' home. Eph happened ter stop in the laurel ter wind up his line, when all in a minit he seen the harnt go by, his face white, an' his eye-balls like fire, an' puny an' one-armed, jes' like he lived. Eph, he owed me a haffen day's work; I holped him ter plow las' month, an' so he kem ter-day an' hoed along cornsider'ble ter pay fur it. He say he believes the harnt never seen him, 'kase it went right by. He 'lowed ef the harnt hed so much ez cut one o' them blazin' eyes round at him he couldn't but hev drapped dead. Waal, this mornin', 'bout sunrise, my brother Bob's little gal, three year old, strayed off from home while her mother war out milkin' the cow. An' we went a-huntin' of her, mightily worked up, 'kase thar hev been a b'ar prowlin' round our corn-field twict this summer. An' I went to the right, an' Bob went to the lef'. An' he say ez he war a-pushin' 'long through the laurel, he seen the bushes ahead of him a-rustlin'. An' he jes' stood still an' watched 'em. An' fur a while the bushes war still too; an' then they moved jes' a little, fust this way an' then that, till all of a suddint the leaves opened, like the mouth of hell mought hev done, an' thar he seen Reuben Crabb's face. He say he never seen sech a face! Its mouth war open, an' its eyes war a-startin' out'n its head, an' its skin war white till it war blue; an' ef the devil hed hed it a-hangin' over the coals that minit it couldn't hev looked no more skeered. But that war all that Bob seen, 'kase he jes' shet his eyes an' screeched

200

an' screeched like he war *de*stracted. An' when he stopped a second ter ketch his breath he hearn su'thin' a-answerin' him back, sorter weak-like, an' thar war little Peggy a-pullin' through the laurel. Ye know she's too little ter talk good, but the folks down ter our house believes she seen the harnt, too."

"My Lord!" exclaimed Peter Giles. "I 'low I couldn't live a minit ef I war ter see that thar harnt that walks Chilhowee!"

"I know *I* couldn't," said his wife.

"Nor me, nuther," murmured Clarsie.

"Waal," said Tom, resuming the thread of his narrative, "we hev all been a-talkin' down yander ter our house ter make out the reason why Reuben Crabb's harnt hev sot out ter walk *jes' sence his brother Joel died,*—'kase it war never seen afore then. An' ez nigh ez we kin make it out, the reason is 'kase thar's nobody lef' in this hyar worl' what believes he warn't ter blame in that thar killin' o' Sam Grim. Joel always swore ez Reuben never killed him no more'n nuthin'; that Sam's own pistol went off in his own hand, an' shot him through the heart jes' ez he war a-drawin' of it ter shoot Reuben Crabb. An' I hev hearn other men ez war a-standin' by say the same thing, though them Grims tells another tale; but ez Reuben never owned no pistol in his life, nor kerried one, it don't 'pear ter me ez what them Grims say air reasonable. Joel always swore ez Sam Grim war a mighty mean man,—a great big feller like him a-rockin' of a deformed little critter, an' a-mockin' of him, an' a hittin' of him. An' the day of the fight Sam jes' knocked him down fur nuthin' at all; an' afore ye could wink Reuben jumped up suddint, an' flew at him like an eagle, an' struck him in the face. An' then Sam drawed his pistol, an' it went off in his own hand, an' shot him through the heart, an' killed him dead. Joel said that ef he could hev kep' that pore little critter Reuben still, an' let the sheriff arrest him peaceable-like, he

201

war sure the jury would hev let him off; 'kase how war Reuben a-goin ter shoot ennybody when Sam Grim never left a-holt of the only pistol between 'em, in life, or in death? They tells me they hed ter bury Sam Grim with that thar pistol in his hand; his grip war too tight fur death to unloose it. But Joel said that Reuben war sartain they'd hang him. He hedn't never seen no jestice from enny one man, an' he couldn't look fur it from twelve men. So he jes' sot out ter run through the woods, like a painter or a wolf, ter be hunted by the sheriff, an' he war run down an' kilt in the road. Joel said *he* kep' up arter the sheriff ez well ez he could on foot,— fur the Crabbs never hed no horse,—ter try ter beg fur Reuben, ef he war cotched, an' tell how little an' how weakly he war. I never seen a young man's head turn white like Joel's done; he said he reckoned it war his troubles. But ter the las' he stuck ter his rifle faithful. He war a powerful hunter; he war out rain or shine, hot or cold, in sech weather ez other folks would think thar warn't no use in tryin' ter do nuthin' in. I'm mightily afeard o' seein' Reuben, now, that's a fac'," concluded Tom, frankly; "'kase I hev hearn tell, an' I believes it, that ef a harnt speaks ter ye, it air sartain ye're bound ter die right then."

"'Pears ter me," said Mrs. Giles, "ez many mountings ez thar air round hyar, he mought hev tuk ter walkin' some o' them, stiddier Chilhowee."

There was a sudden noise close at hand: a great inverted splint-basket, from which came a sound of flapping wings, began to move slightly back and forth. Mrs. Giles gasped out an ejaculation of terror, the two men sprang to their feet, and the coy Clarsie laughed aloud in an exuberance of delighted mirth, forgetful of her shyness. "I declar' ter goodness, you-uns air all skeered fur true! Did ye think it war the harnt that walks Chilhowee?"

"What's under that thar basket?" demanded Peter Giles, rather sheepishly, as he sat down again.

"Nuthin' but the duck-legged Dominicky," said Clarsie, "what air bein' broke up from settin'." The moonlight was full upon the dimpling merriment in her face, upon her shining eyes and parted red lips, and her gurgling laughter was pleasant to hear. Tom Pratt edged his chair a trifle nearer, as he, too, sat down.

"Ye oughtn't never ter break up a duck-legged hen, nor a Dominicky, nuther," he volunteered, "'kase they air sech a good kind o' hen ter kerry chickens; but a hen that is duck-legged an' Dominicky too oughter be let ter set, whether or no."

Had he been warned in a dream, he could have found no more secure road to Clarsie's favor and interest than a discussion of the poultry. "I'm a-thinkin'," she said, "that it air too hot fur hens ter set now, an' 'twill be till the las' of August."

"It don't 'pear ter me ez it air hot much in June up hyar on Chilhowee,—thar's a differ, I know, down in the valley; but till July, on Chilhowee, it don't 'pear ter me ez it air too hot ter set a hen. An' a duck-legged Dominicky air mighty hard ter break up."

"That's a fac'," Clarsie admitted; "but I'll hev ter do it, somehow, 'kase I ain't got no eggs fur her. All my hens air kerryin' of chickens."

"Waal!" exclaimed Tom, seizing his opportunity, "I'll bring ye some ter-morrer night, when I come agin. We-uns hev got eggs ter our house."

"Thanky," said Clarsie, shyly smiling.

This unique method of courtship would have progressed very prosperously but for the interference of the elders, who are an element always more or less adverse to love-making. "Ye oughter turn out yer hen now, Clarsie," said Mrs. Giles, "ez Tom air a-goin' ter bring ye some eggs ter-morrer. I wonder ye don't think it's mean ter keep her up longer'n ye air obleeged ter. Ye oughter remember ye war called a merciful critter jes' ter-day."

Clarsie rose precipitately, raised the basket, and out flew the "duck-legged Dominicky," with a frantic flutter and hysterical cackling. But Mrs. Giles was not to be diverted from her purpose; her thoughts had recurred to the absurd episode of the afternoon, and with her relish of the incongruity of the joke she opened upon the subject at once.

"Waal, Tom," she said, "we'll be hevin' Clarsie married, afore long, I'm a-thinkin'." The young man sat bewildered. He, too, had entertained views concerning Clarsie's speedy marriage, but with a distinctly personal application; and this frank mention of the matter by Mrs. Giles had a sinister suggestion that perhaps her ideas might be antagonistic. "An' who d'ye think hev been hyar ter-day, a-speakin' of compli*mints* on Clarsie?" He could not answer, but he turned his head with a look of inquiry, and Mrs. Giles continued, "He is a mighty peart, likely boy,—*he* is."

There was a growing anger in the dismay on Tom Pratt's face; he leaned forward to hear the name with a fiery eagerness, altogether incongruous with his usual lack-lustre manner.

"Old Simon Burney!" cried Mrs. Giles, with a burst of laughter. "*Old Simon Burney!* Jes' a-speakin' of compli*mints* on Clarsie!"

The young fellow drew back with a look of disgust. "Why, he's a old man; he ain't no fit husband fur Clarsie."

"Don't ye be too sure ter count on that. I war jes' a-layin' off ter tell Clarsie that a gal oughter keep mighty clar o' widowers, 'thout she wants ter marry one. Fur I believes," said Mrs. Giles, with a wild flight of imagination, "ez them men hev got some sort'n trade with the Evil One, an' he gives 'em the power ter witch the gals, somehow, so's ter git 'em ter marry; 'kase I don't think that any gal that's got good sense air a-goin' ter be a man's second ch'ice, an' the mother of a whole pack of step-chil'ren, 'thout she air under some sort'n spell. But them men carries the day with the gals ginerally, an' I'm a-thinkin' they're banded with the devil. Ef I war a gal, an' a smart, peart boy like Simon Burney kem around a-speakin' of compli*mints*, an' sayin' I war a merciful critter, I'd jes' give it up, an' marry him fur second ch'ice. Thar's one blessin'," she continued, contemplating the possibility in a cold-blooded fashion positively revolting to Tom Pratt: "he ain't got no tribe of chil'ren fur Clarsie ter look arter; nary chick nor child hev old Simon Burney got. He hed two, but they died."

The young man took leave presently, in great depression of spirit,—the idea that the widower was banded with the powers of evil was rather overwhelming to a man whose dependence was in merely mortal attractions; and after he had been gone a little while Clarsie ascended the ladder to a nook in the roof, which she called her room.

For the first time in her life her slumber was fitful and restless, long intervals of wakefulness alternating with snatches of fantastic dreams. At last she rose and sat by the rude window, looking out through the chestnut leaves at the great moon, which had begun to dip toward the dark uncertainty of the western ridges, and at the shimmering, translucent, pearly mists that filled the intermediate valleys. All the air was dew and incense; so subtle and penetrating an odor came from that fir-tree beyond the fence that it seemed as if some invigorating infusion were thrilling along her veins; there floated upward, too, the warm fragrance of the clover, and every breath of the gentle wind brought from over the stream a thousand blended, undistinguishable perfumes of the deep forests beyond. The moon's idealizing glamour had left no trace of the uncouthness of the place which the daylight revealed; the little log house, the great overhanging chestnut-oaks, the jagged precipice before the door, the vague outlines of the distant ranges, all suffused with a magic sheen, might have seemed a stupendous alto-rilievo in silver repoussé. Still, there came here and there the sweep of the bat's dusky wings; even they were a part of the night's witchery. A tiny owl perched for a moment or two amid the dew-tipped chestnut-leaves, and gazed with great round eyes at Clarsie as solemnly as she gazed at him.

"I'm thankful enough that ye hed the grace not ter screech while ye war hyar," she said, after the bird had taken his flight. "I ain't ready ter die yit, an' a screech-ow*el* air the sure sign."

She felt now and then a great impatience with her wakeful mood. Once she took herself to task: "Jes' a-sittin' up hyar all night, the same ez ef I war a fox, or that thar harnt that walks Chilhowee!"

And then her mind reverted to Tom Pratt, to old Simon Burney, and to her mother's emphatic and oracular declaration that widowers are in league with Satan, and that the girls upon whom they cast the eye of supernatural fascination have no choice in the matter. "I wish I knowed ef that thar sayin' war true," she murmured, her face still turned to the western spurs, and the moon sinking so slowly toward them.

With a sudden resolution she rose to her feet. She knew a way of telling fortunes which was, according to tradition, infallible, and she determined to try it, and ease her mind as to her future. Now was the propitious moment. "I hev always hearn that it won't come true 'thout ye try it jes' before daybreak, an' a-kneelin' down at the forks of the road." She hesitated a moment and listened intently. "They'd never git done a-laffin' at me, ef they fund it out," she thought.

There was no sound in the house, and from the dark woods arose only those monotonous voices of the night, so familiar to her ears that she accounted their murmurous iteration as silence too. She leaned far out of the low window, caught the wide-spreading branches of the tree beside it, and swung herself noiselessly to the ground. The road before her was dark with the shadowy foliage and dank with the dew; but now and then, at long intervals, there lay athwart it a bright bar of light, where the moonshine fell through a gap in the trees. Once, as she went rapidly along her way, she saw speeding across the white radiance, lying just before her feet, the ill-omened shadow of a rabbit. She paused, with a superstitious sinking of the heart, and she heard the animal's quick, leaping rush through the bushes near at hand; but she mustered her courage, and kept steadily on. "'T ain't no use a-goin' back ter git shet o' bad luck," she argued. "Ef old Simon Burney air my fortune, he'll come whether or no,— ef all they say air true."

The serpentine road curved to the mountain's brink before it forked, and there was again that familiar picture of precipice, and far-away ridges, and shining mist, and sinking moon, which was visibly turning from silver to gold. The changing lustre gilded the feathery ferns that grew in the marshy dip. Just at the angle of the divergent paths there rose into the air a great mass of indistinct white blossoms, which she knew were the exquisite mountain azaleas, and all the dark forest was starred with the blooms of the laurel.

She fixed her eyes upon the mystic sphere dropping down the sky, knelt among the azaleas at the forks of the road, and repeated the time-honored invocation:—

"Ef I'm a-goin' ter marry a young man, whistle, Bird, whistle. Ef I'm a-goin' ter marry an old man, low, Cow, low. Ef I ain't a-goin' ter marry nobody, knock, Death, knock."

There was a prolonged silence in the matutinal freshness and perfume of the woods. She raised her head, and listened attentively. No chirp of half-awakened bird, no tapping of woodpecker, or the mysterious death-watch; but from far along the dewy aisles of the forest, the ungrateful Spot, that Clarsie had fed more faithfully than herself, lifted up her voice, and set the echoes vibrating. Clarsie, however, had hardly time for a pang of disappointment. While she still knelt among the azaleas her large, deer-like eyes were suddenly dilated with terror. From around the curve of the road came the quick beat of hastening footsteps, the sobbing sound of panting breath, and between her and the sinking moon there passed an attenuated, one-armed figure, with a pallid, sharpened face, outlined for a moment on its brilliant disk, and dreadful starting eyes, and quivering open mouth. It disappeared in an instant among the shadows of the laurel, and Clarsie, with a horrible fear clutching at her heart, sprang to her feet.

Her flight was arrested by other sounds. Before her reeling senses could distinguish them, a party of horsemen plunged down the road. They reined in suddenly as their eyes fell upon her, and their leader, an eager, authoritative man, was asking her a question. Why could she not understand him? With her nerveless hands feebly catching at the shrubs for support, she listened vaguely to his impatient, meaningless words, and saw with helpless deprecation the rising anger in his face. But there was no time to be lost. With a curse upon the stupidity of the mountaineer, who couldn't speak when she was spoken to, the party sped on in a sweeping gallop, and the rocks and the steeps were hilarious with the sound.

When the last faint echo was hushed, Clarsie tremblingly made her way out into the road; not reassured, however, for she had a frightful conviction that there was now and then a strange stir in the laurel, and that she was stealthily watched. Her eyes were fixed upon the dense growth with a morbid fascination, as she moved away; but she was once more rooted to the spot when the leaves parted and in the golden moonlight the ghost stood before her. She could not nerve herself to run past him, and he was directly in her way homeward. His face was white, and lined, and thin; that pitiful quiver was never still in the parted lips; he looked at her with faltering, beseeching eyes. Clarsie's merciful heart was stirred. "What ails ye, ter come back hyar, an' foller me?" she cried out, abruptly. And then a great horror fell upon her. Was not one to whom a ghost should speak doomed to death, sudden and immediate?

The ghost replied in a broken, shivering voice, like a wail of pain, "I war a-starvin',—I war a-starvin'," with despairing iteration.

It was all over, Clarsie thought. The ghost had spoken, and she was a doomed creature. She wondered that she did not fall dead in the road. But while those beseeching eyes were fastened in piteous appeal on hers, she could not leave him. "I never hearn that 'bout ye," she said, reflectively. "I knows ye hed awful troubles while ye war alive, but I never knowed ez ye war starved."

Surely that was a gleam of sharp surprise in the ghost's prominent eyes, succeeded by a sly intelligence.

"Day is nigh ter breakin'," Clarsie admonished him, as the lower rim of the moon touched the silver mists of the west. "What air ye a-wantin' of me?"

There was a short silence. Mind travels far in such intervals. Clarsie's thoughts had overtaken the scenes when she should have died that sudden terrible death: when there would be no one left to feed the chickens; when no one would care if the pigs cried with the pangs of hunger, unless, indeed, it were time for them to be fattened before killing. The mare,—how often would she be taken from the plow, and shut up for the night in her shanty without a drop of water, after her hard day's work! Who would churn, or spin, or weave? Clarsie could not understand how the machinery of the universe could go on without her. And Towse, poor Towse! He was a useless cumberer of the ground, and it was hardly to be supposed that after his protector was gone he would be spared a blow or a bullet, to hasten his lagging death. But Clarsie still stood in the road, and watched the face of the ghost, as he, with his eager, starting eyes, scanned her open, ingenuous countenance.

"Ye do ez ye air bid, or it'll be the worse for ye," said the "harnt," in the same quivering, shrill tone. "Thar's hunger in the nex' worl' ez well ez in this, an' ye bring me some vittles hyar this time ter-morrer, an' don't ye tell nobody ye hev seen me, nuther, or it'll be the worse for ye."

There was a threat in his eyes as he disappeared in the laurel, and left the girl standing in the last rays of moonlight.

A curious doubt was stirring in Clarsie's mind when she reached home, in the early dawn, and heard her father talking about the sheriff and his posse, who had stopped at the house in the night, and roused its inmates, to know if they had seen a man pass that way.

"Clarsie never hearn none o' the noise, I'll be bound, 'kase she always sleeps like a log," said Mrs. Giles, as her daughter came in with the pail, after milking the cow. "Tell her 'bout'n it."

"They kem a-bustin' along hyar a while afore daybreak, a-runnin' arter the man," drawled Mr. Giles, dramatically. "An'

210

they knocked me up, ter know ef ennybody hed passed. An' one o' them men—I never seen none of 'em afore; they's all valley folks, I'm a-thinkin'—an' one of 'em bruk his saddlegirt' a good piece down the road, an' he kem back ter borrer mine; an' ez we war a-fixin' of it, he tole me what they war all arter. He said that word war tuk ter the sheriff down yander in the valley—'pears ter me them town-folks don't think nobody in the mountings hev got good sense—word war tuk ter the sheriff 'bout this one-armed harnt that walks Chilhowee; an' he sot it down that Reuben Crabb warn't dead at all, an' Joel jes' purtended ter hev buried him, an' it air Reuben hisself that walks Chilhowee. An' thar air two hunderd dollars blood-money reward fur ennybody ez kin ketch him. These hyar valley folks air powerful cur'ous critters,—two hunderd dollars blood-money reward fur that thar harnt that walks Chilhowee! I jes' sot myself ter laffin' when that thar cuss tole it so solemn. I jes' 'lowed ter him ez he couldn't shoot a harnt nor hang a harnt, an' Reuben Crabb hed about got done with his persecutions in this worl'. An' he said that by the time they hed scoured this mounting, like they hed laid off ter do, they would find that that thar puny little harnt war nuthin' but a mortal man, an' could be kep' in a jail ez handy ez enny other flesh an' blood. He said the sheriff 'lowed ez the reason Reuben hed jes' taken ter walk Chilhowee sence Joel died is 'kase thar air nobody ter feed him, like Joel done, mebbe, in the nights; an' Reuben always war a pore, one-armed, weakly critter, what can't even kerry a gun, an' he air driv by hunger out'n the hole whar he stays, ter prowl round the cornfields an' hencoops ter steal suthin',—an' that's how he kem ter be seen frequent. The sheriff 'lowed that Reuben can't find enough roots an' yerbs ter keep him up; but law!—a harnt eatin'! It jes' sot me off ter laffin'. Reuben Crabb hev been too busy in torment fur the las' four year ter be a-studyin' 'bout eatin'; an' it air his harnt that walks Chilhowee."

The next morning, before the moon sank, Clarsie, with a tin pail in her hand, went to meet the ghost at the appointed place. She understood now why the terrible doom that falls upon those to whom a spirit may chance to speak had not descended upon her, and that fear was gone; but the secrecy of her errand weighed heavily. She had been scrupulously careful to put into the pail only such things as had fallen to her share at the table, and which she had saved from the meals of yesterday. "A gal that goes a-robbin' fur a hongry harnt," was her moral reflection, "oughter be throwed bodaciously off'n the bluff."

She found no one at the forks of the road. In the marshy dip were only the myriads of mountain azaleas, only the masses of feathery ferns, only the constellated glories of the laurel blooms. A sea of shining white mist was in the valley, with glinting golden rays striking athwart it from the great cresset of the sinking moon; here and there the long, dark, horizontal line of a distant mountain's summit rose above the vaporous shimmer, like a dreary, sombre island in the midst of enchanted waters. Her large, dreamy eyes, so wild and yet so gentle, gazed out through the laurel leaves upon the floating gilded flakes of light, as in the deep coverts of the mountain, where the fulvous-tinted deer were lying, other eyes, as wild and as gentle, dreamily watched the vanishing moon. Overhead, the filmy, lace-like clouds, fretting the blue heavens, were tinged with a faint rose. Through the trees she caught a glimpse of the red sky of dawn, and the glister of a great lucent, tremulous star. From the ground, misty blue exhalations were rising, alternating with the long lines of golden light yet drifting through the woods. It was all very still, very peaceful, almost holy. One could hardly believe that these consecrated solitudes had once reverberated with the echoes of man's death-dealing ingenuity, and that Reuben Crabb had fallen, shot through and through, amid that wealth of flowers at the forks of the road. She heard suddenly the far-away baying of a hound. Her great eyes dilated, and she lifted her head to listen. Only the solemn silence of the woods, the slow sinking of the noiseless moon, the voiceless splendor of that eloquent day-star.

Morning was close at hand, and she was beginning to wonder that the ghost did not appear, when the leaves fell into abrupt commotion, and he was standing in the road, beside her. He did not speak, but watched her with an eager, questioning intentness, as she placed the contents of the pail upon the moss at the roadside. "I'm a-comin' agin ter-morrer," she said, gently. He made no reply, quickly gathered the food from the ground, and disappeared in the deep shades of the woods.

She had not expected thanks, for she was accustomed only to the gratitude of dumb beasts; but she was vaguely conscious of something wanting, as she stood motionless for a moment, and watched the burnished rim of the moon slip down behind the western mountains. Then she slowly walked along her misty way in the dim light of the coming dawn. There was a footstep in the road behind her; she thought it was the ghost once more. She turned, and met Simon Burney, face to face. His rod was on his shoulder, and a string of fish was in his hand.

"Ye air a-doin' wrongful, Clarsie," he said, sternly. "It air agin the law fur folks ter feed an' shelter them ez is a-runnin' from jestice. An' ye'll git yerself inter trouble. Other folks will find ye out, besides me, an' then the sheriff'll be up hyar arter ye."

The tears rose to Clarsie's eyes. This prospect was infinitely more terrifying than the awful doom which follows the horror of a ghost's speech.

213

"I can't holp it," she said, however, doggedly swinging the pail back and forth. "I can't gin my consent ter starvin' of folks, even ef they air a-hidin' an' a-runnin' from jestice."

"They mought put ye in jail, too,—I dunno," suggested Simon Burney.

"I can't holp that, nuther," said Clarsie, the sobs rising, and the tears falling fast. "Ef they comes an' gits me, and puts me in the pen'tiary away down yander, somewhars in the valley, like they done Jane Simpkins, fur a-cuttin' of her step-mother's throat with a butcher-knife, while she war asleep,—though some said Jane war crazy,—I can't gin my consent ter starvin' of folks."

A recollection came over Simon Burney of the simile of "hendering the sun from shining."

"She hev done sot it down in her mind," he thought, as he walked on beside her and looked at her resolute face. Still he did not relinquish his effort.

"Doin' wrong, Clarsie, ter aid folks what air a-doin' wrong, an' mebbe *hev* done wrong, air powerful hurtful ter everybody, an' henders the law an' jestice."

"I can't holp it," said Clarsie.

"It 'pears toler'ble comical ter me," said Simon Burney, with a sudden perception of a curious fact which has proved a marvel to wiser men, "that no matter how good a woman is, she ain't got no respect fur the laws of the country, an' don't sot no store by jestice." After a momentary silence he appealed to her on another basis. "Somebody will ketch him arter a while, ez sure ez ye air born. The sheriff's a-sarchin' now, an' by the time that word gits around, all the mounting boys'll turn out, 'kase thar air two hunderd dollars blood-money fur him. An' then he'll think, when they ketches him,—an' everybody'll say so, too,—ez ye war constant in feedin' him jes' ter 'tice him ter comin' ter one place, so ez ye could tell somebody whar ter go ter ketch him, an' make them gin ye haffen the blood-money, mebbe. That's what the mounting will say, mos' likely."

"I can't holp it," said Clarsie, once more.

He left her walking on toward the rising sun, and retraced his way to the forks of the road. The jubilant morning was filled with the song of birds; the sunlight flashed on the dew; all the delicate enameled bells of the pink and white azaleas were swinging tremulously in the wind; the aroma of ferns and mint rose on the delicious fresh air. Presently he checked his pace, creeping stealthily on the moss and grass beside the road rather than in the beaten path. He pulled aside the leaves of the laurel with no more stir than the wind might have made, and stole cautiously through its dense growth, till he came suddenly upon the puny little ghost, lying in the sun at the foot of a tree. The frightened creature sprang to his feet with a wild cry of terror, but before he could move a step he was caught and held fast in the strong grip of the stalwart mountaineer beside him. "I hev kem hyar ter tell ye a word, Reuben Crabb," said Simon Burney. "I hev kem hyar ter tell ye that the whole mounting air a-goin' ter turn out ter sarch fur ye; the sheriff air a-ridin' now, an' ef ye don't come along with me they'll hev ye afore night, 'kase thar air two hunderd dollars reward fur ye."

What a piteous wail went up to the smiling blue sky, seen through the dappling leaves above them! What a horror, and despair, and prescient agony were in the hunted creature's face! The ghost struggled no longer; he slipped from his feet down upon the roots of the tree, and turned that woful face, with its starting eyes and drawn muscles and quivering parted lips, up toward the unseeing sky.

"God A'mighty, man!" exclaimed Simon Burney, moved to pity. "Whyn't ye quit this hyar way of livin' in the woods like

215

ye war a wolf? Whyn't ye come back an' stand yer trial? From all I've hearn tell, it 'pears ter me ez the jury air obleeged ter let ye off, an' I'll take keer of ye agin them Grims."

"I hain't got no place ter live in," cried out the ghost, with a keen despair.

Simon Barney hesitated. Reuben Crabb was possibly a murderer,—at the best could but be a burden. The burden, however, had fallen in his way, and he lifted it.

"I tell ye now, Reuben Crabb," he said, "I ain't a-goin' ter holp no man ter break the law an' hender jestice; but ef ye will go an' stand yer trial, I'll take keer of ye agin them Grims ez long ez I kin fire a rifle. An' arter the jury hev done let ye off, ye air welcome ter live along o' me at my house till ye die. Ye air no-'count ter work, I know, but I ain't a-goin' ter grudge ye fur a livin' at my house."

And so it came to pass that the reward set upon the head of the harnt that walked Chilhowee was never claimed.

With his powerful ally, the forlorn little spectre went to stand his trial, and the jury acquitted him without leaving the box. Then he came back to the mountains to live with Simon Burney. The cruel gibes of his burly mockers that had beset his feeble life from his childhood up, the deprivation and loneliness and despair and fear that had filled those days when he walked Chilhowee, had not improved the harnt's temper. He was a helpless creature, not able to carry a gun or hold a plow, and the years that he spent smoking his cob-pipe in Simon Burney's door were idle years and unhappy. But Mrs. Giles said she thought he was "a mighty lucky little critter: fust, he hed Joel ter take keer of him an' feed him, when he tuk ter the woods ter pertend he war a harnt; an' they do say now that Clarsie Pratt, afore she war married, used ter kerry him vittles, too; an' then old Simon Burney tuk him up an' fed him ez plenty ez ef he war a good workin' hand, an' gin him clothes an' house-room, an' put up with his jawin' jes' like he never hearn a word of it. But law! some folks dunno when they air well off."

There was only a sluggish current of peasant blood in Simon Burney's veins, but a prince could not have dispensed hospitality with a more royal hand. Ungrudgingly he gave of his best; valiantly he defended his thankless guest at the risk of his life; with a moral gallantry he struggled with his sloth, and worked early and late, that there might be enough to divide. There was no possibility of a recompense for him, not even in the encomiums of discriminating friends, nor the satisfaction of tutored feelings and a practiced spiritual discernment; for he was an uncouth creature, and densely ignorant.

The grace of culture is, in its way, a fine thing, but the best that art can do—the polish of a gentleman—is hardly equal to the best that Nature can do in her higher moods.

The name Charles Egbert Craddock is a pseudonym for Mary Noailles Murfree (1850–1922), a significant figure in late 19th-century American literature. Born into a prominent and cultured family in Murfreesboro, Tennessee, Murfree's formative years were steeped in the genteel traditions of Southern society. Her literary voice, however, transcended the conventional narratives of her time by bringing attention to the rugged Appalachian region and its people.

Murfree's early life was shaped by intellectual pursuits despite personal challenges, such as partial paralysis from polio, which left her mobility impaired. This limitation may have contributed to her introspective nature and the development of her writing skills. She initially published short stories anonymously in *The Atlantic Monthly* in the late 1870s, adopting the male pseudonym Charles Egbert Craddock to ensure her work would be taken seriously in a male-dominated literary world.

Murfree's breakthrough came in 1884 with her short story collection *In the Tennessee Mountains*, a vivid depiction of Appalachian life. Her works were widely praised for their detailed portrayals of the region's landscapes and people, earning her a lasting place in the genre of local color writing. However, her depictions often straddled a fine line between realistic portrayal and romanticized interpretation, reflecting both her fascination with the region and the expectations of her urban, Northern readership.

Analysis of *In the Tennessee Mountains*

In the Tennessee Mountains is a seminal work in American regional literature, containing a series of short stories that collectively portray the unique culture, hardships, and natural beauty of the Appalachian region. Murfree's prose is renowned for its detailed natural descriptions, reflecting both her deep observation of the environment and the influence of romanticism. The stories in the collection, such as "The Star in the Valley" and "Drifting Down Lost Creek," reveal her dual purpose: to entertain and to document.

Her narrative style is characterized by its evocative imagery and authentic dialect. Murfree meticulously reproduces the vernacular speech of the mountain people, which adds depth and authenticity to her characters. For instance, in "The Star in the Valley," her use of dialect creates an immersive reading experience, though modern critics have debated whether this device perpetuates stereotypes of Appalachian "otherness."

Murfree's thematic exploration in the collection centers around the tension between tradition and modernity, the isolation of mountain life, and the resilience of its inhabitants. Her characters often grapple with external pressures, such as economic hardships or encroaching industrialization, while maintaining a strong connection to their land and heritage. The stories also emphasize human vulnerability against the backdrop of a sublime yet unforgiving landscape, underscoring themes of survival and stoicism.

Critically, *In the Tennessee Mountains* has been both lauded and critiqued. Contemporary reviewers, such as those from *The Atlantic Monthly*, praised Murfree for her rich, picturesque portrayals and her ability to evoke empathy for her characters. However, later scholars have scrutinized her romanticized lens, suggesting that her status as an outsider limited her understanding of the culture she sought to depict. Nonetheless, her work serves as an invaluable cultural artifact, preserving aspects of Appalachian life during a transformative era in American history.

Legacy

Mary Noailles Murfree's literary contributions helped to shape the local color movement, alongside contemporaries such as Sarah Orne Jewett and Bret Harte. Through the pseudonym of Charles Egbert Craddock, she carved out a space for herself in the literary canon and expanded national awareness of Appalachia.

Her works remain a subject of literary and historical study, offering insights into how 19th-century writers navigated issues of representation, regional identity, and gender constraints. Despite critiques of her portrayals, *In the Tennessee Mountains* endures as a testament to Murfree's narrative skill and her commitment to illuminating a largely overlooked corner of the American landscape.

References

1. Baskin, Mary Harris. *Mary Noailles Murfree: Appalachian Writer of Local Color.* Knoxville: University of Tennessee Press, 1970.
2. Rubin, Louis D. *The Edge of the Swamp: A Study in the Literature and Society of the Old South.* Baton Rouge: Louisiana State University Press, 1989.
3. Foster, Shirley. "Gender and Regionalism in the Works of Mary Noailles Murfree." *American Literary Realism*, vol. 24, no. 3, 1992, pp. 21–39.

Made in the USA
Monee, IL
05 December 2024

72553194R00122